Lyn Ashwood & Rachel Rose

# Comeback

A K-pop Novel

D1496351

First Edition: June 2019

Book Cover Art by Jauni (Lin Xie)
Cover Design by Patrick Knowles

ISBN 978-1-7338115-1-4 (paperback)
ISBN 978-1-7338115-0-7 (ebook)

Published by Ashwood & Rose LLP
www.ashwoodandrose.com
@ashwoodandrose

*To those who turn to K-pop for hope,*
*Trust your dreams and find your strength.*
*Never be afraid to make your own comeback.*
*Shine on!*

## *Comeback*

*noun*

the release of new music by any K-pop artist(s), e.g. single album, mini-album, EP, or full-length album; a comeback is referred to as such no matter the popularity of the artist(s), the level of success for the new song(s), or the length of time in between each release

# Table of Contents

Foreword ...................................................... ix

1: Emery - #AwakenNow ...............................1

2: Alana - #TimeToGo .................................12

3: Emery - #MSlipUp ...................................24

4: Alana - #ImFine......................................42

5: Emery - #YouWho....................................54

6: Alana - #ConfettiConfessions .............65

7: Emery - #HeatWave ...............................80

8: Alana - #MTheHero ................................95

9: Emery - #TrustMe .................................109

10: Alana - #WelcomeToSolar .................122

11: Emery - #ByungNO...............................136

12: Alana - #CallMeEmery .........................148

13: Emery - #ImYourFan .............................164

14: Alana - #DripDrop..................................178

15: Emery - #HoldMeTight ...........................186

16: Alana - #MoonlightAgain .......................198

17: Emery - #YouAndMe ..............................215

18: Alana - #Encore .....................................228

19: Emery - #Reflection.................................248

20: Alana - #Liar.............................................266

21: Emery - #CHICAGLO................................277

Glossary......................................................291

Acknowledgements....................................297

About the Authors......................................301

# Foreword

This book contains words in Korean and Konglish, as well as slang commonly found in the K-pop community. To help ease understanding, each "foreign" term is italicized in text and included in the glossary at the back of the book.

We used our discretion to the best of our abilities when choosing whether to write something in English or Korean. By including some of the more common Korean words and phrases, we hoped that readers would gain a better grasp of Korean life and culture, and by extension the K-pop universe. However, please keep in mind that this type of multilingual storytelling required us to take some liberties with the Korean language to simplify comprehension on behalf of English speakers.

# Emery

## #AwakenNow

Emery had figured wearing all white for today's comeback stage would be tempting fate, but he certainly hadn't expected fate to show up like this.

She slammed into him, tea cascading over the side of the paper cup in her hand and splashing onto his shoes and ankle. Emery winced, not from the pain, but from the thought of damaging his $600 white jeans. His stylists would kill him. Or, no, forget the stylists—President Jo would hunt him down herself.

The girl let out a startled squeak against his chest, stumbling as she drew back. He instinctively reached out to steady her, and his hand latched onto her wrist. With an apology on the tip of his tongue, he looked down at her face just as recognition struck him with alarming clarity. It was *her*. Her.

Wide-eyed and pale, she looked at Emery as if he were a ghost, but *she* was the ghost—an apparition from Emery's past. Memories of the summer two years ago flickered in his mind—her shy smile, the red umbrella, a silver chain—as he watched the panic growing in her familiar light brown eyes. A heartbeat later, she turned and fled without looking back.

"M! Let's go!" called Minhyuk, Emery's manager. "Everyone's waiting backstage."

Emery stood rigid, staring down the hallway in disbelief as the girl vanished around the corner. His heart pounded, its frantic rhythm echoing in his ears. He was used to pressure. He was used to the spotlight. But Emery wasn't used to the kind of emotions now crashing through his mind, threatening to spill over.

Fate had found him in the form of a girl, but it wasn't just any girl. It was *the* girl. He knew her only by the name she had mistakenly left him—*A*, written in a small but graceful script. He couldn't even call it a name. As an initial, it could stand for anything—Ace, Anne, even Apple—but he wasn't one to judge considering his own stage name was *M*. Either way, the simple letter A didn't do her justice. He had pretty much stuck to calling her, well, *Her* in his head.

What was she even doing here? Not here as in Seoul, Korea, but rather *here*, at Music Now. Was he hallucinating? With less than three hours of sleep the night before, the possibility couldn't be ruled out.

He glanced down, taking in the sizable stain on his left pant leg where her tea had spilled. This was real. His imagination wasn't *that* good. There wasn't enough time to return to the bathroom, either. Instead, he crouched down and carefully rolled up his jeans to hide the mark. Once. Twice. Checking his handiwork, he smiled.

"M, now!" Minhyuk said, throwing his arms up in exasperation as he walked towards Emery.

It would only take Emery a minute to catch up to Her. Seconds, if he followed her lead and ran. But it would have to wait, especially since his manager looked like he was preparing to physically drag Emery on stage. He'd seen Minhyuk do it to Sungil once before and definitely didn't need to experience it himself.

"Sorry! Coming, *Hyung*!" Emery answered in Korean. After moving to Seoul just over five years ago when he was fifteen, he could now communicate in Korean without any major problems. It helped that he was Korean American, and had grown up speaking basic Korean with his family and friends in Los Angeles. However, he had still faced a language barrier when he first arrived in Korea, struggling with the formal intricacies of the language. It was frustrating, but after months in an immersive environment, he had achieved an acceptable level of fluency. His brain could now easily switch between English and Korean.

Emery forced a smile and met his manager at the elevator to the live studio. He tried his best to banish Her from his mind, but his thoughts were trapped, held hostage by her haunting image.

Her black hair had grown longer, reaching midway down her back in stark contrast to her pale skin. Her face was sharper than he remembered, more angular, as if she had skipped a few too many meals. But it was more than just her new physical appearance. There was something off in the way she withdrew from him, in the dark emotion that hid behind her light brown eyes.

"Everything all right, M?" Minhyuk asked, stress seeping into his otherwise easygoing tone as they stepped into the elevator. The round-faced manager put a hand on Emery's shoulder, running his gaze up and down, looking for anything out of place.

As he faced Minhyuk, Emery glimpsed his own reflection in the elevator mirror, taking in his dyed brown hair and the blue contacts that masked his naturally dark eyes.

"Spectacular. Never better." The elevator doors opened on the second-floor studio, his lie slipping naturally into place.

Emery caught up to the rest of his group backstage, where they were already going through their last-minute microphone and costume checks while Cocoa Pop's cheerful high notes filled the air. Sungil and Stu were lip-syncing and dancing along, jokingly making up their own version of the girl group's trendy choreography. Jaehyun stood with his back to Emery as a stylist sprayed his bleached blonde hair for what must have been the millionth time that day. Only Yongnam seemed to notice Emery's entrance.

"You okay?" Yongnam mouthed, cocking an eyebrow as he looked over at Emery with mild concern.

Emery gave his leader a double thumbs-up and flashed one of the trademark smiles that made him so popular with the fans. Yongnam frowned, but didn't say anything, and turned his attention back to the stylist adjusting the fringe on his gauzy white shirt. Emery took a deep breath, doing his best to keep his thoughts and racing heartbeat under control.

"NEON, one minute!" a staff member called.

All five members abruptly stopped what they were doing and huddled together in a tight circle, their white outfits glowing even in the dim lighting backstage. Everyone extended a hand to the center, waiting for Yongnam to lead their customary cheer.

"NEON. We are NEON. Light it up!" they chanted in unison. Emery's heart pounded even faster. He savored the nervous thrill building in his stomach and the rush of energy cascading through his fingertips as he took his mic from a waiting staff member. He briefly touched his necklace for luck, anxious to be back on stage in front of his fans.

In the background, Cocoa Pop's song came to an end, and the girl group filed off stage. Emery politely nodded his head to each of the seven girls as they bowed to NEON on their way out.

*Showtime.*

Emery followed his members onto the stage as fans in the audience greeted them with roaring cheers, and the studio cameras moved into position. NEON sat in a circle, back-to-back, waiting for the first of two songs to start. Emery closed his eyes, visualizing the opening choreography in his head while tapping his index finger in time to the anticipated beat.

The music began.

*"Kim Yongnam. Lee Jaehyun. Jung Emery. Shin Sunwoo. Lee Sungil. NEON NEON NEON!"*

Timed perfectly to the opening notes, the chants from NEON's fandom GLO were deafening, even through Emery's custom orange earpieces. He concealed a smirk as he slowly brought the microphone to his lips and crooned the first verse.

*The endless shadows are my home.*
*When I'm with you, I'm still alone.*

In contrast to their powerful title track, this song, "Forever Alone," was more of a rock ballad, emphasizing the group's dynamic voices. Emery loved it. As the group's main vocalist, it was easily his favorite song on the new mini album.

The other members smoothly followed the song's melody as they rose to standing. Emery stepped back from the front as Yongnam and Stu took over with their alternating rap. Stu's fiery red hair stood out as gold light filled the studio stage, reflecting off the silver cross dangling from his ear, while Yongnam's dark features gave him a powerful aura. Today might be their first televised stage for this comeback, but NEON had been practicing their new choreography non-stop for more than a month. The steps had already become second nature.

This was an important time for NEON. Nearly five months had passed since their last single album *Clarity* released, but even the shortest of breaks in the ever-changing K-pop industry could have a significant impact on their career and popularity. With the constant onslaught of new and old groups alike competing for the spotlight, it was time for NEON to reclaim their popularity. It was time for them to release new music. It was time for their comeback.

Dropping their mini album *Awaken* earlier today was only the beginning. Comebacks were always hectic, especially the first week of promotions. "Sleep," "relaxation," and "free time" disappeared from NEON's vocabulary, while live music shows, radio broadcasts, *fansigns*, interviews, and special TV appearances took center stage. Every second of every day was packed to the brim. Just that morning, NEON had arrived at the TV station at 4:00 a.m. for pre-recording, excited but already exhausted. Fortunately, Emery had managed to snatch a thirty-minute nap while the stylists did his hair and makeup. Power naps were basically how he survived a comeback. Well, power naps and iced Americanos.

Emery spun through the intricate choreography, automatically stepping out of Stu's path so Sungil could take the center position. Sungil, better known to fans by his stage name Eagle, was in his element, perfectly hitting his live notes while executing the more difficult dance moves as the song transitioned to the chorus. His sandy brown hair gleamed under the stage lights, highlighting his sharp cheekbones. While he was the youngest member of the group—the *maknae*—at only seventeen, Sungil shone on stage, excelling in not only dancing but singing and rapping as well.

Emery fed off the audience's excited energy. This was the first time GLO was seeing the choreography for "Forever Alone," and judging by the decibel of their screams, they were loving it. The sound of their chants fueled his movements, exhilarating him as his arms flowed through each controlled motion with perfect precision.

Then it was Emery's turn again to take center stage. He stepped forward to harmonize with Jaehyun and Sungil in the chorus. Out of the corner of his eye, he spotted Stu holding back a smirk from the cameras as the fans went wild for Jaehyun's lines. Of course, it might have had something to do with Jaehyun's portion of the song falling in time to the body roll moves of their dance. Jaehyun was often considered the most attractive member in NEON, or the "visual," a fact the eldest member wasn't shy about at all. His hair was bleached this comeback, playing into the more mature, bad-boy image the stylists had designed for him. With the sudden burst of even more piercing cries, Emery suspected that Jaehyun had just flashed his six-pack.

Before Emery knew it, the song was over, and NEON had their backs turned to the audience. The crowd's cheers rang in his ears as the lights faded to black, and NEON moved into place to perform their title track "Enlighten." The pre-recorded version shot at dawn would be broadcast on TV, but they still performed for the audience in the live studio.

While Emery crouched in his starting position, a stinging pain shot through his ankle. Glancing down, he glimpsed the irritated patch of skin under the cuff of his rolled jeans, and the image of her pale, haunted face flashed briefly before his eyes.

The title track started with the distinctive thrum of the bass, forcing Emery back to the present. As their rock-inspired pop song hit its chorus, Emery belted out the high notes, doing his best to ignore the pain in his ankle and the sense that something had changed with Her.

*Wake up. I need to wake up.*
*Enlighten me so I can—*

Emery's voice cut off as his foot slipped. Pitching forward, he stumbled into Jaehyun, nearly knocking them both over in the process. Immediately, they snapped back into step with the choreography, skillfully acting as if nothing had happened, even as the fans gasped in alarm.

*Way to ruin it,* Emery internally groaned.

Smiling sheepishly, he ignored his bandmates' worried glances, and the rest of the performance finished seamlessly. As the song came to an end, a staff member stepped on stage, signaling for NEON to get into place for the final live segment of the broadcast. The award section of the show would begin right after the commercial break.

NEON was the last group to perform, having earned this coveted spot by being the most anticipated in the night's line-up. It still didn't feel real to Emery, that NEON was actually "popular." Just a year before, they were still considered nobodies, *nugus*, more or less fighting with broadcast stations to even get the chance to perform. Now, they were seen as the leaders—the pioneers of K-pop's new sound. He couldn't wrap his head around how fast everything had changed.

*Hoobae* artists, those who debuted after NEON, bowed to Emery and the other senior, or *sunbae*, artists as everyone assembled on stage. More than fifteen groups had participated in the hour and a half show, and Emery quickly spotted Jaden Yang, the main dancer from HI5, and gave him a wave. Technically, HI5 was NEON's *sunbae* group, since NEON had debuted a whole ten days after them. Jaden jokingly never let Emery forget this fact.

"Jaden!" Stu cried, excitedly waving his arms above his head, the long sleeves of his white silk shirt sliding past his wrists to reveal bright silver rings on each of his fingers.

"What's up, Stuart Sunwoo Shin?" Jaden said in English. His mint green hair framed his oval face as he nodded in mock seriousness, only to dissolve into laughter at Stu's disgruntled expression. As Stu crossed his arms and turned his back on Jaden, Emery wasn't the only one grinning when the HI5 member playfully tackled Stu in an apology hug.

While Stu had a Korean name, he much preferred his English nickname, a fact the NEON members learned quickly in their early trainee days when Stu would lash out at anyone who called him Sunwoo. In fact, Jaden was the only one brave enough to call Stu by his full name, and for some reason, Stu let him get away with it. Originally from Taipei by way of Toronto, Jaden had grown close to both Emery and Stu as another native English speaker in the K-pop industry. Surrounded by strangers and away from home, they had bonded together for support as they adjusted to their new lives in Seoul.

Soon all the groups were on stage, and Stu broke apart from his reunion with Jaden to rejoin NEON, who had moved to the side. HI5 stood in the open spot next to Cocoa Pop in the front row. The two groups were going head-to-head as the contenders to win today's show.

Music show winners were crowned based on a combination of album sales, online streams, internet searches of the song, and fan votes. While NEON couldn't qualify for an award until the following week, judging from their performance on the Korean music charts so far, it looked like they would be taking home the trophy on the next Music Now broadcast.

Stu clapped Emery on the back and threw an arm around Emery's shoulders as he waved to the crowd.

"You okay, mate?" Stu said in Emery's ear, his Australian accent lilting his English. "You never make mistakes like that."

"Yeah, you know," Emery shrugged as he glanced down at Stu, who was an inch shorter, even with the lifts he wore in his shoes. "Guess I was nervous about the comeback."

"Mate, you should have seen Jaehyun's face when you

collided. Priceless!"

"He's okay, right?"

Before Stu could respond, the cue music began and all the artists on stage settled into place. The two idol emcees for Music Now—the glitter name tags on their mics designating them as Ginger from LilyRed and Jooyoung from Idyllic—stood in the center, facing the cameras.

"Welcome back to Music Now!" Ginger announced.

"It's the moment you've all been waiting for. Let's check the scores for this week," continued Jooyoung.

The numbers flashed on the screen behind the artists, dramatically tallying the points for each voting category. It looked like it was going to be a close call between Cocoa Pop and HI5.

"Cocoa Pop is currently in the lead," remarked Jooyoung.

"Now finally adding the real-time music show voting, the winner of the third week of June is…" Ginger paused as the scores for the two groups broke even…before HI5's continued to rise even higher, reaching a grand total of 10,629 points.

"HI5! Congratulations!" Ginger and Jooyoung announced in unison as a chorus of confetti cannon pops coated everyone with white and blue ribbons.

NEON's cheers rivaled those of the audience when HI5's leader Ray took the mic to say an emotional thank you to his company, staff, fans, and family for the group's success. Jaden stepped forward to accept the Music Now trophy from the emcees.

HI5 had, until recently, been in a bit of a slump, and it had been more than a year since they had won a music show. But with member Sunghwan's role in the new hit drama *Moonlight, Again*, Korea couldn't seem to get enough of HI5. Emery was glad to see them doing well and excited that their promotions overlapped with NEON's. It was always a relief for him to see some friendly faces to lighten the intensity of their crazy schedule.

The winning song "You, Who" began to play, and HI5 took the extra microphones from the emcees for their encore performance. While the rest of the NEON members playfully congratulated their friends in HI5, Emery's eyes scanned over the crowd, hoping to spot A before he had to leave the stage.

Around three hundred fans stood packed into the studio. They carried lightsticks and banners, passionately promoting their favorite idol groups. Emery was happy to see that more than half of the audience held up NEON's bright orange GLOstick. Their custom lightstick was designed by the NEON members themselves to look like a neon sign within a circular dome that lit up with a fluorescent orange letter N. Solar Entertainment had released a new version of the GLOstick at the beginning of the month to mark their three-year anniversary since debut.

As Emery turned to leave the stage, his chest filled with pride and appreciation for his fans, but he couldn't help but also feel a hint of disappointment. As far as he could tell, there had been no sign of Her in the audience.

# Alana

## #TimeToGo

Shivers ran down Alana's spine as she saw M's carefree smile on stage. Her brief flash of joy twisted with her fear as it all became too much.

She turned her back on the television monitor, effectively blocking out the image of HI5 Sunghwan's tearful face as he sang the opening verse of "You, Who." The fanchants from the studio echoed down through the ceiling into the artist waiting area below.

It wasn't that she was upset about HI5's win. She just felt overwhelmed by it all. Especially now, after everything. It brought too many of her own raw emotions to the surface. Granted, music always had the power to draw out her feelings, allowing them to spill over into her compositions, but it was so much worse now. It was safer for everyone if those feelings stayed locked up. Preferably behind reinforced titanium steel walls ten miles high.

*With a crocodile infested moat*, she thought. Or alligators, perhaps. She wasn't picky. Needless to say, a life of no music had become her new norm. It was all part of her plan.

"Aly! What are you doing? I am not cleaning this up by myself."

Alana glanced over as Stephanie struggled out of LilyRed's dressing room, barely balancing the stack of outfits she carried in her arms.

"Sorry!" Alana shook herself from her thoughts and hurried over to help her cousin.

Stephanie was five foot, five inches of fierce individuality. With an asymmetrical lavender bob, fuchsia pink gel nails, and a bright floral dress, her cousin stood out among the other agency style coordinators, or *coordis*, most of whom—Alana included—preferred a more practical wardrobe of pants and T-shirt. Alana had no idea how her cousin managed to keep both her own appearance and LilyRed's looking so perfect all the time.

"Hold on. I need to rest." Stephanie unceremoniously dropped the clothes on a folding chair and flopped down in the seat next to it. "Who would have thought nine pairs of miniskirts and crop tops could be so heavy?"

"You literally carried them five steps," Alana pointed out.

"Yes, I did! And all by myself, I might add, because somebody was too busy ogling the hotties on screen to do her job!"

Alana blushed, glancing around to see if anyone had overheard. Luckily, while the room was full of staff members, everyone else was too busy with their own cleanup to notice her cousin's antics. Plus, it was unlikely they would have understood, since Alana and Stephanie spoke primarily in English to each other. Alana always appreciated the reprieve from conversing in Korean, which was still difficult at times. Despite growing up speaking it with her family back home in Chicago, her Korean sounded more like that of a ten-year-old kid than a twenty-year-old adult.

Granted, her cousin's accusation wasn't wrong. For the past ten minutes, she had been staring at the monitor in the dressing room waiting area, watching NEON's performance. It hadn't been a conscious decision on her part. She wasn't supposed to watch the music shows at all. It was her own rule, and she had managed to stick to it so well until just now, which was not an easy feat, considering she was practically living at broadcast stations for LilyRed's promotions.

It was all M's fault. She had been on her way back from packing the makeup bags into the van when she remembered Soyoung's tea. It was Alana's job to take care of Soyoung, the main singer of LilyRed, a job which included always having hot tea ready when she got off stage. Alana had detoured to the water cooler in the narrow corridor near the bathrooms, proud that she had remembered on her own. But just as the cup was full, the tea bag already seeping into the hot water, she had turned around and smacked right into a towering figure. Tea spilled onto her right hand and the man's pristine white leather shoes. The smell of cologne and hairspray surrounded her.

*Idol*, she thought in horror.

Startled, she had stumbled back, her hand burning from the tea and her face flaming with embarrassment. Her whole body tensed as she noticed the idol's very white pants had a nice, lightish brown stain at the bottom from the tea she had spilled. On him. Internally cursing her own carelessness, she glanced up, alarmed as his hand clutched her wrist, freezing when their eyes met.

*M.*

Thoughts flew through her head faster than she could handle. Surely, too much time had passed. There was no way he should recognize her, but as Alana had looked into his greyish-blue eyes, she knew. He remembered.

Mortified, she had run away.

It was only once she was safely back in the waiting room that she had allowed her racing thoughts to take over. What in the world had M been doing on the first floor? NEON was supposed to be upstairs and backstage, preparing for their performance. She had purposely avoided the second floor for that exact reason.

Standing in horrified silence, she had stared unseeingly at the reddening burn mark on her hand. As waves of embarrassment engulfed her, she struggled to ignore the small voice in her head whispering how good it was to see him again. Before she could shove her turbulent thoughts behind the walls in her mind, she heard his voice coming from the TV monitor against the wall. Transfixed, she looked up to see M singing the opening verse to NEON's new song and lost herself to their performance.

*They've come so far.* Her heart clenched.

"Hello? Earth to Alana?" Stephanie laughed, and Alana blinked, coming out of her thoughts. "How was NEON's comeback stage? Do you need me to call an ambulance?"

"Don't be ridiculous. You know I don't follow NEON anymore." Alana scowled, glancing back to the monitor. HI5's song had reached the chorus and the Music Now credits were flashing along the bottom of the screen. Panic seized her as she realized that nearly all the other artists had left the stage. She quickly started gathering up the clothes Stephanie had abandoned as the first few idol groups came out of the elevators, their managers and staff hurrying into the dressing rooms ahead of them.

"Please. Your words say one thing while your actions say another." Stephanie gave Alana a knowing smirk. "You've been their fan since debut."

"Things change," Alana said, struggling to pick up a golden

skirt that had fallen to the floor.

"I'm just saying, that level of devotion doesn't disappear overnight."

"It did for me." Alana sighed, forcing a smile to her face. "I've been NEON-free for almost a year now."

Stephanie bit her lip, tucking a strand of purple hair behind her ear as she watched a red beaded shirt tumble from the pile in Alana's arms. Smirking, Stephanie raised one perfectly shaped eyebrow at Alana's flustered motions.

"So you're telling me the fact that NEON's on their way to this room right now is having no effect on you?"

Before Alana could respond, she glanced over in alarm at the sound of the elevator dinging as it returned to the first floor. The waiting room grew louder and more hectic as another round of idols filed through. Alana hurriedly picked up the fallen clothes.

"Are you just going to sit there, or will you help me?" Alana gave Stephanie a pointed look as another skirt slipped from her grasp and fell to the floor.

"Sure, sure, avoid my question," Stephanie said, ignoring the skirt and picking a piece of nonexistent lint off her own dress. "Personally, I think a bit of fangirling would do you some good."

Another *ding* cut their conversation short as LilyRed exited the elevator in a flash of identical red dresses, followed by their head manager Hyungkoo and a parade of staff members.

LilyRed, known for their strong live vocals and playful choreography, was a popular girl group under Red Diamond Entertainment, or RDE. With nine members—after two weeks, Alana finally had their names straight—they had made a powerful impact in Korea with their debut single two years prior, and their quirky dance moves shot them straight to K-pop viral stardom. So far, LilyRed had managed to stay trendy with a perpetual stream of comebacks, around one every three months.

"Eat dinner *quickly*, girls," Hyungkoo barked. "If we are going to make the Chicken Box photoshoot on time, everyone needs to be in the van in fifteen minutes! That means you have until 8:20 p.m." Well-dressed in black pants, blue blazer, and a gold watch, Hyungkoo was—jokingly—considered by *netizens* as better suited for the stage than management.

Hyungkoo spotted Alana and Stephanie in the waiting area as he looked up from his phone. "Stephanie, make sure the girls don't fool around. We don't have time for delays."

"Yes, *Manager-nim*," Stephanie said, stepping forward to help guide LilyRed toward their dressing room. Hyungkoo sighed and rubbed his eyes before fixing his gaze on Alana.

"Is everything in the van?"

"Almost, *Manager-nim*," Alana said. "I just need to take these outfits out and the rest of the girls' things once they finish eating." She threw a nervous glance down the hallway, and her stomach flipped when the elevator dinged again.

"Okay, but hurry," Hyungkoo said, his focus already back to his phone.

Alana didn't need to be told twice. Keeping her head down, she walked as quickly as possible to the exit, dodging a flurry of idols and staff members. It wasn't until she was safely outside in the warm evening air that she dared let out a sigh of relief. In the parking lot, she wove through the sea of black and white company vans, located the two RDE vans, and deposited LilyRed's clothes in the back of the larger vehicle.

Taking out her phone to check the time—8:09 p.m.—she looked back to the broadcast station. Fans were already lining up to catch a glimpse of the artists as they left the building, and she spotted the GLO fandom standing in a group near the parking lot entrance, holding official GLOsticks, fan member signs, and personal electric fans.

Alana winced in sympathy as she watched a GLO hold a water bottle to her forehead. It was hot. The heat in Seoul this summer had been particularly relentless. She had only been outside for five minutes and her black shirt was already wet with sweat on her back. A GLO glanced up from her phone, and Alana reflexively stepped back behind the van.

No matter how many times she told herself otherwise, Alana felt like an imposter. Perhaps it was because Stephanie had gotten her the job after worrying that Alana only rarely left the apartment during her first month in Seoul. Working in the Korean entertainment industry as a style coordinator certainly wasn't the smartest decision Alana had ever made. In fact, it was quite illogical, but at least it fit well into her plan. She would go outside. She would work. She would survive. Nothing else mattered.

As Alana headed back into the broadcast station, she felt a peculiar sadness wash over her. Glancing back at the group of GLO one last time, she stepped into the cool air-conditioned building.

*I don't miss it.*

Alex had always said she was a terrible liar.

Alana made it back to LilyRed's dressing room just as the girls finished their meals.

"I still can't believe **NEON** *sunbae-nim* made a mistake."

Alana looked up from collecting the girls' empty dinner boxes, taking note of the conversation near her.

"It's trending worldwide already," Ginger remarked, her wide eyes sparkling while her long blonde hair framed her slender face. As proof, she showed the screen to the other members seated on the sofa with her.

"#MSlipUp," Soyoung read aloud, her strawberry-colored hair bouncing as she nodded. "Cute."

"Someone even managed to get a *fancam*!" When Ginger held her phone out again, Alana caught a glimpse of the video in question. It was obviously taken by a fan, shakily shot between the raised arms and lightsticks of the crowd. Everything was going fine in the performance—*perfect, actually*—until M slipped. Very noticeably. She watched in horror as M collided into Jaehyun, both catching themselves just in time to continue the next steps in the choreography.

Alana looked away from the video only to spot Stephanie watching her closely. Ignoring the smug expression on her cousin's face, Alana moved to throw the remaining dinner boxes in the trash can.

"M *sunbae-nim* is lucky the performance was pre-recorded," Soyoung commented. "It's bad enough to mess up in front of fans, but at least the mistake wasn't shown on the TV broadcast."

"Okay, LilyRed," Stephanie announced to the group, interrupting the chatter. "It's time to leave. Make sure you have everything."

The girls called out in agreement, packing up their personal bags and collecting the scattered belongings from around the room. In the midst of it all, Soyoung approached Alana and gently tapped her on the shoulder.

"*Unnie*, do you have my tea?" the red-headed idol asked politely.

Alana froze in dawning alarm. She had completely forgotten to go back for another cup after spilling the first one in her encounter with M.

"I'm so sorry, Soyoung. I'll go get it now." Alana backed away, just as Manager Hyungkoo walked in.

"Everyone ready to go? Wait, where are *you* going?" Hyungkoo said, frowning down at Alana as she tried to hurry past him.

"I forgot to get Soyoung's tea. I'll just go really quickly…" Alana's voice trailed off as her manager's eyebrows drew together in anger.

"Really, Alana? Are you stupid? How many times is it now that you've forgotten the tea?" Hyungkoo demanded, his voice echoing in the sudden hush of the room.

"I'm sorry, *Manager-nim*. I'll get it right now. It won't even take a minute." Alana kept her face down, letting her long dark hair hide her frustration. She hadn't forgotten this time. Not completely. She had just gotten…distracted.

"I told you, we don't have time for mistakes tonight! Are you deaf now, too?"

"It's okay, *Manager-nim*," Soyoung said. "It's too hot outside to drink tea anyway."

"Hmph." Hyungkoo looked at Alana for a moment more before turning his back on her. He left the dressing room, holding the door open for the LilyRed members to follow behind him. Stephanie and the other stylists walked over with the last few bags, handing two to Alana.

"Don't take it personally," her cousin murmured. "He's really stressed this comeback. The upper management hasn't been happy with the digital sales this time around." Stephanie paused, evaluating Alana's expression. "You okay?"

"I'm fine," Alana said, staring down at her cousin's bright pink nails. Stephanie gave her a disbelieving look, shook her head, and left.

Alana quietly followed the others to the exit. LilyRed exchanged a few friendly greetings with some of the Cocoa Pop members in the hallway as they made their way through the small groups of chatting artists and staff. They were almost to the exit doors when a shout came from the waiting room.

"LilyRed! Wait!"

A Music Now staff member was running toward them,

and Alana paled when she saw what he was carrying.

"I'm sorry," the man said to Hyungkoo as he caught up with them. "I saw you were leaving and thought you might need this."

He handed a gold leather skirt to Hyungkoo.

"Thank you," Hyungkoo said quietly, scrutinizing the fabric in his hands.

"It's nothing," the staffer carried on casually. "I recognized it from LilyRed's pre-recording this morning."

Hyungkoo waited until the staff had walked away before turning toward the group of *coordis* behind him. "Would any of you care to explain?"

Swallowing nervously, Alana spoke up. "It's my fault, sir. I must have dropped it by mistake."

Hyungkoo's eyes flashed. "Are you *purposely* messing up every task given to you?" he asked tightly. "Or are you really just that incompetent?"

"I..." Her hands tightened into fists around the handles of the bags.

"I honestly don't understand how you could be so bad at your job!" Hyungkoo said, his voice loud and his face red. "Is it too complicated? Is that it? Do I need to simplify things even more for you? You forget every task I assign you. Please explain to me how you are contributing anything to this company?"

"It was a mistake. I'm so sorry, sir," Alana explained softly. The faces around her blurred as she stared down at the burn mark on her hand.

"Oh, so that makes it okay, then? Do you know how much your goddamned mistakes are costing this company?"

Idols and staff crowded the hallway, pausing curiously at the scene. Alana kept her head down, willing herself not to cry.

"Give me one good reason why I shouldn't fire you right

now," Hyungkoo demanded.

"I…" Alana had no idea what to say. Maybe she should be fired. More people were gathering now, their voices echoing in the small hallway, and Alana felt the walls closing in.

"What's going on?"

Alana's heart flipped at the softly spoken question—she would know that voice anywhere.

She looked up to see the hallway packed with people. They stood along the walls on either side, watching, while Stephanie and the LilyRed members gazed at the floor uncomfortably. Halfway down the hall, she spotted him—not only M, but all the members of NEON—standing in front of an open dressing room door and watching the scene she had caused.

Hyungkoo must have noticed the growing audience, too, and his angry expression closed off.

"We'll discuss this later." He let out a long breath. "LilyRed, let's go."

Without another word, Hyungkoo walked out the exit, and the rest of the staff quietly motioned for LilyRed to follow. Stephanie gave Alana an apologetic look as she passed by.

Alana remained a moment longer, her heart pounding as her eyes naturally gravitated back to M, his slender form standing tall and confident in the crowd. She had almost forgotten how truly beautiful he was. His chocolate brown hair was styled back, accentuating his forehead and sharp jawline. She wanted to curse whoever had done his makeup, since it only made his features all the more striking. Shadowed by dark eyeliner, M's eyes stared into her own, searching for answers she wasn't ready to give. Remembering that night, her gaze dropped to his lips, warm and enticing in a natural shade of pink. Even frowning, he took her breath away.

For a fleeting moment, it was as if the past two years had never happened. Seeing him, she felt a flicker of hope in her chest before reality came crashing back. She didn't deserve this. She didn't deserve **M**.

Looking back to the floor, she felt her hair slip forward, creating a curtain of black that hid the scar on her right temple. Shadows swirled in her mind, and she let them push back the memories of that summer, obscuring everything again in a blanket of numbing darkness.

Hyungkoo was right about one thing. There was no time for this.

She turned her back on the sea of faces and walked out the door. It was time to go.

# Emery

## #MSlipUp

"Rock, Paper, Scissors!"

A chorus of cheers and groans filled the van as Emery, Stu, and Yongnam won, covering up Jaehyun and Sungil's Rocks with Paper.

"Now it's a face-off between Jaehyun and Sungil," Stu said in a dramatic voice, stepping in as commentator. "This is an important battle. Practically life or death! Who is going to have to record the extra special morning wake-up call for our beautiful GLO?"

Emery had mentioned the idea as a joke, but he should have known better. One of the key lines of the chorus for "Enlighten" included the English phrase "wake up." He'd off-handedly suggested that someone could record an alarm for fans with the song. Stu, of course, had run with it, announcing the challenge to the thousands of fans watching on their Me-Live broadcast before anyone could stop him.

However, Stu had put a spin on it—now the loser had to sing the lyrics using a cutesy *aegyo* voice. Emery was relieved that his Rock-Paper-Scissors win meant it wouldn't be him. He wasn't sure he had the energy to muster any *aegyo* tonight.

Jaehyun turned to Sungil, who was sitting in the very back row of the van with Emery, and Yongnam shifted the selfie stick so the viewers could see the two members more clearly.

"Okay, let's do this!" rallied Stu from his bucket seat next to Jaehyun. "Loser has to record the morning call. Ready?"

"Rock, Paper, Scissors!"

Sungil let out a whoop of victory when his Scissors cut Jaehyun's Paper.

"Ca-cawww!" Emery, Stu, and Yongnam cried out in unison, causing everyone in the van to laugh. Thanks to the *maknae's* unique stage name Eagle, Stu had started the habit of cawing like a bird each time Sungil did anything noteworthy. The other members and GLO had quickly caught on, and it had grown into a full-blown meme with the fandom.

"Take out your phone, *Hyung*!" Stu said to Jaehyun as he turned toward the camera, his eyes glinting mischievously through his green contact lenses. "Don't worry, GLO. I'll make sure he posts it on the *fancafe* later tonight so you can download it!"

Stu's commentary was interrupted by Jaehyun's abnormally high-pitched voice tearing through the van as he sang into the recorder on his phone. "*Wake upppppppppp! I need to wake up! Enlighten me so I can wake uppp!* Love you, my lovely GLO. Good morning!" The eldest member finished by turning to the camera, closing his eyes, and holding out finger hearts next to his face.

"Awww," the other members chorused while Sungil shuddered in mock horror and Yongnam hid a smile behind his hand, his eyes curving into crescent moon shapes.

"Our little Jaehyunie, so cute!" said Stu in an exaggerated baby voice, pinching Jaehyun's cheeks.

"Yah! Respect your elders!" Jaehyun cried, and pretended to punch Stu, who flew back into his seat and dramatically clutched his heart in response.

While Stu was busy flailing, Sungil sneakily reached out from the seat behind the red-headed member and pinched his cheeks—hard. There was a moment of shocked silence where Stu looked back at Sungil with wide eyes before he burst out laughing, grabbing the selfie stick out of Yongnam's hand to give the viewers a close up of his own face.

"See, GLO? You think Sungil is innocent? Wrong!" Stu pointed an accusatory finger—adorned with a silver skull ring—at the *maknae*.

"What? I'm an angel!" said the youngest, looking straight into the camera as he wrapped Stu in a big hug from behind and leaned his cheek against him.

Emery grinned along with the rest of the members. Reaching over, Jaehyun managed to gain control of the phone, and started to read some of the live comments on the screen aloud.

"'Jaehyun oppa, you're so handsome'—oh, thank you very much—'Please say hi to Brazil'—hello, Brazil—"

"Hi, Brazil!" Sungil echoed in English, waving his hand enthusiastically in front of the camera.

Jaehyun pushed the *maknae's* hand away and resumed reading. "'When are you coming to Paris?'—soon, hopefully—"

"I want to go shopping in Paris," Stu interrupted. "There's this new pair of shoes—"

"You don't need any more shoes," Emery groaned.

"You can *never* have too many shoes," Stu retorted.

"—'NEON *te amo*!'—so many international fans watching today!" Jaehyun continued. "Thank you, *te amo*, we love you GLO—'Is M okay?'—yes, he's fine! I'm seeing a lot of comments asking about M. Don't worry, GLO! We're fine. We'll work hard to make sure the mistakes don't happen again."

Emery let out a quiet sigh, doing his best to keep his smile firmly in place. Over Jaehyun's shoulder, he could see the onslaught of comments telling him "it's okay!" in more languages than he could ever understand.

"'Where's Yongnam?'—he's right here!" Jaehyun turned the camera to show their leader sitting in the front row, and Yongnam reached over to reclaim the selfie stick, positioning the camera to make sure everyone was in the shot again.

"Hello GLO!" Yongnam waved, and at a gesture from Minhyuk, rushed to add, "I'm sorry to say, but we have to go now. Thank you for watching our MeLive! Be sure to tune in tomorrow for our performance on Pop Wave, and we'll meet again on MeLive after the show!"

"Good night GLO!" Jaehyun cried out.

"Thank you for supporting our new album *Awaken*!" Emery called.

"See you tomorrow!" said Sungil.

NEON said goodbye, throwing a mixture of enthusiastic hearts, kisses, and waves before Yongnam pushed the button to end the live video and everyone slumped back in their seats. After all the boisterous talking and laughter, the van felt eerily silent. That was until Jaehyun spoke up, anyway.

"I'm so hungry…" he groaned. "This diet will be the death of me."

As if on cue, Emery's stomach rumbled. He'd barely eaten all day—two apples, a chicken breast, and some almonds. While Solar Entertainment didn't strictly enforce a diet plan for NEON, he wanted to look his best for the comeback promotions, and so he'd cut away any unnecessary calories from his meals.

"Fried chicken," Stu said dreamily. "We're coming for you. Wait for us!"

"Ramen," Sungil countered, his light brown hair hanging messily over his forehead as he looked down at his phone.

Food was a huge motivator for NEON. They would fixate

and plan out their celebratory end-of-promotions meal weeks in advance. Knowing there was an end in sight really helped them endure the strictures of dieting and healthy food.

Emery closed his eyes and forced the image of a big juicy burger out of his mind. He sank further into his seat and let his exhaustion envelop him, wanting nothing more than to sleep for twelve hours straight. Hell, he'd take even six hours of blissfully uninterrupted sleep, but that wasn't likely to happen until after their promotions ended three weeks from now.

He cracked an eye open to check the time on his phone—9:16 p.m. By the time they got home, it'd be close to 10:00 p.m., so even if he managed to jump in the shower first, his head wouldn't hit the pillow until at least 11:00 p.m.

*Not terrible*, he thought. But with tomorrow's 3:00 a.m. wake-up call, he was only looking at four hours of sleep at the very most.

"Soyoung looked hot today," Stu blurted out, breaking the silence in the van.

Emery snorted. Soyoung, from the girl group LilyRed, was Stu's latest crush. Stu couldn't stop talking about her long strawberry red hair and how it almost matched his own. Then again, Stu pretty much changed his love interest on a weekly basis. Emery doubted this one would stick.

"Ginger is more my style," said Sungil, tapping his fingers against the armrest with one hand while scrolling through his phone with the other.

"Bro, Ginger's like five years older than you. There's no way she'd be into a high schooler," Jaehyun pointed out.

"A *world-famous* high schooler," Sungil corrected with a grin. Everyone groaned.

"I wonder what that commotion surrounding LilyRed's staff was about earlier," Yongnam said with a frown, the light of a passing car glinting off his silver hoop earrings.

"Same," said Emery, speaking up for the first time since the MeLive ended. The situation with LilyRed's manager hadn't looked good—with Her somehow at the center of it all. By the time he and the others had stepped out of their dressing room to see what all the yelling was about, she already seemed on the verge of tears. In fact, Emery thought she was crying, until she looked up and met his gaze. There hadn't been a single teardrop on her small, pale face, but the look in her eyes had been even more pitiful.

*Broken.*

Emery's own heart hurt just remembering it. The scene had felt all too familiar to him. He knew what it was like to feel inferior—to be told that he'd never be good enough. It had taken everything he had not to dive through the crowd to protect her and take her somewhere safe, comforting her like she had once done for him. The strength of the fleeting impulse had surprised him.

"That whole thing was weird," Sungil said.

"Somebody was in trouble," Stu said in a singsong voice.

"My money's on the tiny, sad girl," Jaehyun said.

"Obviously. But as long as my sexy Soyoung is okay, nothing else matters," Stu declared.

No one bothered to argue with him, and silence returned as the members focused their attention back to their own thoughts and phone screens.

"Hey, our music video already has eight million views!" Sungil exclaimed. He'd given up tapping the armrest in favor of shaking his leg.

"Yeah, the view count was frozen for a while, but it finally started updating again an hour ago," Jaehyun said.

"How do you know that, *Hyung?*"

"It was in the comments."

Out of all the members, Jaehyun was the most obsessed

with social media. Sometimes it was a good thing, since he kept NEON updated on what their fans were discussing, but at the same time, Emery worried the comments affected Jaehyun too much, especially the hate comments. *Netizens* could be brutal.

"We are trending number one, two, and three worldwide still," Jaehyun added. "#AwakenNow and #NEONForever-NotAlone are number one and two."

Emery internally groaned. He knew what was trending number three—#MSlipUp.

"I'm sorry, guys. For messing up during 'Enlighten.'" Emery's voice was tight with guilt. He figured now was as good a time as any to bring it up. It worried him that they hadn't discussed it yet outside of reassuring the fans on MeLive.

"*Hyung* could have really been hurt," Emery continued, referring to Jaehyun. "I shouldn't have messed up like that when we've been practicing so much. I just wanted to say I'm sorry and I won't let NEON down again."

Emery could feel the others' eyes on him in the silence that followed, but he kept his gaze focused on Yongnam, who had turned in his seat to face him.

"Are you okay?" asked Yongnam.

"Yeah. It was completely my fault. I got distracted."

"Don't beat yourself up," said Jaehyun, giving Emery a reassuring smile over his shoulder. "My beautiful face is fine— that's all that matters."

"Yeah, it's like we said to GLO on MeLive, we're all okay," Stu said. "Besides, you never mess up. It was bound to happen at least once. Now you know how the rest of us feel."

"Just don't go making a habit of it like our dear Australian here," Jaehyun added.

"Hey! Both times this year was because it was raining. You know I don't do well with outdoor concerts," Stu defended hotly.

"And remember that time my shirt ripped right down the center?" said Sungil.

"Come on, we know that was intentional." Stu smacked Sungil's jiggling leg.

"It wasn't, I swear!"

"Regardless, M," said Yongnam, cutting into the debate. "Mistakes happen. All we can do is practice harder."

Emery sighed. There was little point in arguing with his bandmates. Even if they didn't want to blame him, he knew he deserved it.

"Guys, get some rest," Minhyuk called from the driver's seat. His gaze met Emery's briefly in the rearview mirror. "We'll be home in thirty minutes. Take a nap while you can."

Yongnam faced front again, and Emery let his eyes fall shut. His last conscious thoughts were of Her. He couldn't believe she was back. Haunted and broken, but still. She was back.

Once the van pulled up to the entrance of their building, Emery sleepily followed his fellow members as they got out.

NEON lived in a luxury apartment complex that opened a year ago—a gated community, with the highest level of security. Many celebrities and even some other idol groups had moved in as well.

This was NEON's third dorm and their nicest place by far, with wood floors, marble countertops, floor-to-ceiling windows, and a whole room dedicated to their clothes and gifts from fans. Emery still had moments where he doubted the place was truly theirs, as if one day the security guard would fail to recognize them, and he'd wake up back in their cramped pre-debut dorm as a trainee again.

Emery smiled fondly as he thought of the shoebox they

used to live in—the bunk beds in their one bedroom, the single shared bathroom, the clothes line strung from the shoe closet to the fridge with their dance practice clothes drying on every available surface. It had barely fit all five members plus their manager—not that it really needed to, since they hadn't spent much time at home. Back then, they had basically lived at Solar's headquarters, practicing all day, every day, to prepare for their debut.

"Make sure you all get some sleep," Minhyuk called through the lowered passenger seat window, his short black hair sticking up at odd angles and his genial face lined with exhaustion.

"Will do, *Hyung*." Yongnam gave a salute, smirking tiredly at their manager.

"I'll be back at 3:00 a.m. Be ready to get in the van no later than 3:30 a.m."

Sungil, Jaehyun, and Stu gave sleepy waves from the curb, and they all headed into the empty lobby. Behind the main desk, a security guard sat watching a rerun episode of the drama *Moonlight, Again*. He looked up, and everyone nodded in greeting, mumbling a chorus of hellos as they made a beeline for the elevator.

Emery kicked off his shoes at the door as soon as he entered the apartment and collapsed down on the leather couch. The housekeeper had been there earlier, leaving behind a spotless interior.

"I call first shower!" Stu yelled, heading down the hallway, his shirt already off and thrown unceremoniously to the floor.

"Fine! But I'm next," said Jaehyun on his way to the bedroom that he shared with Sungil.

"Third!" the *maknae* called distractedly from the kitchen, where he was systematically opening all the cabinet doors and drawers.

Yongnam flopped down on the couch next to Emery. "M, you can go after Sungil." Yongnam almost always went last. He seemed to prefer it that way, taking his role as NEON's leader seriously, but Emery still made a point to check on him every once in a while. Being the same age, it was easier for them to connect, and Emery never wanted Yongnam to feel alone.

"Thanks."

They both sat in silence, watching Sungil comb through the kitchen. After he finished opening all the cabinets, drawers, and refrigerator doors, Sungil stood back to stare at his options, muttering to himself.

"You sure you're doing okay, M? You seemed a little off today, even before we went on stage," said Yongnam, his eyebrows pulling together as Sungil reached for a can of tuna, a packet of ramen, and jars of *kimchi, gochujang*, and mayonnaise. Carrying his selections to the table, the youngest member began to break the uncooked ramen into large chunks, mixing it in a bowl with the seasoning packet.

"Yeah, I'm all right. Just tired, I guess." Emery ran a hand through his hair, loosening up the stiff hairspray until his fringe fell haphazardly onto his forehead.

"If you want to sleep now, I can wake you when it's your turn to shower."

In the kitchen, Sungil added his chosen ingredients into the bowl of crunchy ramen, stirring it into a reddish-orange lumpy concoction. After pausing to gravely consider his meal, he spun around and grabbed the packet of dried seaweed sitting on the counter, which he opened and then used to scoop up some of the mixture into his mouth. His eyes closed as he chewed, a joyful look on his face.

Emery and Yongnam looked at each other in amusement before Emery responded.

"That's okay. I'll just chill here for a bit."

There was another brief moment of silence, punctuated only by the sounds of Sungil's crunching ramen and the shower running in the distance.

"I'm here if you need anything, okay?" Yongnam placed a hand on Emery's shoulder before heading toward his own room at the end of the hall.

Emery sighed and stretched out on his back. As long as Jaehyun didn't decide to do his full-body three-hour skincare routine—it had happened before during their last promotions and Yongnam had been *pissed*—Emery had about thirty minutes until he could shower. He took out his phone, unable to stop himself from pulling up HeartU, the global social media app. As expected, #MSlipUp was still trending number three worldwide.

**NEON GLO Brigade:** M's face at the end is me when my math teacher catches me streaming K-pop in class #MSlipUp

*Hearts 844, Replies 12, Shares 288*

**Chloe #AwakenNow:** I bet he feels so bad for messing up... Don't worry M we still love you!!! #MSlipUp

*Hearts 529, Replies 64, Shares 112*

**GLO Forever \*STREAM ENLIGHTEN\*:**
Enlighten MV hit 9 million views!! Only 20 hours left to break the record! Keep streaming GLO, we got this!! @neon_solarofficial #NEON #AwakenNow #NEONForeverNotAlone #ENLIGHTEN20M #MSlipUp

*Hearts 276, Replies 24, Shares 54*

**M's Wifeu:** Here's a link to the fancam. You're welcome GLO #MSlipUp

*Hearts 913, Replies 47, Shares 390*

Emery sighed. Edited gifs and memes from the fan-taken video were all that *netizens* seemed interested in talking about at the moment. At least NEON was getting even more publicity for their comeback.

Flipping onto his stomach, Emery pulled up his note app to review what he had written during the day. To anyone else, it would look like a jumbled mess of words and sentences, but to Emery, this was an essential part of his creative process. All of his best songs had begun here, stemming from the stray thoughts and emotions he jotted down on a whim.

He hadn't been able to add much today, just a couple lines for a new track he was working on with Yongnam. Before he could start, his phone buzzed, and "Mom" appeared on the screen. Letting out a frustrated groan, Emery reluctantly accepted the call.

"Hello?"

"Emery! It's been so long. You never call. Have you eaten?" His mom's bright voice filtered through the phone, speaking in her customary mixture of Korean and accented English.

"Yeah, I'm fine, Mom," Emery responded strictly in English, as was his habit. "Busy, but fine."

"Good, good. I just wanted to check in. Your father and I are headed on vacation tomorrow. Remember your dad's friend David? We're going with him and his wife to their time-share in Hawaii. Oh, I can't wait to finally relax. It's been so stressful here. We're in the middle of remodeling the kitchen. It's been such a mess, but I wish you could see it! I finally found the perfect light fixtures to match the countertops!"

LYN ASHWOOD | RACHEL ROSE

"That's great, Mom."

"Wouldn't it be wonderful if you could come with us to Hawaii? Any chance you can ask for some time off? We haven't seen you in more than a year now."

"Mom, we *just* had our comeback today."

"Oh, really?"

"Yeah, type in 'NEON Enlighten' online and the video should come right up. Do you want me to message you the link?"

"No, no. Don't worry, honey. I'll take a look later."

"Okay, Mom." Emery rolled onto his back, covering his eyes with the crook of his arm. He doubted she would actually get around to watching it.

"Your father's doing well, been golfing quite a bit now that he only works on Monday, Wednesday, and Thursday. Oh, right! He was telling me just yesterday about his golfing buddy's son. Remember Richard Kim? He's going to UCLA. Pre-med."

Emery's grip tightened on the phone before he forced himself to relax.

"Honey, we've been wanting to ask you… Isn't it time you thought about college?"

An exasperated breath slipped past Emery's lips, and his mom rushed to continue.

"You've made your point, and we've let this music phase go on, but you're twenty years old now. When are you going to stop playing around?"

"Mom," Emery cut in sharply, unable to keep his frustration at bay.

"Okay, okay, I know. I won't say anything more. But really, honey, you can't do this forever. Just the other day your father told me about an article he read. Did you know that the average career span of a K-pop idol is a few years, at best? I was so shocked! Your father and I are really worried about you."

Emery almost laughed. Sure, his father was worried—about how much face he was losing among his golf buddies for having an idol for a son, because obviously anyone who wore makeup and danced on stage wasn't a "real" man. It didn't matter that Emery genuinely enjoyed performing, expressing himself through his music and interacting with fans. Emery didn't think that his straight-laced, orthodontist father would ever understand him.

When Emery had first expressed an interest in music as a child, his father had assumed he was going through a phase, turning a blind eye to the voice and dance lessons his mom signed him up for. But as the years went by, his father became more and more forthright in his disapproval, pressuring Emery to give up dancing and singing in favor of a more "fitting" activity, one that would make the family proud and contribute to a respectable future. Emery's life became a long series of not-so-subtle criticism and judgement at every turn.

The situation escalated sharply when Emery was selected to become a trainee at Solar Entertainment. After his friends introduced him to K-pop, he had auditioned—with his mom's reluctant permission—for several Korean companies visiting Los Angeles, never thinking that he'd actually make it through the competitive process. Emery still cringed remembering the day he told his parents he was dropping out of school and moving to Seoul. For hours, his father yelled, drilling into Emery's head how much of a disappointment he was to their family. His mom had kept quiet, never once coming to his defense, just like she always did.

In the end, Emery had left home carrying the weight of his father's heavy disapproval with him. So when NEON struggled during their first year after debut, facing the realization they truly were nobody after having such high hopes, his father's last ultimatum came—the family or his dreams.

Emery chose family.

Emery chose *wrong*.

But then again, was there ever truly a *right* choice?

After he had called home to admit defeat, to tell his father that he would be leaving Korea, leaving NEON, leaving music behind, he thought he could finally become the son his parents always wanted. His father had other ideas. Emery would never forget the words his father flung at him that night, each insult ringing in his head until he could no longer hear his own thoughts, his own voice. He was a failure for not finishing school. He was a failure for not having a real job. And, of course, he was the biggest failure of all for disobeying his parents, for being so selfish as to leave in the first place. He should have known. He should have expected his father's reaction. He knew he would never be good enough.

He hadn't spoken with his father since.

Sighing, Emery tiredly rubbed his eyes. "Okay, Mom, I really need to get some sleep. Have a good trip."

"Oh, right. Of course." She paused. "I'll call again once we're back home in a week."

"Night." Emery hastily hung up the phone, resisting the urge to throw it across the room. No, the phone itself wasn't the problem.

In the background, Emery heard Stu exiting the bathroom and Jaehyun quickly taking his place. Yongnam's shout of "keep it short" made a smile tug at the corners of Emery's mouth. His group members didn't know about any of this, not about his family and not about his near withdrawal from NEON. President Jo kept it hushed up; only the top management of the company knew. And now that it was behind them, he was too ashamed to own up to his moment of weakness.

Besides, things were better now.

Letting out another long sigh, he forced himself from the couch and headed to his room, patting Sungil's head as he passed the kitchen table.

In the bedroom, Stu was standing in boxers in front of their floor length mirror, using a hand towel to dry out his red hair. He gave a small nod to Emery before sitting down on the floor to apply his nightly skincare products.

While Stu and Emery both had the same set of dark wood furniture, complete with a double bed, dresser, bookshelf, and desk, that was where the similarities ended. Where Emery appreciated tidiness and order, Stu valued his own "free spirit." The Australian's side was technically *clean*, but Emery wasn't quite sure how he managed to find anything in all the accumulated clutter and precariously stacked piles. The only organized part was Stu's prized sneaker collection, which took up almost an entire wall. Stu called his love for shoes his passion, but Emery thought it was bordering on obsession. Then again, his own collection of Punk the Pomeranian—or Pom— figurines was growing a bit out of control. But at least the fluffy brown dogs wearing studded leather were spread out between his bedroom and his studio at the company.

Emery placed his phone next to the keyboard on his desk and rummaged for some clean sweatpants to wear to bed. After changing, he joined Stu on the floor with his laptop, hoping to distract himself enough so he didn't pass out in exhaustion before showering.

He winced as his leg slid against the hardwood floor. Looking down at his left ankle, he noticed the burn mark from earlier. It now only ached a bit—he wouldn't call it pain—but seeing it instantly brought Her to the forefront of his mind. Before he could resist, Emery found himself searching through Red Diamond Entertainment fan pages, hoping to gain more insight into LilyRed's staff. A few minutes later, he sat back in annoyance. He couldn't find any mention of her among the managers or *coordis*, but he was certainly learning a lot about the LilyRed members, including their hobbies, hometowns, and blood types. The girls even had their own representative animals—Ginger's was apparently a firefly. Emery shook his head. What did that even mean? Further down, he read that Soyoung's ideal type was "a serious, mature man, someone like my father," and Emery held back a laugh. Poor Stu.

"Mate, are you looking at *my* Soyoung?!"

Emery quickly shut his laptop, scrambling to hide the screen from view.

"You were! I can recognize that gorgeous strawberry hair from a million miles away."

Emery held up his hands. "Whoa, Stu. I'm innocent, I swear. I'm not interested in Soyoung."

"You better not be." Stu scrunched up his face, directing a playful glare at Emery through the thin, round frames of the glasses he wore before bed.

Emery laughed and threw his pillow right at Stu's face. "Your woman is safe."

The door flew open, and Jaehyun poked his head in, his blonde hair still dripping onto the towel wrapped around his waist. "M, you're up next after Sungil."

"*Hyung*," Stu cried. "I just caught M looking at Soyoung's photos!"

"What? No way! Is our little Emmie finally interested in someone?" Jaehyun asked, grinning excitedly as he stepped half-naked into the room.

"I wasn't looking at Soyoung's photos," Emery muttered. "But did you guys know that LilyRed's Ginger was almost an Olympic figure skater? That's pretty cool."

Jaehyun and Stu shared a wide smile.

"Ohhh, so you like Ginger then?" Stu said.

"She's a figure skater, huh? Bet she's flexible." Jaehyun raised his eyebrows.

Emery looked around for another pillow to throw. "Get out!"

"It's my room, too!" said Stu.

Ignoring his bandmates, Emery reopened his computer. There wasn't anything online about A, but then again, the Pop Wave music show was tomorrow, and LilyRed would definitely be there promoting—he had already checked the lineup.

So much had changed since the last time Emery had spoken to Her. Had it already been two years? NEON was now on another level, and yet, he had never thanked her for how much she had influenced the whole group's future, particularly his own. Fate had allowed their paths to collide again—he couldn't let her slip away a second time.

# Alana

## #ImFine

"Chocolate or red bean?"

"Hmmm?" Alana looked up from her bowl of ramen. It was still too hot to eat properly, but that didn't stop her from checking under the flimsy paper covering every five seconds. She was starving, having missed dinner because of LilyRed's tight schedule—the Chicken Box photoshoot hadn't ended until midnight.

"Why am I even asking? This is *you* we're talking about. Chocolate it is." Stephanie pulled two chocolate ice cream bars out of the giant freezer and took them to the counter so the clerk could ring them up. They had stopped for a quick meal at the 24-hour convenience store down the street from Aunt Park's apartment.

Thankfully, the rest of Alana's workday had been uneventful after the Music Now disaster. While Hyungkoo had spent the rest of the evening pretending she didn't exist, there had been plenty for her to do on set, and when she wasn't making mistakes and being yelled at, her job wasn't all that bad. She just had to focus harder.

"Is the ramen cooked yet?" asked Stephanie as she joined

Alana at the square table near the window.

"Almost." She peeked under the lid again.

"Oh, what happened to your hand?"

Alana frowned down at the red mark just above her wrist. "I may have spilled tea on it."

"Of course you did. Here." Stephanie handed Alana one of the ice cream bars, before opening up the other and immediately taking a large bite. "Man that's good." She relaxed back into her chair.

Smiling at her cousin, Alana opened her own ice cream. One of the best things about her impromptu move to Seoul was her growing relationship with her mother's family. Before, Alana's contact with her Korean relatives had been minimal, having met them only a handful of times. She had been worried things would be awkward between her and Stephanie, who was three years older and had just finished university in London. However, it helped that Stephanie had attended international schools in Korea, and clicked well with Alana, both culturally and linguistically. Over the past few weeks, the two had grown close working together at RDE. Stephanie's headstrong personality had a way of making Alana feel more secure.

"Don't judge me," her cousin continued, using her ice cream bar to point at Alana before taking another bite. "I haven't had sugar in months."

"I wasn't judging." It was true. Stephanie was always conscious of her diet, usually sticking to the whole grains and vegetables common to Korean home cooking. The fact she was willing to waste a cheat meal on convenience store ramen and ice cream with Alana meant a lot.

"Okay, good. Because extreme times call for extreme pleasures."

"I don't think that's how the saying goes."

"Who cares? My way's more fun." Stephanie winked.

Rolling her eyes, Alana took a bite of her own ice cream, losing herself to the bittersweet taste of chocolate on her tongue.

"There it is," said Stephanie, pulling out her phone to snap a picture of Alana, who completely ignored her cousin to focus entirely on her frozen treat. "Seeing your happy chocolate face was totally worth the calories."

"My what?" Alana looked up.

"Your happy chocolate face. You know, the face you make when you eat chocolate."

"I don't have a happy chocolate face."

"You totally do. Look!" Stephanie showed her the picture on her phone.

Alana frowned. She looked slightly…deranged in the photo. "Everyone looks that way while eating." She hoped, anyway.

"Nope, just you. You look at chocolate like it's your first love."

Alana considered that, then shrugged. "I like chocolate," she said by way of explanation. She swallowed her last bite and looked sadly at the bare ice cream stick.

"Girl, I know." Stephanie laughed. "I'm glad you enjoyed that."

"Thank you, Steph," Alana said. She did feel a little better.

"My pleasure." Stephanie smiled fondly before sadness flickered in her eyes. "He used to love chocolate, too, didn't he?"

And just like that, Alana's good mood vanished. She didn't have to be told who Stephanie was referring to.

"Yes," Alana said tightly, feeling her face shutter. With the first faint touch of panic breaching past her walls, she forced herself to keep breathing.

"I remember seeing pictures of you two with chocolate all over your faces. It must have been for a birthday or something..."

"Halloween." The picture had been a family favorite, her mom sending it out to all the distant family members when Alana was only four and Alex six. It had been on Aunt Park's fridge when Alana visited Seoul two years ago. It wasn't on there now.

Why was Stephanie bringing this up? Hadn't today been hard enough? Glancing away from the look on her cousin's face, Alana stared at the ramen on the table. The noodles should be cooked by now, but she no longer felt hungry. The ice cream sat uncomfortably in her stomach.

"That's right! You were wearing a pink cheerleader costume! And Alex—"

"*Tiki Tiki!*" The ringtone from Stephanie's Tiki Talk messaging app made Alana jump.

"—oh! Sorry, Aly. It's mom. Let me answer this real quick." Stephanie's gel nails clicked against her phone screen as she texted back.

"No worries." With shaking hands, Alana picked up her own phone from the table, opening her email app when she noticed several new messages.

'Summer Special on the New Pinkstone Lip Stain'—*swipe, delete.*

'Half Off the Latest Tiki Talk Emoticons'—*swipe, delete.*

'Regarding Your Leave of Absence'—she paused at the email from her school.

To: alanakim15@soosoo.com
From: registrar@berklee.edu
Subject: Regarding Your Leave of Absence

Dear Ms. Alana Kim,

We have received the extension for your leave of absence through the upcoming fall semester and have updated your student account accordingly.

We would like to remind you that registration for spring courses opens in November if you plan to return to campus this academic year.

We are sorry again for your loss.

Office of the Registrar
Berklee College of Music

With one less thing to worry about, Alana let out a sigh of relief. She hadn't been sure if Berklee would let her take another year off. Seeing the subject of the next email in her inbox, however, Alana felt her lungs constrict with guilt.

To: alanakim15@soosoo.com
From: elizabethkim@soosoo.com
Subject: Miss you

Hi Aly,

That manager of yours yelled at you again at work today? Are you doing okay?? I don't want to pressure you, and I know you said you wanted space, but why aren't you calling home? I miss you. Please just let us know you're doing okay. We love you so much.

Mom

Alana cringed, the tightness in her chest increasing. She knew her parents were worried, which was the main reason she had avoided calling for the past week—the past month, really—doing her best to keep any conversations to a bare minimum when they called her. She felt horrible about it. But how could she possibly convince her parents she was okay if she wasn't sure of it herself?

She had come to Seoul to escape the memories haunting her. Now all she had to do was force herself to get up in the morning and face each day. Force herself to eat and work and *breathe*. Force herself to pretend everything was all right, as if grief weren't ripping her apart from within. Perhaps if she pretended at life long enough, eventually, she would grow strong enough to start living it.

*Wait…* How did her mom know about the incident with Hyungkoo?

"My mom wants to know when we'll be home," Stephanie said.

Alana looked at her cousin, *really* looked at her, and the pressure inside her chest started to morph into something else.

"I'm saying we're on our way now," Stephane continued, finally looking up through the purple strands of her hair. "Why aren't you eating your ramen?"

"You told my parents about what happened with Hyungkoo today." It wasn't a question.

"What? No I didn't."

"You told them." Alana watched her cousin shift in her seat.

"I swear I didn't! My mom…" Stephanie sighed. "She must have told your mom."

"*What* did you tell Aunt Park?"

"Nothing! I just let her know on the way to the photoshoot that we would be late and that you'd had a rough day at work.

Again."

"Why would you say that?"

"She asked about you, and, well, it's true, isn't it? What was I supposed to say?"

"*Stephanie*, you shouldn't have told Aunt Park at all!"

"Why are you making such a big deal about this?"

"You had no right!" The tightness burst from Alana's throat, overwhelming her in a wave of frustration. "Because now my parents know. Because I don't appreciate people talking about me behind my back. Because I came here to escape the feeling of everyone watching me like I'll break."

"Well somebody has to watch you!" Stephanie cried. "You barely sleep, you forget to eat, and you wander around with this lost look in your eyes! I feel like I'm working two jobs, babysitting LilyRed and babysitting *you*. It's no wonder Hyungkoo lost his temper today. Maybe if you didn't worry so much about what people thought, you wouldn't suck so much at your job!"

Shame filled Alana, and she looked down, her long hair falling forward. Stephanie was right. She was stumbling through her life, followed by the dark shadow only she could see.

But she could do better. She *would* do better.

"I'm sorry, Aly. I didn't mean that." Stephanie looked at her, dismayed, her temper immediately cooling. "I'm worried about you. *Everyone* is worried about you. You've changed so much."

Of course she'd changed. Why did everyone expect her to pretend otherwise? Her eyes watered as a feeling of deep exhaustion washed over her.

*Don't cry.*

"I think we need more ice cream," Stephanie said, forcing a smile to her lips.

Alana mustered a weak laugh. "Let's just go."

"Are you sure? You've barely eaten anything." Stephanie looked pointedly at the untouched ramen between them.

"Yeah," said Alana, already standing up to clear off the table.

It was quiet as Alana and Stephanie walked the short block home from the convenience store. Despite it being well past midnight, the air was still hot, and Alana ran her fingers through her long hair, feeling perspiration forming on the back of her neck. She wanted to shower, wash the whole day away, and sleep. Maybe tonight her memories wouldn't haunt her dreams, and she would finally get some real rest.

Alana stood back as Stephanie punched in the door code to her family's apartment, and stepped inside after her cousin, only to find her aunt standing by the entryway shoe closet. Wrapped in a fluffy white robe, Alana's aunt, who she referred to as *imo* in Korean, was a petite Seoulite with pin-straight black hair cut into a stylish bob. Her classy aura was dampened only by the lines of worry around her makeup-free eyes.

"You're finally back," Aunt Park whispered in relief, dropping her arms from where they had been crossed in front of her chest.

"Hi *Eomma*," greeted Stephanie, taking her shoes off before stepping into the hall. "What are you doing up? You should be in bed."

"Speak for yourself." Aunt Park glanced at Alana. "Hi sweetie, how are you doing?"

"Fine, *Imo*. Just need some sleep." Alana gave a tired smile.

"I should imagine so! What is that company doing to you girls? It's horrible. I should never have let you take that job, Stephanie, and I can't believe you dragged Alana along."

"Not this again," sighed Stephanie. "I *want* this job, *Eomma*. I need the experience and connections so I can start my own fashion brand one day."

It was an old argument, one Alana had heard many times before. She automatically tuned them out as she walked down the short hallway into the living room.

"Well, that's great for you, but what about Alana? Why does she need to work herself to death at that awful company?"

*Hi, standing right here*, she thought wryly. Besides, RDE wasn't awful. Not really. Sure, Alana and her cousin were overworked and underpaid, but that was true for pretty much any entry-level job in Korea, and RDE was one of the biggest players in the industry. If Alana didn't want her job, there were thousands lined up behind her, eager to take her place.

"I'm fine," Alana said.

"You're not fine. How could you be fine with that awful manager yelling at you every day?" Aunt Park said.

"I'm *fine*," Alana insisted. Maybe if she said it enough, she'd come to believe it too.

"Well *I* need sleep. Pronto," said Stephanie. "We have to be back at the company for Pop Wave preparations by 9:00 a.m." She turned to Alana. "I'm going to shower, unless you want to go first?"

Alana shook her head and watched as her cousin stumbled sleepily into the hallway bathroom.

"Did you eat, sweetie?" Aunt Park said, turning her attention back to Alana. "Do you want me to heat up some *jjigae* for you? You're still so skinny..."

"Thank you, but I'm fine. Really. You should go to sleep."

"Well, if you're sure..." Aunt Park frowned, and tucked a piece of Alana's hair behind her ear. "Such a beautiful girl. You will tell me if you need anything, won't you?"

"Of course, *Imo*." Alana stepped back, uncomfortable, shaking her hair loose.

"Okay then." Aunt Park turned and padded back to the

bedroom she shared with Alana's Uncle Lim, who was currently away on a business trip in Nanjing.

Uncle Lim worked at Hankang Food, a division of Hankang, Inc., one of the major conglomerates in Korea, where he led the domestic distribution department. Alana's parents, who'd started a small chain of Asian grocery stores in the American Midwest, also worked closely with Hankang products. Food, it would seem, ran in the family. At least, it was supposed to.

Her brother Alex had fought their parents tooth and nail about joining the family business. Alex was the one who had encouraged Alana to follow her own love for music and attend Berklee. He was the one who had inspired her love of music in the first place. Her breath hitched, remembering the late nights they had spent together composing. The way his eyes would light up when he listened to her songs was all the motivation she needed. She had thought he felt the same way about music.

Obviously, she had been wrong.

Alana stepped into the guest room—her room, technically, but it felt more like the room of a stranger than anything else. Leaving the light off, she quietly shut the door. Moonlight from the window revealed bare white walls, a simple twin bed along one side of the room, and a desk, wardrobe, and bookshelf along the other. Alana's eyes passed over the old Korean textbooks on the shelves, left there from her summer in Seoul two years ago, before looking to the empty spot where her NEON albums had once been. She had collected every version of every album, even multiples of their first full-length album *Luminescence*, from back when she had attended their *fansigns*, but the albums were gone now. She had taken them home when she returned to America for her first year at Berklee, and they were now sitting in a pile at the back of her closet in Chicago. Alana couldn't bring herself to throw them away. She would, though. Just not yet.

Since their debut three years ago, NEON's music had been the soundtrack to her life. She had lived and breathed their songs, each one bringing back distinct memories from the time of their release. But she couldn't bear to remember anymore. That was in the past, and all she could do now was focus on the present.

Moving instinctively, Alana plugged her phone into its charger on the desk, the screen lighting up with a new email notification, this time from her dad.

To: alanakim15@soosoo.com
From: benkim67@soosoo.com
Subject: Today

Aly,

I heard from your mother about what happened today. We are worried. Are you sure that's the right place for you to be right now? Alex wouldn't want you to give up everything because of him. We are here for you, and you can always come home if you need to. Call when you get a chance.

Love,
Dad

A small laugh of hysteria bubbled up from the aching tightness in Alana's chest. They didn't understand. She wasn't giving up—not really. She needed to distance herself as far as she could from Alex's memory. How else was she to move on?

Alana curled up in a ball on her bed. Even after all these

months, she couldn't grasp why Alex had decided to quit. His band, his dreams, his life—had all of it meant nothing to him?

She had always thought they were close, even until the end, but it turned out Alex had kept so much from her, burying his pain deep inside. Looking back, she should have dug further, past the perfect brotherly role he always played to the secrets he hid so well. She hadn't known about his band breaking up or his girlfriend cheating on him. She hadn't known that he failed out of college or that their parent's expectations grew too much for him to handle. To her, he had just been Alex—her supportive big brother who helped her with her compositions, ate chocolate bars with her after his late-night gigs, and teased her about her love of K-pop.

It was only after Alex had taken his own life that Alana realized his reality hadn't been so perfect after all.

He had asked her to go with him that night, to what he had known would be his final show, but she had chosen to stay behind, preferring to remain home with her laptop to support NEON's comeback. She should have gone, should have been there for him, but it was too late now.

There was no coming back from death.

Instead, grief took his place in her heart, and she was beginning to forget there was ever a time she laughed so hard her eyes watered or cheered so loud her throat burned. That Alana was gone.

She turned her face into the pillow as tears finally overwhelmed her.

*Now you can cry.*

# Emery

## #YouWho

"Look! It's LilyRed!"

Emery spun around, desperate to see Her, turning so fast his phone slipped out of his hand and flew high over the railing.

"M! Your phone!"

"Wait." Emery looked side to side. "Where's LilyRed?" He didn't see the girl group anywhere.

Stu hit his forehead with the palm of his hand. "Mate, your phone!"

"Huh?" Emery followed Stu's gaze over the railing to where his phone was lying on the lobby floor—four stories below. In a fountain. There was no way it had survived. "Stu, I'm going to kill you!"

"Sorry, M." Stu held his hands up in surrender, grinning sheepishly. "It was a joke. How was I supposed to know you'd freak out and throw your phone to its death?"

"Aghhh," was all Emery could manage before leaving Stu and heading back to NEON's dressing room. He'd have to send Minhyuk to retrieve his destroyed phone later. There were too many fans in the lobby right now.

He clearly needed to be more careful. Stu wasn't the only

member of NEON who had picked up on his strange behavior regarding LilyRed. They had convinced themselves that Emery had fallen for LilyRed's Ginger and were now constantly teasing him about his "crush." He mostly ignored them, but secretly appreciated the excuse to ask about LilyRed's whereabouts.

Thus far, all of Emery's attempts to talk with A had completely and utterly failed. It didn't matter that he had seen LilyRed and their staff almost every day for the past week. Every time he was near her, she wouldn't even look at him, always keeping her head down with her long dark hair hiding her eyes.

At first, Emery had thought he was just unlucky. Last minute schedule changes and extra promotional activities meant he had very little time to spare. Their activities had been tiring, but he was thankful to be performing again at his usual standards. So far, he hadn't made any more careless mistakes on stage, but, try as he might, he couldn't get A out of his head, especially when he kept catching glimpses of her around the different TV stations.

At the recording of Pop Wave last Friday, he had thought his opportunity had come. LilyRed had their pre-recording right before NEON. It should have been perfect. But while he had managed to arrive backstage a good twenty minutes ahead of schedule by forgoing a much-needed nap, there had been no sign of A. He genuinely thought she had been fired—until he saw her abruptly run into the girls' bathroom on his way back to the dressing room. After fifteen minutes of waiting, Emery had gotten pulled away by Yongnam for their next obligation.

It wasn't until the third day of missed encounters that he finally had to admit there was something wrong. Luck had nothing to do with it. She was avoiding him, plain and simple.

The brief sightings continued throughout the week. Emery was exhausted, and it didn't help that at this point, he was pretty much running on Americano fumes. Still, he was also more and more determined to not let A slip past him once again. The more she avoided him, the more he wanted to talk to her. It was ridiculous.

Just yesterday at Show Time, all this evasion nonsense should have ended. His pre-recording had finished early and NEON had a rare two-hour break before the live broadcast started. While the other members napped or played games on their phones, Emery made an excuse about forgetting something in the van and slipped out to search for her. He had spotted LilyRed's purple-haired *coordi* in the hallway, so he figured A had to be somewhere nearby.

When he reached the outdoor parking lot, he froze.

She was standing alone next to a white van parked along the side of the station. He indulged in a moment of triumph before he caught himself with a reminder to approach with great caution. She was looking away from him, busy loading suitcases into the back of the vehicle. No one else was in sight—*perfect.*

"*Hyung!* Wait up!"

Her head instantly snapped up at the sound of Sungil's loud voice. The *maknae* had just left the building and was running to Emery's side.

"Forgot my phone charger," Sungil said as he collided with Emery, throwing an arm around his shoulders.

Before Emery had the chance to respond, she bolted, away from them and toward the parking lot exit, leaving the backdoor of the van wide open. Emery took a step forward, intending to follow her, but stopped when he spotted the sea of fans just beyond the exit gate. She had walked right into the mob, disappearing from his line of sight. There was no way he could go after her now and survive.

"Damnit, Sungil!"

The *maknae*'s eyes widened. "What did I do?"

Emery sighed, shook his head, and put his arm around the youngest member in apology. It wasn't Sungil's fault. "Nothing. Let's get your phone charger."

A day later, Emery's ego was still sore. Not only that, but he was genuinely starting to lose hope. LilyRed would be ending their promotions any day now. His window of opportunity was closing, and he needed to talk to her—to make sure she was all right.

"Good work today, everyone!" Minhyuk said as soon as Emery and Stu reentered the dressing room. They sat down on either side of the sofa, sandwiching Jaehyun in the middle. "Congratulations on your fourth win! I'll have Sohee post your pictures with the trophy in just a bit."

Sohee was the Social Media Manager for NEON. She controlled their main account and made sure the fans were kept up to date on the latest NEON news and activities. Each member also had access to the account, with a few minor restrictions. Jaehyun, for instance, was now limited to posting only one *selca* per day after he spammed the account with more than fifty pictures of himself in a row. Emery smirked just thinking about it.

The Music Kingdom recording had now finished, and the rest of NEON and the staff members were eating a quick dinner before heading to Solar Entertainment. Even though it was Sunday, they had dance practice that evening to work on their choreography for an upcoming festival performance.

"We'll need to leave in fifteen minutes," Minhyuk said, returning to his seat next to Yongnam, who was absentmindedly fiddling with his camera.

Emery scarfed down his chicken breast and steamed

vegetables, leaving the guys to continue their argument over their end-of-promotions meal. Only one week left and they had yet to decide on what to eat.

"Fried chicken! We haven't had it in *months*," said Stu.

"I'm sick of chicken," complained Jaehyun, stabbing his chicken breast with his chopsticks.

"What if we went back to that Japanese place? You know, that one we went to for Sungil's birthday last year? Everyone liked that," offered Yongnam.

"That's boring," said Jaehyun. "We need to actually *celebrate.*"

"Hey! Are you calling my birthday party lame?" said Sungil.

"Yeah, maybe I am." Jaehyun crossed his arms defiantly. "Certainly not the kind of party I would have wanted."

"Ha! You're one to talk," said Stu. "What'd you do this year? Oh right. A MeLive broadcast alone in our dance practice room."

"Not my fault!" said Jaehyun. "We were in the middle of a comeback. If it were up to me, I would have thrown a huge party."

"*But you didn't,*" Stu sang teasingly.

"Good luck getting an invitation to my next party," muttered Jaehyun. He took another stab at his chicken.

"Come on, guys," Emery interrupted. "Why don't we get *samgyeopsal?* That way we get delicious pork belly, all-you-can-eat side dishes, *naengmyeon*, and fried rice at the end!"

"But we always get *samgyeopsal*…" Stu whined.

"And that's a bad thing?" asked Sungil, tapping his chopsticks against the side of his empty dinner box.

"Nah. I suppose I'm always down for some meat," said Stu. "Got to keep my protein intake up for the gym."

"Truth." Jaehyun nodded in approval. Jaehyun and Stu were NEON's resident gym rats. Emery also kept himself fit—it was hard not to, what with all of their dance practices and performances—but he preferred to spend his limited free time in the studio with his music.

"All this talk of food and now I'm hungry again," Sungil said sadly.

"Oh!" said Emery. That reminded him. He grabbed his backpack from under Jaehyun's legs and pulled out the gift he had received at their *fansign* yesterday, a beautiful bright red and orange package of his favorite American snack in all its spicy, cheesy corn puff goodness. Any diehard GLO knew this snack was Emery's favorite, and since they weren't readily available in Korea, he had to rely on fans to supply his addiction.

"M…" said Minhyuk, a warning note in his voice.

"*Hyung*, we'll split the bag," said Emery, flashing a smile. "No big deal."

"Just be sure not to get it on your clothes," said Minhyuk as he turned back to his phone. It was a good thing they were dressed in all black today. Grinning even wider, Emery opened the bag and carefully took a bite, enjoying the taste of the chili pepper powder that coated his tongue.

"We need to tell Ginger about M's addiction. Help a girl out," Stu commented, reaching over to take a handful from the bag in Emery's hand.

"The fastest way to M's heart," agreed Jaehyun, using his chopsticks to grab a piece for himself.

"C'mon, guys. Let's be real. I'm more Ginger's type," said Sungil wryly, eyeing the snack as it made its way around the room.

"You're just jealous," said Stu.

"Hey, don't rain on his parade!" Jaehyun exclaimed. "I kind of want to see M and Sungil battle it out."

"That'd be such an adorable fight," said Yongnam, smirking as he placed his camera carefully back into its case.

59

"Too bad GLO couldn't watch. They'd love that," added Stu.

"You know you're not supposed to be dating, right?" said Minhyuk, playfully stern.

"I'm not dating anybody!" said Emery in exasperation, sliding his hand through his hair. "And I would totally beat Sungil in a fight."

"Sure…" said Stu and Jaehyun in unison.

It was true. Not only the beating the *maknae* part—Emery would totally win—but also the dating part. Emery had never even had a girlfriend before. Sure, he had liked and kissed some girls in Los Angeles before coming to Korea, but it was never anything real. Even now that he was older, Solar had a strict three-year, no-dating policy for all debuted groups. It was literally signed into their contract with the company. While it had just expired for NEON with their third anniversary on June 2, dating was still a largely taboo subject, and it was a huge risk for any celebrity in Korea. It didn't matter who the relationship was with, celebrity or non-celebrity, if Emery were to date anyone, it could ruin his career. Especially since NEON had never had a dating "scandal" before, GLO would feel shocked, perhaps even betrayed. They had dedicated so much love and attention to NEON that the fandom expected the same in return. Dating was more often than not seen as a violation of the bond between fans and idols. Emery couldn't risk breaking it.

"That hits the spot," said Sungil as he emptied the final crumbs from the bag into his mouth.

"*Hyung*, we deserve more rewards," Jaehyun said to their manager. "We got first place today!"

"Which is why I let you eat that silly American snack," said Minhyuk. "And you get more than enough presents from your fans."

Emery smiled, knowing that Solar was running out of space to store all their incoming gifts and letters. That hadn't always been the case. He thought back to NEON's first ever *fansign* after debut. Not even forty fans had shown up. He remembered walking into the auditorium, nervous but excited to meet GLO. He'd never get the image of the numerous empty seats out of his head, each one signaling "FAILURE" before their eyes. It was still painful to think about. But now, thousands competed for the opportunity to attend their *fansigns*. It was a lottery system with only one hundred open spots. The last Emery had heard, fans had to buy at least seventy-five albums for a fighting chance to win a seat.

"Woah! Did you guys see the promo for the *I Can Cook* special?" asked Jaehyun, his eyes lighting up as he scrolled through his phone.

"God, the food looks amazing," said Sungil as he leaned over his shoulder to watch the video. "I want to be on that show just to eat all the delicious things."

"It's more than just the food, Sungil," Jaeyun said, scowling at the *maknae*. "They always have the best guests. Imagine being part of the cast. I could learn so much from experienced actors and comedians…"

"You're doing it again," said Stu. "Why don't you just ask Solar if they can get you a spot on TV already?"

"I have. So far, nothing's worked with our schedule."

"Don't worry, *Hyung*. Something will come up," added Sungil.

Minhyuk looked up to give Emery a pointed look, and the idol glanced away, barely stifling a groan.

Just a few days ago, Emery had been offered a role on the aforementioned *I Can Cook*, but he had instantly turned it down. First of all, he *couldn't* cook. And second, he had no time. When he wasn't on stage, his job was to make music and put NEON first. As their main composer, he needed to focus on their next album. While he knew there was value in gaining publicity for NEON on screen, he also didn't see the point of wasting his time on variety shows. He wanted to be known as a musician, not an entertainer.

Stu or Jaehyun would be much better suited for the role, but the studio insisted. Apparently, they were looking for an "American" and no one else. Emery was still "considering the offer," according to Solar's president, but there was no way he would accept.

"I'm finished eating," Emery said quickly, wanting to leave the conversation behind. "I'll head down to the vans first." He stood up and grabbed his backpack.

"Oooh, are you going to find Ginger?" Stu teased as he took another bite of his chicken. "Tell Soyoung I say hello!"

Emery sighed and turned back to look at their manager. "Oh, by the way, *Hyung*, Stu owes me a new phone. Be sure to get me the newest, most expensive one and charge it to his account."

The Australian immediately stopped smiling.

"And Stu, be sure to let *Hyung* know where he can find my broken phone." Emery flashed a wide grin at Stu's disgruntled face as he exited the room and headed toward the artist lounge in the hopes of finding A.

But she wasn't in the lounge, and she wasn't in LilyRed's crowded dressing room, either—the door had been open when he walked by.

*If I were a* coordi noona, *where would I go?* Emery hummed in thought, heading out toward the parking lot. He pushed the button for the elevator, anxious not to waste any more time, but as the elevator doors opened, he was left momentarily speechless by his stroke of luck.

He had found Her.

She didn't notice him at first, and he couldn't help but observe that she looked frazzled and overworked. Dressed in dark jeans and a simple black T-shirt, she wore her hair down, hanging lank past her shoulders. Dark circles stood out under her eyes. She looked positively dreary, especially in contrast to the bright pink cake she was holding. Obnoxious yellow letters spelled out "Congratulations LilyRed" amidst a wreath of multi-colored heart cake pops. One hundred percent of her attention was on the cake in her arms; she looked terrified of dropping it. She stepped out of the elevator and was now just inches from him.

"Hi…" Emery said hesitantly, keeping his voice low, hoping not to startle her.

Her gaze shot up from the cake, her eyes locking with Emery's and widening in a shocked and almost fearful look that reminded him of an abandoned puppy. He fought back the sudden urge to scoop her up in a hug. Instead, he reached a hand out to steady the cake, which had taken an unsettling dip to the right.

Clearing his throat, he addressed her again in English, "Hey… I'm M."

She continued to stare at him.

"You know, from NEON?"

His last words seemed to bring her back to life, but not in the way he had expected, although he probably should have, given her actions over the past week. The next thing he knew, she turned on her heel and was practically running down the hallway.

"Hey, wait!" Emery cried before chasing after her.

She avoided the main dressing rooms and headed straight for the backstage area of the studio. The bright pink cake helped ensure he never lost sight of her. A few crew members were walking around, giving them strange looks as they passed by, but no one said anything. Emery refused to give up, even as they ventured deeper and deeper backstage, winding through Music Kingdom's set graveyard. Emery spotted a large wooden sign that spelled out NEON propped up in the corner. It had been part of their stage last week.

"Hey!" Emery called again. She finally looked back over her shoulder before turning sharply down a small hallway to her right. By the time he made it to the corridor, he saw her struggling to close a black door behind her. "I just want to talk!"

Without thinking, he grabbed hold of the door and pushed himself into the room with her. Before the cake could come crashing down, he reached out to steady it, gripping the cardboard base with both hands.

"What are you doing?!" she cried in English as the door clicked shut behind them. Frantically, she released her hold on the cake, passing it to Emery, before bolting toward the door. In her haste to wrench it open, she unexpectedly ripped the rusty doorknob off, effectively sealing them both in the room.

Emery couldn't help but smile.

# Alana

## #ConfettiConfessions

Alana stared at the broken doorknob in disbelief. It was metal and surprisingly heavy in her hand. Adrenaline coursed through her veins from the chase through the halls. Her breathing quickened as she helplessly tried to reattach the doorknob, only for it to fall to the ground with a clunk on the linoleum.

"I don't think that's going to work," M said.

Alana tried prying the door open with her fingers, getting more frantic as the door didn't budge. She couldn't breathe. Her heart pounded with her desire to get out, *out, OUT.*

"Here, let me try."

She felt him come closer and immediately spun around to face him.

"Whoa, careful!"

M yanked the cake back, balancing it above and away from her. His triumphant grin faltered when he looked at her face.

"Hey, are you okay?"

She struggled to inhale, her breathing rapid and shallow. "I-I think…I need to sit down."

"Right. Okay." M looked around. As far as Alana could tell, they seemed to be in some sort of storage closet, as there were shelves and boxes along the walls. It was dark, the only light coming from the slight crack under the door.

"Here. Sit here." M set the cake carefully on the floor before arranging a few sturdy boxes against the wall. He looked over to her expectantly.

Alana just stared at him, the reality of the situation hitting her hard. She was trapped in a dark room. With M—NEON's main vocalist *M*—who was making a chair out of storage boxes. For her. This could not be happening. Her legs gave out and she slowly slid to the ground, the strap of her bag falling limply off her shoulder.

"Oh, okay. Or you can sit there…"

She could feel his eyes on her as she held her head between her legs, trying to catch her breath. At the sound of movement coming toward her, she froze.

"Easy. I'm just sitting down over here. Everything's going to be okay—ummm, A? I feel like an idiot. I don't even know what to call you…" his voice trailed off as she focused on taking slow, deep breaths.

"I chased you through the halls," he said after a pause. "Who does that? I'm sorry. That was dumb. I just wanted to speak with you… But why did you run? It's not like I thought you were a crazy fan stalking me or something. Not that I would have thought you were crazy. Now I'm the one who sounds like the crazy stalker. God, I'm sorry," he repeated.

She slowly calmed, breathing and listening to the rhythmic sound of his voice. Her heart skipped when his words began to register. This was M. Apologizing to her when he had nothing to be sorry for.

"Alana," she said shakily, looking up to meet his eyes. He was dressed in all black today—black jeans and a flowy black silk shirt. It made him difficult to spot in the dark, but she could tell he was sitting on the ground, leaning against the box across from her.

"What?"

"My name. It's Alana," she said, her voice stronger.

"Alana," he spoke her name softly, and shivers ran up and down her spine. "I'm M—er, Emery. Emery Jung."

She felt her lips twitch into a smile. "I know."

"Right. Obviously, you know. I know you know." He hesitated, and Alana's lips twitched again. "You feeling better now?"

She considered that. Her breathing had returned to normal, mostly, but her heart still beat wildly in her chest. She figured it had less to do with panic and more to do with the person currently sitting just a few feet away.

"I'm fine," she said in surprise, realizing it was true.

"Good." M seemed genuinely relieved.

Alana swallowed as sudden shame overwhelmed her. "I'm sorry."

"What for?"

She could just make out his frown in the darkness. "For panicking on you. For running away. For injuring you…"

"You don't have to apologize…" M muttered. Alana heard a crinkling noise as he shifted about. "Do you have panic attacks a lot?"

"Sometimes."

He was quiet for a moment. "I—wait. What do you mean you injured me?"

Alana tried to get a better look at his expression. "For spilling tea on you. I'm sorry if it burned you—made you slip on stage. I'm so sorry."

"Oh, right. That." He paused. "That wasn't your fault. None of this was your fault. Is that why you've been avoiding me?"

"Maybe."

"Well you can stop now." He laughed. "I've been trying to talk to you all week."

That explained why M kept turning up everywhere she went, even when she had been trying so hard to keep her distance. What could the idol possibly have to say to her? She was afraid to ask. Looking at the floor, she said, "Could you call someone to open the door? I left my phone charging in the dressing room."

Alana wasn't so sure Hyungkoo would worry about her absence—he probably thought she was lost on the way to get the cake—but she knew M would be missed, and it wouldn't be good for them to get caught together in a dark room, or closet, or...wherever they were.

There was an awkward pause. "I don't have my phone on me either," M said. "It broke." He sounded slightly embarrassed.

"Oh." Alana's heart faltered. "But someone will come looking for you. They know you left, right?"

"Yeah... I'm sure someone will notice, don't worry."

Alana would have felt better if his last statement sounded a little more convincing. She winced when she remembered her cousin waiting for her in the dressing room. Her family was going to freak out if she didn't come home tonight.

"I have to get out of here," she said into the darkness.

Silence stretched on. Then M quietly asked, "Why are you avoiding me?"

She opened her mouth to deny it, but stopped. She *had* been avoiding M. She didn't trust herself to stay in control around him. He was tied too strongly to her memories, pulling too painfully on her heart. She couldn't tell him that though. "I was...embarrassed." It wasn't a lie.

"Embarrassed?"

"No one likes being yelled at in public, but especially not in front of people they used to idolize." Out of everyone, M was the last person she'd want to see her at her worst. It was stupid, but she couldn't seem to deny the instinct to run every time M came close. She hadn't thought he would notice or even care. Sitting trapped in this closet together with him obviously proved her assumptions were a little off. That was the thing, though—why had he followed her? Why *did* he care?

"Used to idolize," he repeated her words slowly.

She felt the blood leave her face. "That's not what I meant! I mean, yes, I haven't really kept up with NEON recently, but it's not just you. I don't listen to any music anymore…" Alana trailed off weakly.

"I understand," M said abruptly. "Life gets busy. I get it." He paused for a moment before continuing. "But I'm surprised. Weren't you going to study songwriting at school?"

She winced. "I'm taking a break from college."

"So then you came to Korea to work for RDE?"

"Not exactly."

"But you *do* work for LilyRed, right? I mean, you're carrying their cake around, so I assume you still work there."

She felt her cheeks warm. "I didn't get fired, if that's what you're asking."

"Right. Good." M cleared his throat. "You know, your manager was an asshole for yelling at you like that."

Alana covered her burning face with her hands. "No, he's not a bad guy. It was my fault. I'm not exactly great at my job."

"That's hard to believe."

"It's true! Multitasking is difficult for me. I tend to…forget things when I'm not focused." Why was she telling him this?

"Okay, never mind, I can see that." Hearing the amusement in his voice, she dropped her hands to see his attention directed at the cake beside her.

"Hey, I didn't drop it!"

"Uh-huh," said M. He was laughing. She felt her own mouth start to curl into a smile.

"What's with the cake anyways?"

"It's a gift from the GILD, LilyRed's fan club. We're celebrating their last day of promotions." She was supposed to deliver the cake in time for the girls' MeLive broadcast, which must have started by now. Hyungkoo was going to kill her.

"Just in time," M muttered.

"What?"

"Nothing."

Alana could feel M studying her as she avoided his gaze, letting her eyes wander around the room until they fell back onto the cake. Her stomach rumbled, loudly, making her cringe.

"I haven't eaten yet today," she rushed to explain.

"At all? Not even breakfast?"

Alana shook her head. What with trying to keep track of all the LilyRed members' things and actively avoiding M, there had never been a good time to eat. "I forgot."

"How do you forget to eat?" The horror in his voice was almost funny. She watched him curiously as he reached for his backpack, searching through it, but coming up empty handed. "Sorry, I don't have anything to eat in here." His focus turned toward the cake on the floor. "I won't judge if you want to steal a piece."

Now it was Alana's turn to be horrified. "I'm not eating LilyRed's cake! I'm trying *not* to lose my job."

"Oh, come on. I doubt they will notice if you eat one of those heart things sticking out of the top." As if to prove it, he reached over and plucked out a heart-shaped cake pop and offered it to her. "Here."

Alana felt her mouth fall open as she stared at him incredulously.

"Well, if you won't eat it…" M shrugged and took a bite, chewing thoughtfully. "Tastes familiar. I think GLO has gotten NEON a cake from here before. What was that place called again?"

She blinked. "Are you crazy? I'm going to get in so much trouble! Now the decorations are lopsided. It's…asymmetrical!"

M snorted. Before she could do anything, he snatched another heart from the cake and held it out to her. "There. Fixed it."

"Hey!"

"Come on, Alana. I'm offering you my heart here."

She felt the blood rush to her face. "Ha. Ha. Very funny." But when her stomach growled hungrily again, she scowled. "Fine. But only one."

As she leaned forward to take the cake skewer, his fingers brushed against hers, and her heart skipped a beat, her warm cheeks flaming even brighter. She was grateful for the dark room as she quickly drew back and took a bite, aware of his eyes on her. The taste of rich chocolate and sweet frosting filled her mouth and she held back a sigh of content, polishing off the treat in just two bites.

"You should eat more," said M. He leaned forward to defile the cake once again, but Alana was ready this time. She quickly reached her hand out and yanked the cardboard base out of his reach. In the dark, she felt more than saw the no-doubt devilish grin that spread across his face.

"Nooo," she said. "The cake is not ours to eat!" She moved to put herself between M and the cake, and he pulled back abruptly to avoid colliding into her. Steadying himself, he grabbed onto the base of the shelves, which swayed ominously for a second before one of the boxes at the top lost its battle with gravity and tipped over the edge, landing mere inches from where M sat with a thud.

Alana's eyes widened as bright golden flakes rained down on them both, reflecting off the scarce light. She squinted closer at the scattering of gold decorating the floor before realization hit her.

"Confetti!" She laughed, startling herself, the sound foreign to her ears.

"No way!" There was definite amusement in M's voice as he opened one of the large boxes next to him. He grabbed handfuls of the contents and stared, mesmerized, at the confetti in his hands before letting it flutter back down.

She looked around. "We're in a closet full of confetti?"

"Seems like it." M's broad smile was just visible in the dark. "You have a piece on you."

Alana froze as he reached out to gently brush the golden paper from her hair. She ducked her head, pulling away from his touch, acutely aware of the scar on her temple as her hair fell forward to hide her expression.

M cleared his throat and leaned back once again. "Well, I guess there are worse places to be trapped."

Despite his words, the reality of their situation began to truly sink in, and they debated ways to escape. Unfortunately, yelling for help didn't work, and they decided they would just have to wait. As the minutes ticked by, Alana soon gave in, devouring the rest of the cake pops and leaving behind tiny holes in the frosting. M didn't say anything, but she could hear his quiet laughter each time she took another bite of chocolate. Meanwhile, the idol opened almost every box in the room, seemingly fascinated by all the different types of confetti and streamers each one held. Sadly, none of the boxes contained anything useful to help get them out, and Alana was starting to go crazy.

"How long do you think we've been in here?" she said when M returned to his spot on the floor for the fifth time.

"It's hard to tell. An hour? Maybe two?" M guessed as he distractedly played with a handful of confetti from the ground.

"Aren't you worried at all?"

He looked up at her, letting the golden flakes fall from his hands. "Someone will find us. My manager is probably looking through CCTV footage right now to see where I ran off to."

"Shouldn't he have found us by now? Maybe we should try shouting for help again?" she said, fidgeting with the strap of her bag.

M sighed, standing up slowly and approaching her. Alana inched even closer to the door.

"What are you doing?" she squeaked. Her breath hitched as he crouched down in front of her. This close, she could see the light reflect off a chain he wore around his neck. The deep smell of his cologne overwhelmed her with notes of oranges, sandalwood, and spices.

"I'm just trying to get a better look at this door you broke. Maybe I can pick the lock." He flashed a teasing smile at her.

"Oh." She quickly scooted away, giving him space to inspect where the handle had broken off. "Can you see what's wrong?"

"Huh." M's face was visibly focused as he looked closely at the door. She watched as he carefully slid his hands underneath where their scarce light shown through and pulled. With a soft click, the door slowly swung open.

"How…" Alana blinked at M as light flooded the room, dispersing the darkness. She looked between him and the door, then back at him again.

For a moment, M seemed just as astonished as she was before he burst into hysterical laughter. "It wasn't locked!"

"W-what?"

"The door was never locked!" M repeated, struggling to

breathe through his mirth.

"You've got to be kidding me."

"We just sat in an unlocked closet for *hours!*" Regaining some of his composure, he looked at the expression on her face only to burst out laughing again.

"I tried opening the door!" Alana was mortified. "I swear it wouldn't open!"

"If you say so," M gasped out, wiping a tear from his eye and holding his hand out to her. "Let's get out of here."

She looked into his brown eyes, sparkling with the remnants of his laughter, and stopped thinking. She took his hand, and he pulled her to her feet, smiling for a moment before letting go. While he walked over to pick up his backpack, she hid her hand behind her back. It tingled where he had touched her.

Alana looked around the closet. There was gold confetti scattered across the floor but everything else remained intact. She sighed inwardly and picked up her bag and then the cake, minus the heart decorations.

"Ready?" M flashed her another smile, and she felt herself smiling in return.

Alana took a deep breath as they stepped outside the deserted station, staring into the night sky. There was a rare summer breeze in the air, cool against her skin.

"The vans are gone," M said from beside her.

She glanced at the spot where the idol vans were usually parked. M was right. They were gone.

"I don't believe it. Did they *forget* me?" M stared in shock at the empty parking lot.

"I'm sorry," Alana said miserably.

"Why are you sorry?" M frowned at her. "Your company left you too. How are you getting home?"

"There's a bus stop on the corner."

"*You* can't take the bus. It's late! Are the buses even running?"

Alana laughed. Again. She couldn't remember the last time she had smiled or laughed so much. Her cheeks hurt. "Yes, it shouldn't be a problem."

"Is it safe? I'll take the bus with you."

"You can't take the bus!" She echoed his earlier protest. "You're an idol. What if someone recognizes you? Besides, do you even know which bus takes you home?"

"I'm not going home. We were supposed to have dance practice tonight." He paused, combing his fingers through his dark hair. "I can't believe they forgot me! It's not like we are one of those groups with sixteen members. There's only five of us! You'd think my disappearance would be rather obvious."

"Well, you can't take the bus with me. I'm not heading to Gangnam."

M considered her statement briefly before pulling a notebook and pen from his backpack. After quickly writing something down, he ripped the paper out and folded it, tucking it into the outer pocket of her shoulder bag. Alana looked down at the note curiously.

"My Tiki ID," he explained.

Alana gawked at him. "You can't give me this. Take it back!" She balanced the cake in one arm and reached for her bag with the other.

"Promise that you will message me when you get home, Alana."

"I can't message you," she choked out, leaning just a bit too far to the side in her attempt to snatch the note. "I can't—"

The cake slipped from her grip, falling as if in slow motion before splattering onto the pavement in a kaleidoscope of pink and yellow frosting. She gasped and reluctantly met M's eyes to see a matching look of alarm on his face, his arms stretched outward as if he had tried to stop the cake's inevitable fall.

The sound of a car pulling in distracted them both. Headlights flooded the parking lot, and Alana blinked at the sudden brightness.

As the vehicle came to an idling stop beside them, NEON's manager jumped out, rushing to where they stood.

"M!" the manager said, relief evident on his round face. "*Here* you are."

He paused as he took in the scene, his eyes glancing from M to Alana and then to the cake on the ground. Alana abruptly straightened, watching the manager warily.

"Oh my god," M said in dismay, switching back to speaking in Korean. "You did forget me!"

"We didn't *forget* you," the manager spluttered. "I came back as soon as we got to the company and realized you weren't there. Why didn't you get in any of the vans?"

"The better question is how did no one notice I was missing? I'm hurt, *Hyung*."

Alana stared down at the remains of the cake, shifting uncomfortably. Her movement distracted M's manager, and he looked at her curiously.

"Uh, *Hyung*, this is Alana. She works for RDE. She's been keeping me company since you left me here to die."

The manager sighed, shaking his head at the idol, before looking back at her.

"N-nice to meet you," she greeted in Korean, nodding her head politely.

"Your accent... You're not Korean?" he said in surprise, his gaze shifting between M and Alana again.

"No, I'm American. My parents live in Chicago, but I also have family here in Seoul." She avoided looking at M. "I should probably head back. It's late, and they will be worried about me."

"Of course. Thanks for keeping an eye on M for us."

With one final glance to the ruined cake, Alana took her leave. She could feel their eyes following her all the way out of the parking lot.

★ ★ ★ ★ ★

The apartment was quiet when Alana finished her shower, the automated hallway light her only illumination as she stepped softly into the guest room and shut the door. She froze when she saw Stephanie sitting on her bed, a furious scowl on her face.

"Where the hell have you been?!" her cousin demanded in a furious whisper.

Alana winced. When she had first arrived back at the apartment, she had found Aunt Park panicking while Stephanie was still out looking for her, terrified that Alana had seemingly disappeared into thin air. Her cousin must have returned while she was getting ready for bed.

"Steph, I'm so sorry—"

"I can't believe you! What happened?"

"I got stuck in a closet…"

"You…what?"

"Seriously. I was trapped at Music Kingdom—well, I thought I was trapped, anyway—and my phone was gone."

Stephanie reached into her pocket and pulled out Alana's phone. "I'm gluing this to your hand. You're never allowed to go *anywhere* without it. I better not see it abandoned in the dressing room ever again. Understood?" she bit out.

"It's not like I forgot it on purpose…" Upon seeing her cousin's glare, she hastily added. "I promise, Steph. I don't want a repeat of tonight."

"Good. I covered for you by the way. Told Hyungkoo that

the cake hadn't been ready and you got stuck at the store. He thinks you just went home from there."

"Thanks, Steph. I owe you."

"*Never again*, Alana. I mean it."

"I know, I know. I'm sorry."

Stephanie sighed, standing up from the bed. "Remember, be ready to leave by 8:00 a.m. tomorrow."

"Will do."

Her cousin's gaze softened. "I'm glad you're okay, Aly."

"I really am sorry."

Stephanie nodded. "Now get some sleep. You look like crap." With that parting remark, her cousin left the room, gently closing the door behind her.

Alana let out a shaky breath, glancing at the phone in her hand as the events of the day caught up to her. She looked over to see a hint of M's notebook paper sticking out of her purse. In a daze, she took the paper out of the bag and unfolded it, staring at his Tiki Talk messaging ID.

She shouldn't add him. She *really* shouldn't message him. He was an idol, and she was nobody. What she ought to do was throw the paper away. Whatever this was between them, it was over.

Unmoving, Alana continued to stare at the slip of paper with M's handwriting. She thought back to how he had talked her down from her panic attack in the dark. He hadn't judged. He hadn't tried to *fix* her. Rather, he had listened with kindness and understanding. None of his actions made any sense.

She ran her fingers over the paper. All he had asked was that she let him know when she made it home. It was only a message. That wasn't asking too much. Alana could do it.

*Don't be a coward*, she told herself.

She quickly entered his ID into her phone and typed out a

message. The memory of him smiling warmly in the darkness flashed in her mind. Without thinking, she hit send.

### *June 30*

**Alana (11:22 p.m.)** Hey, it's Alana. I'm home.

# Emery

## #HeatWave

Emery rested his head against the window, aimlessly watching the rice fields pass by in a green blur. Thoughts swirled in his head, jumping from topic to topic without settling. Alana. His parents. Today's festival choreography. NEON's next album.

He opened the note app on his new phone, jotting down his observations and reflections as he brainstormed new lyrics, until the phone buzzing in his hand startled him from his thoughts. "Alana" appeared on his screen, and his heart gave a small lurch.

### July 13

Alana (10:13 a.m.) Just arrived

Emery smiled. It had been over two weeks since he'd last seen her, the day they'd been "locked" in the closet together. He had been relieved when she messaged him the first time, then worried that she would continue to run. But they hadn't lost contact; in fact, they'd been texting daily ever since then. Or rather, *he* texted *her* daily and she occasionally replied. He couldn't quite call their messages conversations, per se. They were more like a running list of updates from his down time in between activities. But he knew she looked at them—the "unread" tag always disappearing within minutes. That was enough.

He scrolled back through some of their texts once again. By now, he had practically memorized her responses.

*July 1*

Emery (7:01 a.m.) Good morning!!!

Emery (11:51 a.m.) I know you read that… It's okay if you don't respond. Just know I'm probably going to spam you with lots of texts and cat pictures

Emery (11:52 a.m.) Starting…NOW!

Emery (2:34 p.m.) Wow still no response?

Emery (2:35 p.m.) Hmmm maybe 53 cat pics was one too many

Emery (2:35 p.m.) TT

Emery (5:42 p.m.) Okay, let's start over…

Emery (5:43 p.m.) How are you today?

Emery (5:48 p.m.) This is where you'd say, "Fine, and you?"

Emery (5:49 p.m.) Thanks for asking! I'm great :)

Emery (9:53 p.m.) You know, I have 12,544 more cat pics in my arsenal…

Alana (10:16 p.m.) Wow haha you really don't give up, do you?

Alana (10:17 p.m.) Also, dog pics are preferred lol

### July 4

Emery (8:42 a.m.) Happy 4th of July!

Emery (8:43 a.m.) I figured you'd actually care. Stu didn't. I swear, any time it's an American holiday he becomes 10x more Australian

Emery (8:43 a.m.) Ah man, now I want to see fireworks

Alana (10:46 p.m.) I miss the fireworks, too :) Happy 4th!

### July 6

Emery (5:20 p.m.) We FINALLY decided on what to eat for our celebration tomorrow. Only took us three weeks… We suck at making decisions. But we're getting *samgyeopsal!* SO EXCITED

Alana (5:21 p.m.) Lol I can tell

Emery (5:21 p.m.) OMG YOU RESPONDED!!

Emery (5:21 p.m.) Hiiiiiiii

Alana (5:21 p.m.) Um hi lol?

Emery (5:22 p.m.) This is such a big deal! I feel so honored!!

Alana (5:22 p.m.) Right. Forget I said anything

Emery (5:22 p.m.) Don't go! I'll be good, I promise!!

Alana (5:22 p.m.) Okay…

Emery (5:23 p.m.) So how are you? Things good with work?

Alana (5:25 p.m.) Well there haven't been any more cake casualties, if that's what you're asking

Emery (5:25 p.m.) That's a relief

Emery (5:26 p.m.) Gah, time for Show Time broadcast. I'm so sad to leave this miraculous moment TT

Alana (5:26 p.m.) Lol go do your work~

### *July 7*

Emery (4:12 a.m.) It's our last day of promotions! I finally have a day off tomorrow :)

Emery (5:45 a.m.) Wow it's been a week since we were stuck together. Being back at Music Kingdom feels strange

Alana (5:46 a.m.) Ugh go away. Too early

Emery (5:47 a.m.) Morning to you, too! I wonder if they ever fixed the doorknob

Alana (5:47 a.m.) Stop messaging meeeee

Emery (5:47 a.m.) I'm going to check!

Alana (5:48 a.m.) I'm going to block you

Emery (5:52 a.m.) Lol the closet's exactly as we left it! Confetti's still all over the floor

Emery (5:52 a.m.) Should I tell someone?

Alana (5:52 a.m.) Turning my phone off now

Emery (5:53 a.m.) I left the door propped open. Hopefully a staff member notices

Emery (10:16 a.m.) Well, we had confetti during our pre-recording so I think everything's okay?

Alana (10:18 a.m.) That's good lol

Emery (10:19 a.m.) And I got an hour nap in! Just the live performance left

Emery (5:17 p.m.) Freedom is so close

Alana (5:30 p.m.) You can do it! *Fighting!*

Emery (7:24 p.m.) OMG we got a cake!

Emery (7:24 p.m.) And yes, it looks almost the same as LilyRed's :) It has to be from the same place!

Alana (7:25 p.m.) Ahh no way! Haha any good?

Emery (7:40 p.m.) YES! Go check out NEON's HeartU account. We just posted a picture of us with the cake!

Alana (7:44 p.m.) …um why is Jaehyun shirtless?

Emery (7:46 p.m.) Because it's Jaehyun lol best not to question him

Alana (7:46 p.m.) Lol I should've known

Emery (7:47 p.m.) I made sure to eat a heart cake pop in your honor! But it was vanilla cake this time

Alana (11:45 p.m.) That's so sad. GLO should know chocolate is always the superior choice :)

Alana (11:46 p.m.) And congrats on finishing your promotions!!

*July 8*

Emery (2:06 a.m.) OMG so full. That *samgyeopsal* was AMAZING!

Emery (2:07 a.m.) Sorry in advance - drank LOTS of *soju* :)

Emery (2:10 a.m.) You there???

Emery (2:34 a.m.) Alanaaaaaaaaaaaaaaaaaaaa

Alana (10:40 a.m.) Lol looks like you had fun. How are you feeling this morning?

Alana (3:26 p.m.) Enjoying your day off?

**Alana (5:49 p.m.)** Hello…?

**Emery (6:22 p.m.)** I'm alive!!! Sorry!! Our manager took our phones away last night TT You can blame Jaehyun. He almost spammed our account with videos of his drunken rapping again. Minhyuk was not pleased

**Alana (6:24 p.m.)** LOL probably for the best

Emery enjoyed seeing her slowly open up, growing more and more comfortable chatting with him over the passing days. Yet, as if by some unspoken agreement, they never mentioned the past. Emery knew he would get more of a response out of her if he kept the topics casual and light, hiding his worries about her changed behavior and appearance. She wasn't the same girl he had met two years ago, and after her reactions in the confetti closet, he was hesitant to push her too quickly. He wanted to help her, just like she had helped him when he had needed it most, but first, he needed to gain her trust. Spamming her with cute dog photos would have to do for now.

He smiled at the thought of finally seeing her today. Both NEON and LilyRed would be performing at the "Beat the Heat" Music Festival in Daegu. Not that he and Alana would have much of a chance to talk, but at least he could check up on her and see how she was doing, even if from afar. She had grown quiet over the last few days, and it made him uneasy. Fortunately, she started responding again just last night and confirmed she would be there at the festival today.

*"Tiki Tiki!"*

Emery looked down at his phone with a smile, thinking Alana had sent another message, but the amusement drained from his face when he saw who it actually was from.

## *July 13*

Mom (10:35 a.m.) Hi honey. Why haven't you returned my call? I can't wait to tell you all about our vacation. And our house looks amazing, the remodeling is almost done. Let's do a video chat so I can show you all the changes! Your dad and I are still up. Love, Mom

Emery sighed. His mom had called him that morning at 4:00 a.m. Korean time, waking him up from a rare moment of deep sleep. Ignoring it, he had quickly rolled over and turned his phone on silent but had been unable to fall back asleep. He chose to get some work done in the few hours before dawn instead, wishing his mom would stop pretending everything was normal—that the Jung family had a happy and healthy relationship.

Emery (10:37 a.m.) Sorry, Mom. I'm working right now. I'll call when I get back home tonight. Promise

"Wake up, guys," Minhyuk's voice broke through the silence of the van. Everyone but Emery had been fast asleep. "We'll be there in about five minutes."

Groans and mumbles emerged from the very back of the van as Sungil and Jaehyun began to stir.

"Wake up, Stu," said Emery as he gently reached over to shake his shoulder. Stu groaned and opened his eyes, reluctantly removing his noise-canceling headphones as he looked around sleepily.

"I just got off the phone with Yena," said Minhyuk. "She says that fans have started to gather, so prepare yourself if you don't want to be photographed just yet."

"Yes, sir," Sungil said with a mock salute before covering his mouth to yawn.

Emery pulled out his favorite hat and black cloth mask from the front pocket of his bag. Without his usual makeup, his face was shiny, and a quick glance in the rearview mirror confirmed that his hair was sticking up in the back. They had left their dorm just after 7:00 a.m., jumping right into the van to head to Daegu, a city located three hours to the south of Seoul.

"Once we arrive, you'll be heading straight to sound-check," said Minhyuk. "The rest of our staff is already there, so let them know if you need anything."

"Which one makes my face look smaller?" said Jaehyun while holding up an orange beret and a camo bucket hat.

"Neither. You're doomed," Stu said with a grin.

"Ignore him. Either one is great, *Hyung*," said Sungil.

"Don't worry. I never listen to Stu," said Jaehyun with a look of intense concentration as he stared at the hats.

"The camo one's brand new, right?" said Emery. "Maybe wait to debut it the next time we go to the airport."

"Good call, M." Jaehyun carefully put the bucket hat back into his bag before spending the next minute perfecting the beret's placement on his blonde head.

"And it's hot today," Minhyuk added. "Already 33 degrees, might get up to 38 this afternoon. Don't forget to drink lots of water."

It took Emery a second to mentally convert the temperature to Fahrenheit. No matter how long he lived in Korea, he still thought of temperature in terms of the U.S. system. He groaned. The temperature would be in the 90s and reaching close to 100. Performing today was going to be brutal.

As the van slowly made its way toward the staff parking lot, Emery could see fans walking around outside the window, carrying giant cameras, signs, and even ladders. Some were peering at their van, straining to see who was inside, and Emery felt a wave of gratitude for their blackout windows.

"Sorry, guys. Looks like this is as close as we can get. Security will help escort you backstage. Don't come out until I open the side door." Minhyuk stopped the car and got out.

"Wow, I didn't think so many fans would be here already," said Yongnam.

"Ah, man, maybe I should have gone with the bucket hat," said Jaehyun, a look of regret etched onto his face.

"Stop whining. You look great," said Stu as he adjusted his glasses in the rearview mirror. "Why didn't I bother to put on some BB cream?"

"I have an extra facemask if you want." Emery dug into his bag and pulled out another black mask.

"You're a lifesaver," said Stu. He quickly pulled it on, covering up his face.

Emery was the first to exit the van once Minhyuk opened the sliding door. He pulled down his black cap to make sure it was in place and followed the security guard toward the backstage entrance. The crowd cheered behind the roped-off path, and the click of camera shutters filled the air. Thousands of fans would see these pictures online within minutes. Emery was always blown away by how fast fansites worked.

"Ahhh, so handsome!"

"M! M! Over here!"

"I love you, Stu!"

"Did you eat?"

Emery waved to the fans, excited to see so many there to support NEON. Clearly loving the crowd's attention, Jaehyun threw finger hearts and kisses to everyone he passed. Stu was going down the right side of the path, greeting fans along the barrier, while Sungil and Yongnam brought up the rear, waving and posing for pictures along the way as fans shouted "ca-caw" at the *maknae*. Emery saw a woman holding a small child, maybe three or four years old and dressed adorably in

NEON orange. He made his way to their side and offered his hand out to give the little girl a fist bump. She hesitated for a moment, but quickly overcame her shyness, excitedly tapping her fist to his. The air filled with a chorus of "awwws," making Emery laugh.

Finally, they made it backstage, high walls hiding the area from outside view. Emery couldn't see the fans, but he could still hear them, their screams rising even louder with the arrival of another idol group. There were white tents set up to act as dressing rooms, arranged in neat lines with different names displayed on the front. The security guard led them to the first tent on the right labeled "NEON."

Emery opened the flap to see their stylists already inside waiting for them. Large electric fans were running on full blast to help relieve some of the intense heat. He bowed and politely greeted everyone before putting his bag down in the corner, removing his facemask, and taking a seat on one of the folding chairs near the makeup stations. He took out his phone to text Alana while he waited for the other members to get situated.

Emery (10:49 a.m.) I'm here :) We have rehearsal now, but I'll come find you after!

"*Noona*, where's the bathroom?" Sungil asked his stylist.

"I saw it next to the medic tent, Sungil. I'll go, too." Yongnam said, gesturing to follow him, before the two left the tent together.

"Our fans are the best," Jaehyun said as he adjusted his hat in the mirror.

"Aren't they?" Stu said proudly, retying the laces on his sneakers. "M, that little girl was so cute! I wouldn't be surprised if you started to trend."

Emery let out a nervous laugh. "Well, I guess that would

be better than the whole slipping thing."

"Here," Yena interrupted, holding a stack of name tag bibs against her denim dress. "You'll need these for soundcheck."

Yena was the head stylist of NEON, supervising each member's personal stylists and working closely with the group's managers for events. She had been with Solar for more than two years, helping to sculpt NEON's image along-side their rise in popularity. With her brown hair cut short and tucked behind her ears, the no-nonsense stylist began passing out name tags to the members.

Emery accepted the bib with his name on it and tied it to his chest. Idols wore the bibs during rehearsal so the cam-eramen would know who they needed to focus on during the actual performance.

"*Noona*, do you know who's on stage now?" Emery asked Yena.

"I think it's LilyRed. I heard their song playing just before you got here."

A smile automatically came to Emery's lips.

Stu, who had also perked up at the mention of LilyRed, was quick to notice the expression on Emery's face. "Oooh, thinking of Ginger already?"

"Dude, you've been acting all mysterious lately," Jaehyun said, playfully nudging Emery's arm. "What's up?"

"None of your business," Emery defended, fighting back a blush.

"Awww, he's turning red," said Stu.

"Our little Emmie is growing up so fast," Jaehyun said while pretending to wipe away a tear.

"Oh, stop being so dramatic." Emery wished he had something to throw at them.

"Is that why you won't do the TV show? Afraid you won't have time with your precious Ginger?" Stu said while giving

Emery a sly glance.

Despite his outright refusal to appear on *I Can Cook*, he was still under pressure to take the role. A few days prior, Min-hyuk had deliberately let slip the news about the casting offer to the rest of NEON, and now Stu and Sungil were constantly bringing up the show. In comparison, Yongnam supported his decision to focus on music. Only Jaehyun was strangely silent on the subject.

Thankfully, Solar could say he was "considering" the role for only so long. Sooner or later, the show would have to find someone else to take the part. Emery just wanted the casting deadline to pass already.

Minhyuk entered the tent to a chorus of "hello's" from the staff members.

"You guys ready to go?" He looked around the tent. "Where's Yongnam and Sungil?"

"Bathroom. Should be back soon," said Jaehyun.

"Good. LilyRed is about to finish. Head to the stage first and I'll wait for them here."

Emery, Jaehyun, and Stu made their way outside the tent, their entourage of personal stylists following behind them. The bright sunlight blinded Emery momentarily, and the hot air engulfed him. He pulled his hat further down, hiding his face from the sun.

"Urgh, so hot. I hope we can chill in the van later with proper AC," said Stu.

"What kind of Australian are you? This should be noth-ing for you," said Jaehyun.

"Yeah, but we have AC and know when to stay inside."

"*Heol*, and here I thought Australians were tough."

"I'll show you tough—"

"Come on, let's go," said Emery quickly before their ban-ter could turn into an argument.

As they made their way toward the massive outdoor stage, Emery kept his eyes out for Alana. He hadn't seen any of the LilyRed staff yet, but he could hear their song "Ta-Da" playing over the speakers. She should be close.

He turned the corner and spotted the bright purple hair of one of LilyRed's *coordis*. His eyes automatically moved behind her to the girl dressed in black, struggling as she lugged a heavy container of water toward the stage.

Alana.

She looked awful. Her skin was unnaturally pale, and sweat matted the hair framing her face. Every few steps she would pause to cough into her shoulder. Emery frowned.

"*Alana!*"

Emery looked up in alarm at the angry cry from LilyRed's manager.

"You forgot the suitcase with the stage shoes?! I knew I couldn't trust you with this." The manager blocked Alana's path, arms crossed and face livid. "Mistake after mistake. I can't believe I've put up with you this long."

Emery stood transfixed, narrowing his eyes as he watched Alana. She still carried the water, but with the way her arms shook, he didn't think she could last much longer.

"Your job is to *help*. But what have you actually helped with? Do you even try?"

Alana didn't move.

"I've had it with your crap. I'm not dealing with this anymore."

The manager's voice grew quiet, and Emery strained to hear what was said next.

"You're fired."

Alana finally lost her grip, and the case of water went toppling to the ground. A few bottles sprang loose from the packaging, rolling feebly on the dusty pavement.

"*Manager-nim*, what's going on?"

Emery saw the girl with purple hair streak back to Alana, stepping right in front of her while Alana stared at the ground, her eyes glassed over and unfocused.

"What happened to Alana?" the girl said, her tone accusing.

"What *happened*?! Just *another* mistake. I'm done. I've had it. She's been worthless since day one," the manager replied.

"What mistake? Whatever she's done, I'll fix it. Just please stop yelling at her!"

Alana took a few unsteady steps back, distancing herself from the growing argument. The color had completely drained from her face. Closing her eyes, she used the back of her hand to wipe her forehead.

Something was very wrong.

A crowd had started to gather, but everyone seemed focused on the dispute, not on Alana. Emery glanced to Jaehyun and Stu for support, but they were also sucked into the yelling match that had broken out between the two LilyRed staff members. Emery felt paralyzed, his mind racing to find a way to help her.

Finally, Alana opened her eyes. She looked dazedly around at the crowd before spotting Emery. For a moment, she seemed to steady, a spark flashing in her light brown eyes. Then her gaze faltered, and she collapsed.

# Alana

## #MTheHero

Alana was hearing voices.

They surrounded her, but remained distant, just past the point of comprehension. With her mind veiled in darkness, she felt calm, almost peaceful. She would have liked to stay longer, completely surrendering herself to the soothing void, if not for the voices. They were growing steadily louder and harder to ignore.

*"What were you thinking? How many people saw you carry her?"*

*"She collapsed! Was I supposed to just leave her there?"*

*"The girl was surrounded by people. Why did it have to be you?"*

*"I don't know. I didn't think…"*

*"Well, you need to start thinking! This is how you ruin your career…"*

The voices faded away, leaving Alana confused. What language was that? The words weren't making any sense, but the tone of them worried her, sounding panicked and defensive. She tried to move, to see something, anything, through the darkness, and her heartbeat sped up as pain throbbed in the back of her head. Her whole body ached.

*"Your cousin is suffering from heatstroke, and she's showing symptoms of a cold…"*

*"Only Aly would catch a cold in summer…"*

That was Stephanie's voice. That, at least, she recognized. Slowly, her memories started coming back to her—the music festival. Her cold. The heat.

*"What are you doing here?"*

*"I just spoke with the management at Solar. They want to meet with Alana as soon as she wakes up."*

Was that Hyungkoo, too? Oh God, she was in so much trouble. He had been furious. Then again, he was always angry with her.

*"Great. I'll let her know. Oh, and in case it wasn't clear, I quit."*

*"What?!"*

She drifted off again, sounds coming and going through the haze.

Suddenly, Alana saw white. As she squinted at the abrupt brightness, it took her eyes a moment to adjust before the sloping fabric ceiling came into focus above her. Not a hospital, then—she felt a small sense of relief.

"Good. You're awake."

Alana glanced over to find her cousin standing next to her cot in the otherwise empty tent. For once, Stephanie's appearance lacked its usual shine. Her yellow dress was wrinkled and her hair had been pulled back in a messy ponytail, loose purple strands escaping to haphazardly circle her pink cheeks. Her makeup failed to mask the worry on her face.

Alana opened her mouth to reply when a coughing fit seized her.

"Somebody's been busy keeping secrets," Stephanie said, raising an unimpressed eyebrow.

"W-what happened?" Alana asked when she finally caught her breath.

"You fainted."

As the fuzzy conversations Alana had overheard began

to register, she sat up, accidentally pulling at the IV taped to her arm.

"Woah! Not so fast. The medic said you hit your head pretty hard when you fell."

Alana groaned. That explained the hammering at the base of her skull. She lay back down on the cot, her head spinning with pain and questions.

"Oh, and before I forget, Solar Entertainment wants to speak with you. I'm not so sure that's a good idea, with you being sick and everything, but I promised to let you know."

"Solar? Why?" Could they have discovered her texts with M?

When Alana had first messaged him, she had assumed that would be the end of their strange relationship, having done what he asked. They would return to their designated roles—he, an idol, and she, a staff member. She certainly had no intention of continuing contact, but then he surprised her with an onslaught of messages and GIFs. At first, she had tried to remain distant, reading everything he sent but resisting the temptation to respond. With each passing day, however, she found herself looking forward to M's creative attempts to draw her into a conversation. His updates amused her, but more than that, talking to M grounded her, giving her a bright and safe place to be herself, away from the shadow of Alex's death.

Before she knew it, they were actually conversing, exchanging messages with frightening regularity. Emotions she'd thought were lost—excitement, playfulness, curiosity—slipped past her walls, and laughter was no longer foreign to her lips. With every message, she could forget momentarily the incessant ache of grief in her chest. M helped her forget. Yet at times he also forced her to remember with devastating clarity. M, after all, was a part of NEON, the idol group tied closely to her own loss.

The worst had been two days ago, on the anniversary of Alex's death. Waking up that morning, guilt consumed her as she read M's messages, and her reality came crashing down. A full, excruciating year had passed since Alex had died. Her brother was truly gone, and she had missed the chance to save him—that was never going to change. When the realization hit her, she had avoided contact with everyone for the rest of the day, turning off her phone so she wouldn't be tempted to take solace in M's bright demeanor. She didn't deserve to forget.

"You're the one who needs to explain why Solar's suddenly interested in you," said Stephanie. "I can't believe there was something going on between you and that NEON guy, and I didn't notice! It certainly explains a lot."

"I don't know what you're talking about…"

"Uh-huh. Then why did NEON's M swoop down to save you and carry you all romantically in his arms?"

"M did *what?!*" Alana hadn't realized her voice could reach that pitch until now.

"You heard me." Stephanie crossed her arms.

"Yeah, but I don't believe you. You've seen too many K-dramas. Besides, why would he do that?"

"I'm telling the truth. Ask anybody. M wasn't exactly subtle when he carried you here." Stephanie smirked. "He must really like you."

"Don't be absurd," Alana muttered. "Wait… People saw him carry me?"

"Like I said, it wasn't subtle. He definitely made a scene."

"Hold on, rewind. What exactly happened after I passed out?"

"Well, you got fired… You do remember that, right?"

"Yeah, I got that part," she huffed. Honestly, she was rather surprised she lasted as long as she did at RDE. Leaving now was probably for the best.

"It was totally unfair, by the way. You didn't even forget the shoes this time, just so you know. They're in the van. Manager Hyungkoo was completely out of line."

Alana sighed. "It wasn't like it was my first time forgetting something…"

"No, whether you made mistakes in the past or not, it's not okay for him to yell at you. I won't allow it. *Especially* not while you're already sick and overworked. I can't work with someone who thinks it's okay to treat his employees like that."

"You can't quit, Steph."

"Too late. Already did." Stephanie stuck out her tongue.

Outwardly, Alana only frowned at her cousin's flippant behavior, but inside, she felt sick. Well, she *was* sick, but this was different. Once again, she had made a mess of things. "But why? I know what that job means to you."

"You're more important than a stupid job. I'll find another one. This isn't the end."

Their conversation cut short when two women entered the tent. One was obviously a medic. She wore a dark blue uniform with a large medical insignia on the sleeve. The other woman Alana recognized as one of NEON's *coordis*. Her hair fell just above her shoulders around her angular face. She looked at Alana with a warm smile paired with dimples in her cheeks.

Alana tried sitting up again, slower this time, as the medic stood by her cot.

"Hello, I'm Ms. Kang. How are you feeling?" the medic said, checking her pulse.

"Okay." Alana automatically switched to answering in Korean.

"Are you experiencing any dizziness or nausea?" Ms. Kang stepped back, her eyebrows coming together in concern.

Alana's head was pounding, her chest ached from constant coughing, and her whole body felt chilled, but it wasn't anything she couldn't handle. "Just tired. When can I leave?"

"You can leave now if you'd like. But it might be a good idea to go to the hospital—"

"No, I'm fine. Thank you for everything." Alana gestured to the IV in her arm and the medic silently removed it.

With Stephanie's arm for support, Alana carefully swung her legs to the floor and stood. The world darkened around the edges momentarily and her ears rang, but the dizziness faded after some deep breaths.

"Let's get you back to Seoul," Stephanie said.

"Wait!" said the NEON *coordi* from her place near the tent's entrance. "Before you go, my boss needs to speak with Miss Alana."

"Are you serious right now?" Stephanie's voice rose. "Alana is sick and needs to go home. Nothing at your company has anything to do with her."

"I'm sorry. It won't take long, I promise. We wouldn't ask if it weren't important." Behind the *coordi*'s professional demeanor, Alana could sense a hint of desperation.

"I'll go." Alana's chest constricted, and she coughed into her shoulder.

Stephanie threw her arms up in exasperation. "Can you even walk on your own?"

Alana took a wheezing breath and a hesitant step away from the cot. "Apparently," she said before succumbing to another coughing fit. With a sigh, Stephanie opened a water bottle from her bag and handed it to her.

"This is idiotic," said Stephanie, as if Alana weren't already aware.

"We're just heading to our company van," the *coordi* said quickly, glancing briefly at Alana in concern. "Our manager got permission to pull one of the vans around backstage, just behind the tents. It's not far, and it's air conditioned."

"I said I'd go," Alana said as her breathing calmed. She took a small gulp of water.

"Thank you!" The *coordi* smiled in relief, flashing her dimples again.

"Take it easy and get some rest," the medic said as she followed the three girls to the entrance of the tent. "You should go to the hospital once you get to Seoul."

Alana shuddered. She *really* didn't like hospitals.

"I'll be sure she gets medicine," Stephanie promised, taking in the expression on her cousin's face.

After thanking the medic, Alana stepped outside into the blaring sunlight and overwhelming heat. She swayed, and felt Stephanie's arm loop through hers as they weaved their way through the rows of white tents backstage. Alana shot her cousin a grateful look, and Stephanie had the grace not to say anything.

When they rounded the corner behind the artist tents, Alana spotted NEON's black company van idling on the yellow grass. The windows were too tinted to see who was inside. Alana reluctantly approached with Stephanie in tow as the *coordi* knocked on the van's side door before sliding it open, causing a burst of cool air to hit Alana in the face.

"*Manager-nim*, here is Miss Alana," said the *coordi*, and Alana could see NEON's manager sitting in the driver's seat. M was in the bucket seat behind his manager, scowling at the headrest of the seat in front of him, but at the sound of Alana's name, he looked up. They made eye contact briefly, and Alana caught a glimpse of some unnamed emotion before he averted his gaze.

"Alana, thank you for coming. I'm Minhyuk Jang, NEON's head manager. Please sit down."

"I'll wait for you just outside," said Stephanie, a frown creasing her brows.

Alana nodded at her cousin before stepping into the van. The sound of the door closing behind her had an ominous finality to it. The transition from loud, hot festival preparations to silent, cool van was abrupt.

"How are you feeling?" Minhyuk asked. He had turned in his seat to face her.

"All right…" She shifted uncomfortably in her chair. A quick glance to her left revealed that M was back to staring at the seat in front in him. He wore black sweatpants and a fitted white T-shirt, a black cap hiding his brown hair. Alana recognized the logo on his clothes as the sportswear company that NEON modeled for. Their advertisements were plastered all over the subways and buses in Seoul.

"Well, I'm sure you want to get home to rest, so let's get this meeting started," Minhyuk continued.

"Okay." Her voice hitched as the urge to cough hit her again. She shivered in the cool air conditioning of the van and tried to discreetly wipe the sweat from her brow.

Minhyuk cleared his throat. "I have Solar Entertainment's upper management and PR team waiting on the phone. Now that you're here, I'll put them back on speaker and we can continue the call."

With alarm, Alana noticed the cell phone sitting on the van's console, the word "President" reflecting back to her on the screen. She took a shaky breath, trying once again not to cough as Minhyuk hit the button for speaker phone.

"President, I have Miss Alana here with us now."

"Okay, thank you for coming, Alana. I hope we can have your full cooperation in managing this situation as quickly as possible," said President Jo, the CEO and President of Solar Entertainment.

President Jo was famous for breaking boundaries in the Korean entertainment industry. Formerly known as Yongsun, the leader of the girl group Celestial, she went on to become a famous solo artist when her contract ended under JW Entertainment. Not only had she successfully written, composed, and produced all her own music, she went on to use her contacts in the industry to create her own company eight years ago, making her the first female CEO of an entertainment company in Korea.

"Manager Choi has just informed us that the incident is already trending number one in Korea," President Jo continued, not waiting for a response. "Unfortunately, a few fans managed to capture photos and even videos. I suspect ladders were involved. Anyway, we need to address this as quickly as possible to control the news as it spreads worldwide."

*Shit.*

"We are prepared to do whatever's necessary," Minhyuk said. Alana was impressed by the genuine respect in the manager's voice. In fact, everyone she had met who worked for Solar Entertainment spoke of their president with obvious regard. President Jo's efficient way of taking control of the situation was not at all how the Korean media painted her—a retired girl group member "cutely" trying her hand at management. No, President Jo was not playing around.

"First, we need to know if there is any truth to the rumors spreading online," a male voice said, presumably Manager Choi. "My team has already prepared a statement denying all allegations, but it's important we are aware of any mitigating factors that could refute our claims."

"Basically, Alana, what is the extent of your relationship with Emery?" said President Jo.

The shock of that statement caused Alana to lose the battle with her lungs, and she dissolved into a coughing fit. She turned her head away from M and into her shoulder as her lungs punished her for daring to breathe.

"This is insane," M said over Alana's coughing. "She has nothing to do with this, President."

"If that were the case, we would not be having this conversation right now, Emery." President Jo's voice softened when she added, "Look, I know how dating in the industry works. The fact of the matter is, whether you two are in a relationship or not, the images I'm seeing online of this girl in your arms makes it *look* like something is going on."

Alana concentrated on taking shallow breaths while her coughing subsided. M's expression looked bleak.

"I work—" Alana winced. "Well, I *worked* for RDE. I saw M a few times at the broadcast stations during LilyRed's promotions, but we really only spoke in person once, after Music Kingdom a few weeks ago." It was all technically true, if she ignored their time together two years ago… That didn't count, right?

Minhyuk grimaced. "I can confirm that Alana was there when I picked Emery up that night. It was the first and only time I have seen them together."

"We haven't run into each other since," Alana confirmed truthfully. She swore she heard M snort and pointedly kept her expression blank.

"Hmm. You aren't from Seoul, are you?" President Jo asked. "You speak Korean with a slight accent."

"I'm Korean American. I grew up in Chicago," she said.

"President, is this really needed right now?" M asked politely. "I know I messed up. What do I need to do? I'm assuming I have to sit out for today's festival performance."

"Not necessarily," the unidentified male voice spoke up again. "Sitting out is practically admitting there's something going on."

"Then what am I supposed to do?" M asked.

"We will get to you in a minute, Emery," President Jo

said. "First, we are going to deny all dating rumors." A hint of amusement crept into her voice. "Then we are going to change the narrative."

Alana glanced at M in confusion. His face was carefully blank as he stared at the phone on the console.

"What does that mean, President?" Minhyuk asked cautiously.

"Just that it was perfectly reasonable, even admirable, of Emery to carry one of NEON's new *coordis* to the medic tent when she fainted. It showed great character and humility on his part for caring so much about his staff."

"Ah," Minhyuk said, nodding.

Alana's cold must have been worse than she thought, because the president's words weren't making sense.

"We have already spoken with Red Diamond Entertainment, and they will confirm our version of events. It's the best for all involved. What do you say, Alana?" President Jo asked.

"I'm sorry… I'm not quite sure what this means."

"Right, let me be more clear. You're hired."

Alana saw M start in his seat out of the corner of her eye.

"What?!" he said.

"I have the contract sitting on my desk as we speak," President Jo continued, ignoring M's interruption. "You can sign it when you come to our company for your first day of work. How does a week from Monday—July 22—sound?"

"You're serious?" Alana said, her mind spinning. She was just *fired*, for crying out loud.

"The official start date at Solar will be left out of the public statement, but as of today, consider yourself a new Assistant Stylist for Solar Entertainment, at least until the rumors fade. In the meantime, you two will be seen as working together, but in a strictly professional capacity. Any other relationship between you two ends now. Are you agreeable to these terms?"

Alana felt trapped, all her carefully laid plans spinning out of control. She needed to turn her back on M and the K-pop industry as a whole, not step further into it. Her mouth twisted. It was truly ironic. Her former self would have died of happiness, but now all she felt was dread.

This truly was insane. Because Solar didn't even know the half of it. Even disregarding their secret text conversations over the last few weeks, Alana *knew* M. A working relationship with him would cross too many boundaries to count. If they were forced together like this, she didn't think she could remain distant—the red thread of fate felt poised to lead her even further astray. She didn't want this. She *couldn't* want this.

"Um, I mean... Is there no other way?" Alana asked, dreading the answer.

"For you? Not really," President Jo said. "If you don't agree, Emery will have to take a break from public appearances, at least for now. Depending on the repercussions, we're prepared to pull him from NEON's upcoming world tour, if needed."

So she really didn't have a choice. Her refusal would hurt M. In spite of everything, she could never risk harming him, not when she had the power to help. Protecting his reputation meant more than her own issues. She would manage. She would find a way to survive.

Perhaps, with this unexpected offer, she could fix more than one mistake.

Decision made, Alana took a deep breath, doing her best to ignore the alarm bells sounding in the back of her mind. "Okay. I'll join Solar."

"Great. Manager Choi, distribute Solar's official statement at once across—"

"I have one condition, though," Alana interrupted. Silence greeted her as everyone realized what she had done, speaking over not just a company superior, but the *president*. Feeling a blush reach her hairline, Alana tried to stay calm as she waited.

"Yes?" President Jo finally said.

"I'll only join if you also hire Stephanie Lim. She's my cousin and has experience working in the industry. It's my fault she quit RDE, and I couldn't stand it if I was still a stylist and she wasn't. Please—you won't regret it. She'd be a perfect addition to Solar. She's really qualified. Not like me—er, not that I can't do the job. I can! But she actually studied this stuff in college and wants to be a designer one day…" Alana trailed off, embarrassed. She felt both of the other occupants in the van staring at her, and she looked everywhere but at the idol sitting next to her.

"I see," President Jo said, amusement clear in her voice.

"Would this be the girl standing outside next to our Yena?" Minhyuk spoke up.

"Er… Yes, that's her."

"President, I've seen her around," said Minhyuk. "She's made a name for herself as a respected *coordi* for LilyRed."

"Hmm."

There was a pause, and Alana squirmed in her seat.

"I guess I don't see a problem with this new addition," President Jo finally said. "If your cousin is agreeable, have her join you on your first day. I'll have another contract drawn up."

"Thank you," Alana said as relief washed over her. At least, Stephanie would still have a job.

"That's settled then. Manager Choi, I'd like an updated report on my desk in the next hour."

"Yes, President."

"Perfect. Now, Emery." President Jo sounded almost indulgent. "You are performing tonight with NEON as planned.

If asked, you were just helping a staff member. Nothing more. But otherwise, try not to mention anything."

"I understand, President." M let out a soft sigh.

"Good. We are also going to take advantage of this unplanned media attention."

"Okay…" M's voice wavered. Alana resisted the urge to look at him again.

"You will be appearing on *I Can Cook*. Since the dating rumors are false, we have no fear in pushing you further into the spotlight. Ultimately, this will be great for your image and reputation."

"I'm not so sure that's actually a good idea…" Emery paused to take off his hat and nervously smooth back his hair before he continued. "You know I'm not the best at reality shows. Wouldn't it be better to let the rumors cool off first?"

"Nonsense. Besides, it's only the filming that starts soon. I spoke with the show producers, and the episodes won't be aired until after *Chuseok* at the end of September. That's more than two months from now."

"But—"

"I'm not asking this time, Emery. You are doing the show." The friendly, conversational tone fell away from President Jo's voice.

Alana held her breath.

"Yes, President," M said quietly.

"Okay, I have another call to make. Minhyuk, keep me updated on events at the Daegu Festival."

"I will, President," Minhyuk instantly agreed.

"Great, I will see you all when you return to Seoul. Oh, and Alana?"

"Yes…President?"

"Welcome to Solar Entertainment."

The phone screen faded to black as President Jo hung up.

# Emery

## #TrustMe

"You looked dope. Like you came straight out of a K-drama," said Jaehyun.

"K-dramas are *dope?*" Stu asked with a smirk, causing Jaehyun to glare back at him.

"More like a superhero movie," Sungil said.

"Ha, I bet we'll be seeing memes about Emery's 'heroic' actions from GLO soon," Stu said, letting out a soft chuckle.

"How could you, M?" Jaehyun said in a mockingly hurt tone. "You know I'd look much better in a cape. Such a shame."

"What should his superhero name be?" asked Sungil.

"Spider-M," said Jaehyun without hesitation.

"Ven-M." Sungil looked proud of himself.

"Iron M, no wait. I got it. Captain M-erica," said Stu, and Sungil gave him a high five.

"Super M," Jaehyun said with a smirk.

"Wrong universe, *Hyung. Bat-M* is cooler," said Sungil.

"*Em em em em em em em em em Bat-M,*" Stu sang cheerfully.

Emery looked up from underneath his black hat in relief as Stu, Jaehyun, and Sungil burst out in laughter.

After Emery and Minhyuk had returned to the tent, it had taken time to calm the rest of the group down—particularly Stu, who kept pestering them for more details—but everyone was now up to speed about Alana's new position. Yongnam still looked concerned, but gave an understanding nod when he met Emery's eyes.

Minhyuk's phone buzzed and he took it out from his back pocket. "Okay, guys, your soundcheck was rescheduled for 3:00 p.m. I want you to stay here until I come back to get you in an hour. The *coordis* will be bringing some food soon. *Please* don't go anywhere. We don't need any more excitement today." He turned to leave, but stopped before opening the door flap. "Oh, and congratulate M on his new role. He's officially joining *I Can Cook*."

"What?! *Baksu!*" Stu stood up to excitedly clap his hands in applause while Minhyuk exited the tent.

"Ah, that's awesome, M! You'll be great," Sungil said.

"Wait, what?" Jaehyun said, eyes narrowing. "You cause a scandal and they reward you by letting you star on the show?"

Emery was surprised, and rather hurt, by the bitterness in the oldest member's voice. He thought it was clear that *I Can Cook* was a punishment, not a reward.

"I really don't want to talk about it," Emery said, rubbing his eyes. He felt a headache coming on and just wanted some space to think.

"Ah, come on," Stu whined. "We know you're not giving us all the details."

"Let it go," Yongnam said tiredly, and a weighty silence settled among them.

"I'm going to get some rest," said Emery. "Let me know when it's time to go." He walked over to his bag in the corner, grabbed his headphones, and sat down in an empty chair on the far side of the room. Headphones in place, he hit play and closed his eyes, letting the events from earlier replay in his mind.

He hadn't hesitated. One moment Alana was falling, and the next he was at her side, the world blurring around him as he scooped up her limp form and held her tightly to his chest. She had felt surprisingly light in his arms, fragile and defenseless. He couldn't recall his surroundings for the life of him. Had anyone else tried to help? It didn't matter—he didn't care. In that moment, Emery had overtaken M, cameras and consequences be damned. She'd needed help, and he'd felt an irresistible need to help her. That had been the only thought in his mind.

Emery sighed. He couldn't afford to let her get any closer. She was a risk. There was no denying it. He was becoming too attached—he should have seen it coming. It was exactly what had happened two years ago, after all. He reached up with his hand to hold his necklace, a silver USB hanging on the chain around his neck. His thumb automatically traced the engraved A—a well-worn and practiced motion.

That summer night had almost been the end. NEON's failed comeback. The sympathetic smiles and forced optimism. The defeat, the disillusionment, the guilt—it had writhed through him, churning into an inexplicable rage attacking him from within as he stood motionless in the rain at the Han River. The pressure had been building for months, but it was that final phone call with his father that had sent him over the edge. Everything boiled over until he had nothing left. He pummeled the concrete light post over and *over* again as fury overwhelmed his senses.

He remembered relishing the pain, grateful for the distraction and release from the torment in his mind. How many punches had he thrown? Ten? Twenty? Enough to leave his knuckles a torn and bloody mess. No matter how hard he hit, however, his rage only grew stronger, brighter, as if feeding off the destruction of his life.

He had failed as a musician—*punch*.

He had failed as a son—*punch*.

He had failed at beating the crap out of the freaking lamp post—*punch, punch*.

His head swam, and he gasped for air. Crumpling to his knees, he surrendered to the storm as rain beat down on his face. It was all over.

It was at that moment *she* found him.

He would never forget the sight of her red umbrella, as bright as the blood on his fingers. She was standing above him, protecting him from the rain, as he fought for breath. Then she crouched down. Her arm wrapped around his waist, tugging him, urging him to his feet. He gave in, leaning against her warmth as she silently led him to a nearby bench along the river.

He had been shaking—from distress or the cool rain, he wasn't sure—but she took her white headphones off from around her neck and placed them gently over his ears. The world faded as he listened. Complex melodies wove in between steady beats, and his racing heart slowed as the lyrics of a soft voice registered. He closed his eyes, letting the unfamiliar sounds wash over him.

She held the umbrella against the rain, waiting patiently as his breath calmed. After five, ten, maybe fifteen minutes, he finally looked at her, taking in her small face and damp hair as she stared thoughtfully into the distance. Perhaps sensing his gaze, she turned her head, and his heart stilled as he looked into her stunning light brown eyes. They almost seemed to glow when she smiled shyly back at him.

With quiet movements, she gestured for him to take the umbrella. He blinked, freed from her magnetic pull as she reached into her bag, taking out a small case to reveal bandages, disinfectant, and tissues. He slipped the headphones off, and she gently took hold of his free hand, treating his wounds with special care. He felt his cheeks burn with embarrassment, but also gratitude. In the light from the street lamp, he could make out the Punk the Pom design on the bandages. A small, genuine smile formed on his lips. Finally, she spoke.

"Your other hand."

Caught off guard by her use of English, he complied, switching the umbrella to his bandaged hand. He watched her delicately clean the blood from his knuckles and felt compelled to apologize, suspecting she had seen too much of his violent breakdown.

"I'm sorry."

At his words, she looked up, and he was once again captured by her strange eyes. Yet, again, she remained silent. She didn't probe and she didn't push. She just waited.

"It all just hurts," he choked, horrified to realize he was crying. "I don't understand... I thought they would be happy with my decision—but no, it's not good enough. I'll never be good enough."

She finished wrapping his hand, placing it lightly on his lap. Ashamed, he glanced down, blinking away his tears, but then he felt her cool fingers wrap around his other hand, gently reclaiming her umbrella with a reassuring squeeze.

"It'll be okay," she said.

Suddenly, he was compelled to share truths he no longer wanted to disguise, and before he knew it, he was telling her about his family, things he had never spoken aloud to anyone. Throughout his rambling and ranting, she listened without judgement, offering quiet words of comfort in the broken pauses.

He felt free, unburdened in the presence of a stranger.

Eventually, his words ran out, and as the rain gentled around them, he grew curious about the girl beside him. He asked her about the songs he'd heard through her headphones and was surprised to learn they were her own. She'd written them herself.

"—when I'm at Berklee in the fall. I can't wait. There's this one songwriter workshop—you'd love it, M—but it's almost impossible to take as a freshman—"

*M.* She knew him.

He looked at her closely. She hadn't seemed to realize that she'd slipped up, calling him M before he ever introduced himself, and suddenly he recognized her.

She was his fan, a GLO. He'd seen her at their recent music shows and *fansigns*, waving her GLOstick and wearing a bright orange headband. Before the panic could set in—what had she seen?—he paused, taking in her unassuming manner. He felt he could trust her. She knew who he was, what he was, but she treated him as if he were an ordinary person. With a conscious decision, he let his idol mask fall away. For that night, he let himself be just Emery.

They chatted for more than an hour under her red umbrella. Emery listened as she spoke of her dreams, her carefree ambition twisting his heart. He had once been like her, ready to fight and pursue his passion for music, no matter the obstacles. Was he truly ready to let it all end? To say goodbye to M, to NEON, to GLO? As he looked at her, her bright energy and determination cascading off in waves, he finally had his answer—*no.*

Cutting her off mid-sentence, he had kissed her.

It was spur of the moment—typical Emery—but as their lips touched, it was as if a bolt of electricity struck his brain, short-circuiting his rationality. After a moment of frozen surprise, she returned the kiss, the umbrella slipping from her hand and hitting the ground, and he reached up to cup the back of her head as the kiss deepened, digging his fingers into her silky hair and savoring the taste of her soft lips against his own. His anger and pain melted away. It was bliss.

But as suddenly as it began, it ended. She pulled away sharply, gasping, and stood up. Emery felt a tug as the chain of her necklace caught around his fingers, breaking. She ran. Emery watched her shadow disappear down the path, the rain wiping away all trace of her. He sat there, numb, and looked down at the discarded umbrella at his feet, and then the broken necklace in his hand. Holding it up to the street lamp, he examined the silver charm with the letter A engraved into its surface. Only later did he discover it was a USB stick containing her compositions, songs he would come to cherish as he worked on NEON's breakthrough album.

That night seemed like a dream now.

He fought back the impulse to message her. *No.* He needed to stop. He couldn't drag her into his life. His hand clenched even tighter around his necklace. If he messed up again, they would both pay. He would have to ignore her—pretend she didn't exist. He felt a pang in his chest, ironically wishing he could ask her for some tips.

*I hope she's okay.*

"Who's winning?" asked Emery, smiling.

"No one, 'cause they both suck," said Jaehyun as he lazily stretched out on the sofa, and adjusted the sheet mask on his face.

They had returned to their dorm immediately after the festival, getting back well past 11:00 p.m. Even though they still had a week left of music show promotions, their concert preparations were well underway. When not at music broad-cast stations, NEON spent all their time at Solar's headquar-ters. For Emery, that meant he was either at dance practice or in his music studio, trying to make progress on their next album before the world tour started. For tonight, however, NEON was enjoying a few hours of freedom at their dorm.

"Yah! We told you to shut up." Stu had a look of intense concentration as he gripped the controller, his glasses threat-ening to slip off his nose at any moment.

They were playing a racing game with only twenty sec-onds left on the clock. Sungil was in the lead, but Stu was doing everything he could to catch up. Before Stu could make a final move, Jaehyun threw a pillow at the back of Stu's red head, knocking his glasses clear off his face and allowing Sungil to clench his win.

"*Hyung!*" cried Stu in frustration, throwing the pillow back at the eldest, who deftly dodged out of the way.

"Can we watch *Moonlight, Again* now?" said Jaehyun, re-moving his mask and patting his skin delicately. "I'm dying to know if Somin will ever wake up from her coma."

"Watch it on your phone or something. I need a rematch," said Stu as he jammed his glasses back in place.

"Nah, I'm up for some *Moonlight*," said Sungil. "I totally forgot about that cliffhanger." He put his controller down and joined Jaehyun on the couch. Stu made a huffing noise, but moved to switch the TV to play the drama.

"You want to join us, M?" Sungil said, patting the free space on the sofa to his right. "This should be a good one."

Emery looked at Jaehyun, who was avoiding his eyes. Jae-hyun had been acting coldly toward him all day, ever since the scandal was covered up, and Emery didn't blame him. He just hoped he could regain his trust soon. It was all such a mess.

"Thanks, but I still have some work," Emery said with a

regretful smile. "Try not to spoil it for me. I'll probably watch it tomorrow."

"No promises, mate," said Stu as he sat down on the floor. "Okay, I'm pushing play. M, could you get the lights?"

Emery turned off the main light, glancing over at his members who were already engrossed in the show. His guilt from earlier crept back. Today could have been so much worse.

Resigning himself to the conversation to come, Emery forced himself to walk toward Yongnam's room at the end of the hall, cautiously knocking on the closed door and waiting for an answer. After a moment, he knocked again, this time with more force, entering at the sound of Yongnam's deep voice.

"Hey." Emery closed the door behind him. Wearing a comfortable black sweatshirt and basketball shorts, Yongnam was seated at his desk with two monitors fired up and large headphones covering one ear. Emery wasn't the only one still working tonight.

Over the years, Yongnam and Emery had developed a tag team style when it came to NEON's albums. Emery focused on songwriting, while Yongnam took charge of polishing and post-production, both simultaneously pouring their own thoughts and experiences into NEON's music. The idol group was lucky in that regard. After years of training and teaching Emery and Yongnam about the inner workings of album production, Solar trusted them to create their own music, unlike many of the other K-pop groups in the industry. The company's production department supported their creative process and growth, and it took the efforts of the entire team to create the tracks that continued to push them to fame.

Yongnam swiveled his chair around, gesturing for Emery to take a seat on his bed. Emery removed his slippers and pulled his legs into a crossed position on the soft, green comforter, his usual spot when they worked together in Yongnam's room.

"I got stuck on the third track and needed a break. What are you up to?" Emery asked while looking over Yongnam's shoulder at the computer screens.

"I'm still fiddling with the title track. The intro has been bothering me. Can you listen and let me know what you think?"

Yongnam turned his chair back around and hit play. They listened for about twenty seconds before Yongnam paused it again.

"I don't know. The distortion of the bassline seems off." Yongnam's eyebrows pulled together in intense concentration as he stared at the digital audio workstation on his screen.

"Maybe instead of changing the bass, try tweaking the piano?" said Emery, a thoughtful expression on his face.

"I'll give it a shot." Yongnam grabbed a pen and wrote in the notebook next to his keyboard.

Emery shifted his gaze to the framed photographs on the walls—Yongnam with his younger sister, another of his parents, a beautiful beachside sunset, and, of course, many with and of the NEON members.

"Is that new?" Emery pointed at a photo on Yongnam's bookshelf that wasn't in a frame. In the image, NEON stood in a dressing room, Stu holding a trophy over his head while everyone posed around him. Yongnam's face was hidden behind his camera while he used the room's mirror to capture all five of them at once. Everyone looked so happy.

"Yeah, just got it developed. You like it?"

"Of course," said Emery with a genuine smile.

Besides music, photography was Yongnam's next great passion. He carried his prized 35mm film camera with him practically everywhere, snapping photos whenever he got the chance. Yongnam was easily the most sentimental of the group—not that he'd admit to it. He made sure all the special moments were documented. Emery cherished every single photo Yongnam had given him. They weren't just photographs, but frozen moments of their shared history, their shared family.

"I'm sorry," said Emery, looking at the back of Yongnam's head.

"Hmmm? Why's that?" asked the leader as he made more notes about the album track.

Emery looked down at his slippers, unsure of how to continue.

"Is this about earlier?" said Yongnam, turning his chair around to face Emery again. "You don't have to apologize for helping someone."

"What would you have done?" asked Emery, genuinely curious.

"Hard to say," Yongnam said, playing with an earring as he considered the question. "But I'm proud you helped her. Someone had to."

"But would you say the same thing if the scandal had been worse?"

"Yes, of course," he said without hesitation, eyes locking with Emery's.

"I just wanted to help her. I wasn't thinking."

"I know," Yongnam said cautiously. "Seriously, M. You don't have to keep apologizing. What is this really about?"

Emery paused. He couldn't tell his leader about Alana—not the full story, at least. The world didn't need to know what secrets he kept behind his mask. His shame was too personal to share, even with Yongnam. He couldn't bear to see the look of disappointment on his friend's face if he found out about his family—or about his near withdrawal from the group. But he still wanted—*needed*—to talk about Alana. The situation today had gotten too far out of his control. He knew he could trust

Yongnam with this, as long as he chose his words carefully.

"I-I need some advice."

"Sure, go ahead."

"What would you do if someone you knew changed? Like if Stu stopped making jokes or if Jaehyun stopped looking in the mirror."

"Ha. Don't see either one of those happening anytime soon," said Yongnam with a smirk.

"Okay, maybe not the best examples," Emery agreed. "But let's pretend. What if someone's personality did a complete one-eighty? What would you do?"

"It depends," said Yongnam, his expression thoughtful. "Are these changes for the better or worse?"

"Just different, I'd say. Darker. As if that person's bright energy were taken away."

"Do you know what caused the change?"

"No idea. We're not very close."

"Is this anyone I know? Maybe I can try and help."

"No. Just a girl… I met her awhile back."

Yongnam didn't say anything, a frown forming on his face, and Emery quickly explained, "She's actually a fan of NEON. Or at least she used to be, until…well, I'm not sure." Emery ruffled his hair, unsure of how much he should say. "I recognized her a few weeks ago and couldn't get her out of my head. I was curious. I needed to know her story."

"So then what?"

"Well… At first she ignored me. Even flat-out ran the other way when she saw me."

"At least *someone* was thinking straight." Yongnam gave a sly grin.

"Ha ha, very funny. But seriously, the more she avoided me, the more I had to speak to her."

Yongnam leaned back in his chair, resting his hands behind his head. "Is this why you've been acting strangely these past few weeks?"

"I guess." Emery shrugged. "I was trying to find a way to talk to her."

"Did you?"

"Well, only after we got locked in a confetti closet together…" Emery's voice trailed off.

"Confetti closet? What's that mean?"

"Don't worry about it," Emery said hurriedly. "Basically we finally talked and exchanged Tiki IDs."

A flicker of emotion flashed in Yongnam's eyes, but it was gone before Emery could identify it.

"But she's no one," said Emery, still in a rush. "We're just friends."

"I'm not judging." Yongnam held his hands up in defense. "Just be careful, okay? You seem overly interested in this girl."

"It's all in the past, I swear. You know my focus has always been on NEON."

"You say that, but sometimes I don't know where your head is at."

Emery fought back a wince. Yongnam knew him too well.

"I'm here whenever you need to talk, M," the leader said quietly. "You aren't alone, okay?"

"I know," Emery said as he stood up, suddenly feeling exposed. He put his slippers on, ready to escape back to his own room. "I need to sleep. Don't stay up too late."

Just as Emery reached the door, Yongnam spoke up once more.

"M, just warn me if anything changes, all right?"

"Don't worry," said Emery, pausing at the door. "You can trust me."

# Alana

## #WelcomeToSolar

Alana peered up at the Solar Entertainment headquarters. Large posters of NEON and their *sunbae* group NEPTUNE hung from the side of the building, spanning close to five stories. M's enlarged face inevitably drew her gaze as the banner fluttered in the wind. She forced herself to look away.

The street was quiet. Luckily for her, there weren't any fans lined up outside. She had been to the company before as a fan herself, taking touristy pictures in front and hoping to catch a glimpse of NEON from outside, but this was entirely different. Today, she was going *inside*.

She took a long, deep breath and stepped up to the frosted glass doors, heart pounding in her chest, as Stephanie rang the doorbell on the intercom.

They were early, even after circling the block twice—Stephanie teasing her the whole time—and getting coffee at a nearby shop. It was still only 9:35 a.m., and work didn't start until 10:00 a.m. Aunt Park's apartment in Sadang was thirty minutes from the company, but Alana had already been dragging Stephanie onto the bus by 8:30. She didn't want to be late for their first day.

*"This is Solar Entertainment. Please state your name and business."*

Alana jumped at the rough, male voice coming from the intercom, the Korean slightly muffled through the speakers.

Stephanie cleared her throat. "Yes, I'm Stephanie Lim, here with Alana Kim. We're recently hired stylists and supposed to start work today."

*"Please wait."*

"Okay," Alana squeaked into the intercom, prompted by Stephanie's elbow in her side. God, why was she so nervous? The worst they could do was fire her, and truly, that would be a blessing. She couldn't believe she had agreed to this.

*"Please proceed to the fourth floor. Someone will meet with you both shortly. Welcome to Solar Entertainment."*

"Thank you."

The doors slid open, and Alana entered the building with her cousin, looking around at the white walls and tiled floor of the small entryway. There was an elevator to their front and a guard's desk to the left. A small hallway led from the elevator to another frosted glass door. Nodding politely at the security guard, they walked quickly to the elevator.

Alana darted anxious glances around the room, scanning everything from the surveillance camera in the corner to the orchid on the security guard's desk. She took in her cousin's bright turquoise dress and hot pink sneakers. The colors complemented Stephanie's short hair, now a smoky grey instead of lavender, with sideswept bangs falling across her face. In contrast, Alana wore her usual black jeans and T-shirt, hoping to blend in as best she could. Walking side by side with her cousin, the differences between them couldn't be more obvious. Stephanie exuded brightness, strength, and confidence—everything Alana had lost.

This was a mistake. She didn't belong here.

"Relax, Aly," Stephanie said, smirking when Alana jumped.

"Excited to see a certain member of NEON?"

In their week off, Alana had broken under The Stephanie Inquisition, spilling to her cousin about her recent interactions with M—the tea accident, her attempts to avoid him, the confetti closet, and even their text messages. Rather than being upset with Alana, however, Stephanie had been miffed M hadn't done more in their "relationship." No matter how many times Alana insisted there was nothing going on between them, her cousin would just raise her sculpted eyebrows in a suggestive look.

As Alana was about to respond, the elevator doors opened, revealing none other than Hyojoon Kang, the lead dance instructor and choreographer at Solar Entertainment. Alana recognized him instantly from all the behind the scenes footage of NEON in the dance studio.

"Ah...h-hello." She stammered before bowing her head low in respect.

Stephanie coughed to hide her laughter at Alana's high-pitched greeting, and Hyojoon nodded politely to them as they joined him in the elevator. Dressed in black sweats and white shirt, with his long hair pulled back in a simple ponytail, the only color adorning his look was his pristine red designer tennis shoes. When the elevator arrived on the fourth floor, Alana stepped out behind Stephanie, fighting the urge to turn and double check that she had really shared an elevator with *the* Hyojoon Kang.

They stood alone in the modern waiting area. Two white couches surrounded an industrial grey coffee table facing the elevator, and the walls were bare except for a large painting of Saturn. Alana was unsure of what to do or where to go. Hallways splintered off the main room, leading to a series of doorways, and she could hear voices in the distance. Stephanie plopped on a couch, and Alana tentatively joined her.

"This is fun," Stephanie said brightly. "You're so cute when you're on edge."

"Urgh. I should have never gotten you this job." Alana buried her face in her hands.

"Too late now." Stephanie smiled and leaned back on the sofa. "I still can't believe you *bargained* with the president of Solar to hire me."

Stephanie had initially been skeptical when Alana told her about their new jobs, making her describe the conversation in the van over and over again. She even went so far as to call Solar for more details, and it wasn't until she spoke to Manager Choi that the news really began to sink in. Alana smiled, remembering how Stephanie had tackled her with a grateful hug.

"Of course. I owed you. And besides, you're perfect for this job."

Stephanie grinned happily. "I am, aren't I? But really, thanks for this, Aly."

Alana's smile morphed into a yawn. Fortunately, the worst of her cold had passed—the week of sleep and her aunt's cooking leaving her feeling much more human—but her mind had been too wired to get much rest the night before.

As they waited, Alana looked down at her phone. Her finger automatically gravitated to her HeartU app, and she refreshed the now go-to hashtag: #MTheHero. Since the incident, the tag had grown to over two million posts. No matter how hard she tried, she couldn't stop scrolling through the messages, videos, memes, and GIFs. It was like a train wreck she couldn't look away from.

**JaeJae:** I KNEW it! She's not M's girlfriend. Idols treat their staff with respect. M is a really good person!! All you GLO blowing up my feed for nothing lol WHY

YOU ASSUME?? O.o #MTheHero
*Hearts 1,467, Replies 499, Shares 683*

**GLO Forever:** Guys remember to keep streaming
Enlighten MV! We are so close to reaching 100 million
views!! Don't give up now!!!! @neon_solarofficial
#NEON #MTheHero #ENLIGHTEN100M
*Hearts 281, Replies 12, Shares 102*

**EmNam Trash:** Searches "How to be NEON's staff?"
#MTheHero
*Hearts 2,438, Replies 231, Shares 798*

**NEON GLO Official Trans:** M's such a gentleman!!!
My heart can't handle it!!! I hope that girl is okay though
>.< #MTheHero
*Hearts 1,311, Replies 754, Shares 487*

**Save Yongnam's Forehead:** I had a test last week and
I missed everything!! What's going on??!?!?! I keep seeing
photos of our Emery carrying a girl O.O #MTheHero
*Hearts 41, Replies 15, Shares 2*

**Stu Stan Stew:** I don't care if NEON dates. I just want
to know they have people to make them feel safe, loved,
and supported <3 #MTheHero
*Hearts 3,534, Replies 809, Shares 921*

**MnMnMs:** I'm sorry. I don't see staff here. All I see is
FAMILY <3 #MTheHero
*Hearts 2,192, Replies 862, Shares 2,632*

**HI5xNEONxFYRE Stan:** All y'all over here worrying about M dating some coordi, and I'm just like, DID YOU SEE THE HINT OF ABS WHEN HE PICKED HER UP?!?! M's been holding out *SWOONS* #MTheHero

*Hearts 1,975, Replies 492, Shares 521*

Luckily, to the fans, Alana had remained nothing but a nameless staff member. While most were jealous of her situation, it was a playful kind of jealousy, not the vindictive, fear-for-your-life sort—an important distinction.

"Hi Alana, Stephanie. It's good to see you both again."

Alana looked up, startled, to see the NEON *coordi* they had met at the festival standing in front of them.

"I don't think we were introduced properly. I'm Yena Park, the head stylist for NEON." Now that Alana was no longer knocked out from her cold, she saw Yena more clearly: a few inches taller than her, with a slender build. She was dressed in black, like Alana, but with white, beaten up sneakers on her feet.

Alana put her phone away and stood, bowing to Yena.

"Hello. Nice to see you again."

"You too." Yena smiled warmly at them. "If you will both follow me."

The trio walked into a small conference room at the end of the main hallway, surrounded by frosted glass. A long white table with eight chairs spanned the entirety of the room, and a whiteboard on the far wall was covered in pictures and bullet point lists. Upon closer examination, Alana saw that there was a column for each NEON member, detailing various stage outfits and styles. In the top right corner, "D-75" was outlined in bright orange.

"I'm not sure how much was explained to you about your

positions here at Solar," Yena said once they settled down in the chairs, "but you will both be assisting me, as well as the other coordinators for NEON. Stephanie, I plan to have you help with product acquisition from designers, while Alana will be aiding with tasks on set."

Over the next hour, Yena talked them through Solar's policies and history. It was surreal to learn about the company's founding from an inside perspective, how President Jo had created the company through the formation of NEPTUNE, a seven-member girl group modeled largely after her own experiences in the industry. After two years of moderate success with NEPTUNE, Solar debuted NEON.

As Alana knew well, NEON's popularity had been slow to develop, hindered by intense competition from other new groups under the top entertainment companies, as well as by NEON's deviation from the more mainstream pop music sound in Korea. It also hadn't helped that just after their debut, President Jo had been involved in a dating scandal with a producing director fifteen years older than her, casting a negative light on the entire company when the media portrayed her as a conniving opportunist sleeping around for industry favors.

"I don't know what you've heard about President Jo, but we here at Solar trust the work she's done for us," Yena said. "She's great at what she does and always honest with her staff. Fortunately, the media is catching on. Every once in a while we still get negative press about President Jo's relationship—which is still going strong, by the way—but after NEON's success with *Requiem*, the media has come to grudgingly recognize our president's talents."

Alana let out a shaky breath. None of this was new to her. The release of NEON's second full-length album *Requiem* coincided with the night she lost her brother, after all.

"Okay, then," Yena said, standing up and motioning for Stephanie and Alana to do likewise. "Since it's getting close to lunch, I'll show you two around the building and introduce you to some of the other staff. Later we will visit HR to sign your contracts."

Alana followed Yena through the tour in a daze, desperately trying to memorize all the new information being thrown at her as they were introduced to the different office administrators, managers, coaches, producers, dancers, and stylists. She met PR Manager Choi in person, as well as the Social Media Manager Sohee Ahn, who led the creation and posting of all official NEON content.

During the tour, Alana discovered the building contained seven floors, including the basement. The first two floors of the building housed mainly administrative and office staff, while the president and her executive assistant were located on the top floor, along with the main conference rooms. The artists themselves mostly spent their time in the basement, working in the dance and vocal practice rooms. However, when it came to the creation of musical content, idols like M and Yongnam could usually be found in the studios on the fifth floor, which was also home to the company's state-of-the-art recording studio—or so Alana was told. Their tour didn't include the fifth floor, unfortunately.

When they weren't on site with NEON, Alana and Stephanie would be working mainly on the fourth floor, which held a common waiting area, the meeting conference room, space for idols to get their hair and makeup done, and some additional rooms for filming and storage. They also got to peek into the main inventory closet, which was a stylist's dream come true, judging by the way Stephanie's eyes lit up with excitement.

Finally, Yena ended the tour on the third floor—not coincidentally where the company cafeteria was located.

"I hope you both are hungry, because the food in our cafeteria is pretty famous," Yena said, leading them past the long rows of tables and chairs to the short line at the counter. When it was Alana's turn, she stared wide-eyed at the array of food.

Today's lunch menu was *bulgogi*, served with seaweed soup, multi-grain rice, and several side dishes, including *kimchi*, bean sprouts, and chicken fingers. Her mouth was already watering as she carried her tray to a table near the windows that overlooked the ritzy Cheongdam neighborhood in Gangnam. Sitting down across from Yena and Stephanie, Alana took a bite of her *bulgogi* and felt her heart lift at its taste.

She looked up at Yena's laugh to find the stylist watching her in amusement. "Told you it's good."

Swallowing her food, Stephanie said, "This is honestly the best *bulgogi* I've ever had!"

Alana nodded her head in agreement and took another bite, closing her eyes in happiness.

"It's all good for you too," Yena said. "Our president likes to make sure the food is healthy, so the artists can eat in the cafeteria without feeling too guilty."

Alana set her chopsticks down. "The idols eat here?"

"Of course! Speaking of, here's NEON now. They must be taking a break from dance practice."

Alana's head snapped up from her tray and followed Yena's line of sight to the entrance. NEON had indeed just walked in, dressed casually in sportswear and sneakers. As they drew closer, she noticed that they wore no makeup, all of their faces flushed and sweaty from exertion. Despite the black cap hiding half his face, M instantly caught Alana's eye. He was laughing at something Eagle said, his arm casually thrown around the *maknae*'s shoulders, when he looked up. Their eyes locked from across the room, and everything around Alana seemed to fade as they stared at each other. She felt heat rush to her cheeks looking at the way his shirt clung to his slender figure. All expression dropped from M's face as Eagle spoke into his ear, and he carefully averted his eyes.

Alana let her own gaze fall to her tray, staring at her meal as disappointment settled uncomfortably in her stomach. Out of the corner of her eye, she saw the NEON members file through the growing cafeteria line, making casual jokes with each other and the kitchen staff. As they picked up their dishes, Alana spotted Stu attempting to steal a piece of chicken from Eagle's plate.

"*Hyung!*" Eagle's cry echoed throughout the cafeteria, making more than one staff member glance over in interest.

"It was just one piece!" Stu said, laughing as he quickly blocked Eagle's attempt to steal a piece back in revenge.

"They are going to make a mess if they keep that up," Yena muttered in exasperation.

While Stu was distracted with Eagle, Yongnam, who was last in line, casually reached out to grab all the chicken off Stu's tray and place it on his own.

"Here you go, Sungil," said Yongnam, handing a piece over Stu's head to the taller *maknae*, who abruptly stopped wrestling with Stu to accept the chicken from his leader with all the seriousness of a soldier taking orders from his general.

Stu looked at Yongnam in shock when he realized his own food was missing. "Yah! You stole my chicken!"

"Yup." Yongnam's mouth curved upward, his eyes smiling.

Alana felt her own grin threaten to form and knew she wasn't the only one. Half the staff in the cafeteria sported amused smirks at NEON's antics, while the other half, like Yena, just looked completely done. Alana got the impression this wasn't the first time NEON messed around at lunchtime.

"You won't think they're so cute after working with

them," Yena muttered to Alana. "I swear, those boys live to drive me crazy."

Thanking the kitchen *ajumma* politely, Yongnam turned away from the counter and carried his tray nonchalantly after Jaehyun, M, and Eagle.

"Yah!" Stu repeated, looking disbelievingly around at the entertained staff, his eyes lighting up when he zeroed in on Yena. "*Noona*! Yongnam *hyung* took my food!"

The other members paused halfway to a table in the back, watching Stu as he approached the head stylist. Alana saw M's eyes tighten when Stu plopped his tray down at their table, sitting in the chair right next to Alana.

"I'm aware," Yena said dryly. "Next time, don't steal food that's not yours."

"You wound me, *Noona*. I would never steal." Stu put his hand to his heart in mock pain, before noticing Alana and Stephanie watching him warily. "Hello there, ladies. You believe me, don't you?"

"Uhhh." Alana looked helplessly to her cousin, who was eyeing Stu critically, taking in his fiery red hair and playful smirk.

"Not a chance." Stephanie snorted.

"Wow," Stu said, laughing. "I like you. You must be new."

"We both are." Stephanie gestured to Alana.

The other members of NEON approached the table. Eagle looked at Alana curiously as he sat down next to Stu, and Jaehyun followed suit, taking the chair on her other side. Yongnam and M held back momentarily before sitting in the open chairs to Stephanie's right.

"Ohhh, right!" Stu snapped his fingers, staring at Alana. "I knew you looked familiar. You're her!"

"The fainting girl from the festival!" Jaehyun grinned in realization. "I was so shocked! One second you were standing there and then—*bam*—you were on the ground and our

Emmie was carrying you away all heroically."

Alana blushed, glancing uncertainly at M, who was quietly frowning at his lunch like it had somehow offended him.

"Hey guys," Yena said. "This is Stephanie Lim and Alana Kim. You'll be seeing them around Solar from now on."

NEON greeted them with polite nods.

"You're going to be working with us?" Eagle asked after introductions were made, eating a chicken finger in one big bite.

"That's the plan," Alana said carefully.

"How old are you? Should I call you both *noona*?" Eagle said.

"I was born in '96," Stephanie said, "but my little cousin here was born in '99."

"Oh, Alana *noona* is the same age as M *hyung* and Yongnam *hyung*!"

"Just 'Alana' is fine. I'm American," she said, hoping that offered enough explanation.

"Are you feeling better?" Yongnam watched Alana closely. "You were sick, right?"

"Yes, I'm much better. Thank you." She held herself back from fidgeting under his intense gaze. Even without makeup and styling, NEON's leader was uncommonly attractive, his dark black hair falling messily across his forehead and obsidian eyes.

"Good." Yongnam started eating his lunch.

Stu watched pathetically as his leader took a bite of chicken. "*Hyuuuung.*"

Yongnam ignored the redhead, continuing to eat calmly.

"*Hyung*, pleeeease. My chicken," Stu said in a sad, child-like voice. He leaned forward with his hands together in a pleading gesture while staring at Yongnam with big eyes, reminding Alana of a cartoon character.

Yongnam pushed his tray forward, wordlessly offering the

coveted chicken back to Stu. Rather than take it, however, Stu started sending heart gestures to Yongnam, ranging from a small heart with his hands to a giant heart with both arms above his head. Yongnam watched the antics expressionlessly, but as Stu moved a finger heart steadily closer in front of the leader's face, Yongnam lost control of his serious expression and burst into laughter.

"I love you, bro," Stu stated solemnly in English.

Yongnam hid a smile behind his hand as he responded in Korean, "I love you, too. Now take your chicken before I let Sungil have it all."

Stu glanced suspiciously at the *maknae* before snagging the chicken with his chopsticks from Yongnam's tray and eating it with exaggerated passion. Alana felt herself smiling broadly at the exchange, until she noticed M watching her with an inscrutable expression. She quickly looked away only to meet Stephanie's amused gaze.

Alana largely kept to herself as everyone ate, listening as the conversation turned to NEON's morning dance practice. They must have been working with Hyojoon, because Stu wouldn't stop talking about their *seonsaengnim*'s red sneakers. Apparently they were custom made by the brand's designer, engraved with a special symbol and serial number. Stu was dropping hints left and right about his upcoming birthday. He was so obvious it was almost painful.

"NEON, almost finished?" said Minhyuk, who had en-tered the cafeteria and approached their table.

"Finishing up now," said Yongnam with a salute after looking around at everyone's trays.

"Good. Hyojoon's waiting in the studio. He wants to get started on the new choreography." Minhyuk nodded to Alana and Stephanie, noticing them at the table, before turning to M. "Don't forget you have a meeting with President Jo at 3:00

p.m. We need to go over the details for the first *I Can Cook* shooting on Thursday."

"Got it, *Hyung*," said M, picking at the leftovers on his tray with his chopsticks.

Stu crossed his arms. "If only that *fake* Australian didn't get cast. I would have been perfect!"

"We know," Jaehyun and Sungil said in unison.

"I bet he doesn't even know what a lamington is. Living in Sydney for two years does not make you Australian. Stupid show with its stupid rules."

"Drop it, Stu," Jaehyun said, annoyed. "Apparently only M is good enough for reality TV."

Alana saw confusion cross M's face before it went blank once more.

"You guys set? Let's go." Yongnam stood up from the table with his tray.

"See you later," Sungil said cheerfully to Stephanie and Alana. Everyone else nodded goodbye as they stood up, except M, who quickly grabbed his tray and left the cafeteria without acknowledging them.

"You finished with your lunch, Alana?" Yena moved her leftover food into her rice bowl, tidying her tray.

Alana sighed. If M wanted to ignore her, that was fine—perfect, even.

"Yeah, I'm finished," she answered, giving Yena a small smile.

"Good. Let's go sign your contract."

# Emery

## #ByungNO

"You have fifteen minutes to buy ingredients," said the emcee, playfully waving a white flag with the logo for *I Can Cook*.

Emery looked down their makeshift starting line in front of the town's Joongang Market. The teams were lined up and ready to go, each pair wearing matching colored shirts. Cameras were everywhere, ready to document their every move.

The cooking mission today was to use Gangneung's famous tofu, *chodang soondubu*, in a Korean dish of their choice. Thankfully, the show's staff had warned them about the mission a few days in advance, giving Emery enough time to brainstorm some recipe ideas. He had been practicing in NEON's dorm kitchen every chance he got. He wasn't brilliant, but even Jaehyun had said his dish was passable.

Byung Ho Kim, the famous comedian, stood to Emery's right, a confident smirk on his face. Despite Emery's height, Byung Ho still towered over him, standing almost a head taller with broad, wide shoulders. He was a thickset man, his black hair shaved short while sporting bushy, dark eyebrows. As Emery's teammate, Byung Ho wore the same bright yellow shirt, but while it hung loose around Emery's fit form, the yellow fabric could barely contain his teammate's girth.

For better or worse, Byung Ho was competitive. As Emery's *sunbae* in the industry, it was Emery's job to follow Byung Ho's lead, listen to his instruction, and take his advice while they filmed their segments. Byung Ho loved peppering their scenes with teaching moments and comedic tips, and Emery had certainly been "learning," but perhaps not in the way the comedian had in mind.

Filming of Episode One had been exhausting, an eighteen-hour overnight shoot that had scraped away every ounce of Emery's patience. While the whole thing hadn't been *horrible*, he still wasn't looking forward to another round of shopping and cooking today. If only it had been a singing competition. Emery could have held his own without a problem.

As the "International Edition" of *I Can Cook*, four celebrities with experience abroad were paired with four of the show's main cast. In addition to Emery, Jaden from H15 was also on the show, thanks to his Taiwanese-Canadian roots. Cocoa Pop's Japanese member Ayaka Yamamoto and the Korean actor Hyun Soo Jun, who had lived in Australia for a few years—much to Stu's consternation—rounded out the international cast. During the show's three-episode arc, they were expected to learn more about Korean cooking, while bringing some of their own country's influence into the cuisine.

While Byung Ho and Emery worked fine together on camera, Emery rarely interacted with his teammate outside of shooting. Once the cameras stopped, Byung Ho gravitated to the other regular cast members, leaving Emery to mostly hang with Jaden and the Solar staff on set. Not that Emery minded. He couldn't pinpoint why, but Byung Ho rubbed him the wrong way with his constant jokes and overblown smiles. It didn't help that Byung Ho's nickname for Emery—*kiddo*—

had stuck, and now all the older cast members refused to call him anything else.

They were more than an hour into shooting, having just finished the short opening segment, which took about ten run-throughs until the show's writers and producing director, Junghwan Ku, were happy.

*Just keep smiling,* Emery told himself for what must have been the hundredth time that day. He made sure to look straight at his assigned camera, giving the biggest smile he could muster. His role had been clear from the beginning. He was to play the typical "boy next door," charming housewives with his good manners and good looks while they mentally married him off to their daughters. His smile needed to stay firmly in place.

"Ready. Set. *Go!*" cried the emcee with a flourish of his flag.

All four teams ran off in different directions through the market. Emery followed Byung Ho's bulky figure down the narrow aisles lined with vendors, past stall after stall of dried seafood and grains, items that wouldn't be of much use to them today. In other circumstances, when he wasn't trailing Byung Ho, Emery loved the cozy feeling of Korean tradition-al markets. Colorful signs and overflowing stalls gave way to a vibrant atmosphere brimming with life.

Emery's plan for today's show was to keep the menu plain and simple. Since tofu was the main ingredient, he figured they could just make a tofu stew or *dubu jjigae.* Even his mom, who couldn't find her way around the kitchen no matter how much she remodeled it, had made that type of soup when he was growing up. Creating a *jjigae* dish, along with serving some *banchan* of *kimchi,* bean sprouts, and radish, should be more than enough to help them survive the cooking round. He just hoped the result would be good enough for Byung Ho.

Unfortunately for Emery, he had cost his team valuable

points on the quiz part of the show in the last episode. They were currently in last place and had the smallest budget for grocery shopping: only 15,000 Won—about thirteen dollars— to buy everything they needed. Byung Ho remained unfazed on camera, boasting how the market *ajummas* would be lining up to give them good deals, but afterwards, when the cameras weren't on, Byung Ho's glances—perhaps better described as glares—made Emery squirm with guilt.

Byung Ho abruptly stopped in front of a specialty *hotteok* stall, and both Emery and the two cameramen almost toppled into him. Out of the corner of his eye, Emery saw the Korean rapper DrowZee and Ayaka, both wearing blue shirts, haggling two stalls away.

"Kiddo! I bet you wouldn't know, but this place is famous. Their *hotteok* is *de-li-cious*," Byung Ho said, exaggerating each syllable, another one of his trademark quirks.

Emery obediently looked at the menu, seeing not just the traditional sweet, brown sugar flavored *hotteok*, but also mozzarella cheese *hotteok*, chocolate almond *hotteok*, and even ice cream *hotteok*. They smelled fantastic.

"*Ajumma*, good afternoon." Byung Ho smiled brilliantly at the older woman with short, curly black hair behind the cart, puffing up his chest and dramatically putting his hands on his hips. "Kiddo here has never tried *hotteok*—"

Emery just stopped himself from rolling his eyes at the false assumption.

"—he's a *foreigner*," Byung Ho said by way of explanation, the word "foreigner" spoken like a shameful secret.

"How many you want?" the *ajumma* barked out, completely unfazed.

"Two ice cream *hotteok*," said Byung Ho, his smile wide as he looked down on Emery.

A crowd had started to gather. Even though they were in

the small city of Gangneung, their celebrity status held strong, perhaps even stronger than in Seoul. This was a big day for Joongang Market, one that would surely be immortalized with photos of the celebrities visiting the different stalls on the show.

The *ajumma* got to work preparing fresh *hotteok* for Byung Ho and Emery, keeping her head down as she assembled the dough and placed it on the grill. While waiting, Byung Ho's focus shifted to Ayaka, who was picking out ingredients.

"Looks like Team 3 is using octopus for their *jjigae*," said Byung Ho, his expression focused. "We'll need to prepare something more complex—"

"*Omo!*" the *hotteok ajumma* said in an enthusiastic voice, having finally noticed Emery's presence. "You're M! From NEON! *Omo!* My daughter loves you. Can I get a picture?"

Emery obligingly moved forward to pose for the picture, even adding his signature to the stall's main sign as the *ajumma* continued to talk directly to M, gushing about NEON, her daughter, the weather, and anything else that came to her mind.

"Kiddo, give her the money!" Byung Ho interrupted tersely.

"Oh no!" said the *ajumma* as she warmly handed over their *hotteok* topped with vanilla ice cream. "This is on me. I'm so happy you stopped by."

"So kind of you," Byung Ho said while pulling Emery in for a tight side hug and ruffling his hair in a very unflattering way.

With *hotteok* in hand, they continued their journey further into the heart of the market. They passed by more food stalls and stores before coming to the main grocery section. Vendors had fruits and vegetables lined up along the center aisle, leaving two pathways on either side for shoppers. Along the edges, more established stalls sold meat and seafood. Emery spotted Jaden and his teammate, the beautiful actress Jiwoo Song, a few stalls over. They already had bags full of ingredients and were now bargaining with a shopkeeper. Byung Ho immediately switched into action mode, clearly frustrated with their team's lack of progress.

"Okay, I'm going to get the *dubu* and seafood," said Byung Ho. "You can try bargaining for vegetables. We need mushrooms, spring onions, and lettuce. Keep 6,000 Won and I'll take the rest. Let's meet back here in five minutes."

Emery obediently headed to the first vegetable stand he saw, anxious to get this stage of the show over with. The cooking part would take place later in the afternoon.

After a few minutes, Emery returned to find Byung Ho holding a plastic bag over his meaty shoulder. Emery was rather proud of the amount of specialty vegetables he'd managed to purchase for only 6,000 Won. He'd taken pictures and signed autographs until the store owner had finally taken pity on him and handed over way more than he should have for the small amount of money Emery had.

"Kiddo! You're going to love what I got." Byung Ho's wide mouth spread into a sly smile. "I just hope you didn't mess up." He looked into Emery's bag. "That will do, I guess. Lucky for you, I know what I'm doing."

Byung Ho opened up his own bag to reveal a massive amount of seafood and tofu, double the size of Byung Ho's round face. They could practically supply the entire cast.

"You're not the only one who can charm *ajummas*," Byung Ho said with a smirk.

Emery stood alone outside the hotel, thankful for the brief moment alone.

After wrapping up at the market, the cast and crew had

relocated to film the cooking portion of the show. For the past few hours, Emery had been in the ballroom of a luxury beachfront hotel, doing his best to keep up with the show's various games and challenges, but his team was still behind. Emery had messed up again on the quiz section, thanks to his limited Korean cooking vocabulary and knowledge. But seriously, when was he supposed to have learned that Koreans first started eating kimchi in the 12th century? It wasn't a subject that had come up in between NEON's dance practices and world tours. Regardless—Byung Ho wasn't happy and had stormed off as soon as Director Ku yelled "cut," muttering something about a smoke break. If they lost today, their team would have to sleep in a tent outside as part of the show's "punishment." Emery let out a sigh.

The hotel's ballroom overlooked a manicured courtyard with a winding path that led down to the ocean. It was peaceful and serene, a stark contrast to how Emery felt when he was on set. At every turn, there were certain expectations for him—from PD Ku, from Byung Ho, from Minhyuk, and even from the other cast members. Needing to escape, he slipped off set during the break in filming, searching for some peace and quiet. Only Alana had seemed to notice, nodding to him as he walked past her and out of the room.

Despite himself, Emery smiled, thinking of Alana. She was here today as part of his support staff. Both of them had kept their promise to Solar, remaining distant from each other with an extra dose of avoidance. Emery had yet to speak a direct word to her since his texts the day of the festival, but from what he could see, she was adjusting to her new job at Solar without too many issues. Still, she looked troubled and listless, keeping her eyes down even with the other staff members.

Emery stared at the path scattered with pebbles and debris. He kicked a sizable stone near his foot, sending it skittering across the concrete.

"Why am I so useless?" he muttered, following the stone and kicking it again. He wanted to talk to her—just once—to make sure she was okay. Surely, that wouldn't be so bad.

With another kick, the stone went flying down the path. No, he couldn't do that. He had caused enough trouble. He wouldn't drag her into his life any more than he had already done.

He wound up again, frustration and guilt coursing through him, and kicked the stone with all his might.

"*Aish!*" a deep voice cried out. Startled, Emery looked up to see Byung Ho further down the path, clutching his shin, the stone just before him.

"You little brat," Byung Ho spat out.

Surprised by the venom in his senior's voice, Emery hurried to Byung Ho's side, bowing deeply in apology. "*Sunbae,* are you okay? I'm sorry! I wasn't paying attention."

Emery looked around. While lost in his thoughts, he had apparently made his way back to the courtyard. The hotel was just a stone's throw away, the building's ocean-view balconies protruding overhead.

"You did that on purpose, didn't you?" Byung Ho demanded, holding a cigarette in one hand and rubbing his shin with the other.

Emery felt his eyes widen. "No! I was just thinking. I didn't know you were even out here..."

Byung Ho snorted. "Good thing you're just as weak as you are stupid."

"Ah, good one, *Sunbae,*" said Emery, trying to play Byung Ho's words off as a joke even as he hid a cringe.

"No. Seriously, why are you such a sissy?" Byung Ho sized up Emery's appearance from head to toe, and Emery self-consciously stepped back. "Not that I ever expected much from a

Flower Boy like you in the first place."

"I don't—"

"I've been on hundreds of these variety shows, and you're the worst teammate I've ever been stuck with. You're just so *bad*."

Emery flinched, but kept his face respectful. He *had* messed up earlier, but it hadn't been on purpose.

"Worthless, that's what you are. You're dragging me down with you. I've never been in last place before, let alone twice. Did you know that? My reputation is on the line!"

"I promise to do better. We still have the next round—"

"Ha! Yeah, right. I know your type. You're just here for the quick boost in fame. You don't care about anyone else."

"That's not—"

"*You're* the one using *me*." Byung Ho's face grew redder as he continued. "I'm an established celebrity while you're this newbie from nowhere. What are you giving me in return? Nothing. This industry is all about give and take. The sooner you figure that out, the better."

Emery forced his gaze to the pavement and kept his head down as he seethed internally.

"You think you're so cool because people like you now? Well guess what, *kiddo*, you're in for one hell of an awakening when everyone loses interest in what you're selling. Your manufactured songs and smiles aren't going to get you anywhere in the long run. Because that's all you are—a trend. I give you one more year before people forget you ever existed in the first place."

Emery's whole body tensed as he struggled to rein in his burning anger. He spotted the rock he had been kicking lying just beside Byung Ho, and his foot twitched with the temptation to kick it again, this time right into Byung Ho's ridiculous face.

"You're in NEON, right? The 'underdogs rising to sudden

fame' story. Ha. Heard that one before. Tell me, how'd you make that happen? What special *favors* did you give? Or did President Jo whore herself out all by herself?"

"How dare you," Emery snapped, abruptly switching to informal Korean speech as he raised his head to glower at Byung Ho. "I don't care if you're my *sunbae*." He practically spat the title with his disgust. "You're out of line."

Byung Ho's expression, already red with snide judgement, twisted in outrage. "You!" he said, pointing an accusatory finger at Emery. "You have no right to speak to me like that! That's not how this industry works. I could ruin your career with just a snap of my fingers."

Emery took a step forward, refusing to back down. "You don't deserve my respect, you manipulative—"

Emery's vision spun as the momentum of Byung Ho's backhand struck him across the side of the head. He stumbled back, his eyes watering and his temple throbbing painfully, only just managing to stay on his feet.

"And there's more where that came from, you worthless piece of shit," Byung Ho sneered. "I will make you regret this."

"Is that all you got?" Emery righted himself and gave Byung Ho a mocking grin, while keeping his "senior" in his line of sight.

But just as Byung Ho lunged for Emery, the door from the hotel flew open, revealing none other than Director Ku. The short man was dressed in his customary khaki shorts and polo shirt. Emery had never seen him wear anything else.

"Byung Ho! Do you have a light?"

"Director! Of course," said Byung Ho, instantly turning his charm back on, his vicious demeanor evaporating. Emery blinked.

"Oh, M. I didn't see you there. Do you smoke too?" Director Ku looked at Emery with concern.

"No, I—"

"M was just keeping me company," Byung Ho cut in, putting an arm around Emery's shoulder and pulling him in for a tight side hug. "Right, kiddo? Some team *bonding*."

Emery grunted in agreement. They didn't need to get the director involved. This was between him and Byung Ho, no one else.

"So glad to see you two getting along," said the director, lighting his cigarette with Byung Ho's lighter. "We were a bit worried when we paired you together, but everything is going so well, isn't it? I bet we'll even have a ratings spike for these episodes."

"Yep, nothing to worry about here," Byung Ho said. Emery shuddered at the sickly-sweet smile spreading across Byung Ho's too-wide mouth.

"Well, I think M and I better head back inside. We need to strategize before the next shoot."

"Sure. Can't wait to see what you guys cook up." The director left to head further down the path, exhaling smoke as he went.

Instead of letting Emery go, however, Byung Ho tightened his grip, his fingers digging painfully into Emery's shoulder, and whispered into his ear, his words laced with malice. "One word and I'll destroy your career. Don't test me, *kiddo*." Then he released Emery, threw his cigarette to the ground, and stormed off for the hotel without another word.

Emery stared down at the glowing cigarette butt at his feet, the ashes crumbling to the pavement as the light slowly died. The side of his head throbbed dully.

The deck was stacked against him. There was no way he could win against Byung Ho. No one would believe his story. *A hoobae* didn't question his *sunbae*—that just didn't happen in the industry. If anything, Emery would be the one blamed for speaking disrespectfully to his senior.

Emery rubbed his pounding head, taking a few deep breaths and willing his smile back into place. He could do this. A few more hours and the shoot would be over.

*Just keep smiling.*

# Alana

## #CallMeEmery

Alana took another sip of her drink.

The rest of the cast and crew from *I Can Cook* were consuming more impressive alcoholic beverages like beer and *soju*, but Alana stuck to her Japanese sweet peach drink. With only three percent alcohol content, it was a safer choice.

Normally, Alana didn't drink. Even though it was perfectly legal for her to consume alcohol in Korea, it still felt scandalous at the age of twenty, since the U.S. laws she had grown up with were so ingrained in her psyche. But legality aside, there was also the whole "lowering your inhibitions" part. The idea of not being in control of her thoughts and actions terrified her.

Tonight, though, she figured she could use it, hence the peach drink. The magical, fruity elixir. The bubbly, buzzy goodness. Alana snorted softly.

The alcohol wasn't doing its job, however. Wasn't it supposed to make her relax? *Lies.* She was still royally pissed off. She scowled at the unintelligible Japanese label on her can before taking another sip.

"You doing okay, Alana?" Yena asked, her cheeks dimpling

as she smiled. The head stylist had taken Alana's addition to Solar in stride, never wavering as she calmly kept track of Alana's rather...*unfocused* ways. After Hyungkoo's volatile mood swings, Alana found Yena's steady management style comforting.

Alana was sitting next to Yena at a table with some of the other *coordis*, while most of the managers, cast, and crew congregated by the hotel bar. Everyone had gathered to celebrate and relax after the day of filming had ended. The room was beautiful, full of elegant tables and chairs with floor-to-ceiling windows overlooking the ocean. If only Alana weren't so angry, she might actually be enjoying it.

"It's not working." Alana took another sip of her drink, politely turning her head away from the table. As she drained the final drops from the can, her eyes wandered over to Yena's beer. "Maybe I should switch to something stronger?"

The head stylist unsuccessfully tried to hide her laughter. "Maybe you should switch to water. How many of those peach things have you had?"

"Not enough." Alana's hands gripped her can tighter at the thought of Yena taking her drink away.

Loud laughter at the bar distracted her, and she looked over to see Byung Ho drunkenly guffawing at something Director Ku said. Evidently, while M and Byung Ho were technically supposed to sleep in the losers' tent in the courtyard outside the hotel, once the show had gotten the required shots of them suffering, no one really cared that the comedian had come up to the hotel bar to drink. Alana's scowl morphed into a full-on glower. She hoped he choked on his *soju*.

"O-o-okay, someone has definitely had enough." Yena's eyes widened at Alana and the death glare she was directing at Byung Ho.

At first, Alana had thought she might be overreacting in

her dislike for the comedian, that maybe his brand of humor was getting lost in translation. It wouldn't be the first time a Korean joke had gone over her head. But today had disproved that. Byung Ho was a two-faced, lying piece of crap.

"What's her problem?" said Seungyeon, the *coordi* for Ayaka.

"He made a *big* mistake," Alana explained around another swallow of fruity sweetness.

"Huh? Who did?" Seungyeon looked back and forth between Alana and Yena for an explanation.

"Just ignore her. She's drunk," Yena said quickly.

"You know it's true. I can't wait to watch GLO rip him apart." That reminded Alana. Pulling out her phone, she smiled savagely as she logged into an old social media account. It was one she had created for award show voting back in the day, not that it had done much good. At the time, NEON just didn't have enough fans to win any awards. But not anymore. No, only an idiot messed with NEON now that their fandom had grown to global proportions. Which, of course, explained Byung Ho's actions.

"He's an idiot," she shared helpfully as she created a new post and attached the video.

Mikyung giggled nervously, pushing a piece of her bobbed hair behind her ear as she took a sip of beer. She was the *coordi* for Jaden and very shy. If Alana was the kind of girl people found quiet, Mikyung took it to a whole new level.

"Who are you messaging, Aly?" Yena frowned at Alana's rapid typing on her phone.

Ignoring the question, Alana finished adding all the necessary hashtags and handles before sending her post out to the social media universe, a thrill of triumph running through her.

"She's probably drunk texting an ex," Seungyeon commented, flipping her long, dyed-brown hair behind her shoulder. "I thought Americans were supposed to be good at drinking."

Catching that last part, Alana turned a scowl on Seungyeon. "I thought you were supposed to be smart, but you know, there's an exception for everything."

"Yup, time for bed." Yena hastily started gathering the empty bottles and cans over Seungyeon's angry spluttering.

"What's her problem?" Seungyeon demanded, staring at Alana like she had never seen her before. Which was unsurprising. She probably *hadn't* noticed Alana before tonight. It wasn't like Alana's current policy of keeping her head down and her work mistakes to a minimum was anything noteworthy. She was enduring. She was surviving. She was *trying*. But to what end?

"I need some air." Alana was on her feet before the thought had fully registered.

Yena looked up from wiping down the table in surprise. "I'll go with you."

"No, it's okay. You stay here and have fun. I'll see you back in the room."

"Are you sure? I don't think—"

Alana didn't wait to hear the rest. She was already heading for the exit, giving the bar a wide berth, but still casting one last glare at Byung Ho on her way out. Returning to the lobby, Alana let out a long sigh. The hotel was located near Anmok Coffee Street, right along the ocean. It was late and the lobby was quiet, but she could hear the sound of the waves crashing outside.

When she stepped out into the hotel courtyard, she couldn't help but glance over at the sad little yellow-and-navy tent erected near the doors. The "I Can't Cook Tent." More like the "Byung Ho Is An Idiot Tent."

Stupid challenge. Stupid comedian. Stupid cold. It was all

her fault M had been forced to appear on this ridiculous show in the first place.

The stillness of the tent bothered her. She figured M was asleep. Before she realized what she was doing, Alana was next to the tent, pressing her ear to the side, trying to hear…something. Was he not breathing? She leaned in closer but heard nothing but the sound of the ocean.

"Shut up, beach! Bitch? Beach!" She stood to direct the full destructive power of her glare on the offending waves when she noticed movement along the shoreline.

She froze, her breath catching—did Korea have bears?—until she noticed the outline of the figure in the dark. Human. Probably. She blinked a few times, squinting to make out any identifying features.

Moving closer, she crossed the street from the hotel courtyard to the sidewalk barrier along the beach. The figure was walking slowly away, disappearing farther down the coast. There was something about the tenseness of his shoulders, the way he kept his head down—because she could tell it was a he now—that struck a chord of déjà vu.

It was M.

Replace the ocean with the river, and all that was missing was the rain. Had it really been two years since she had spotted him outside a convenience store, where she had been editing photos from NEON's *fansign*? M had been walking slowly, heading toward the river, seemingly oblivious to the rain drenching his clothes. Ignoring her initial delight at her stroke of fangirl luck, Alana had let the sadness of the scene drive her to action. Picking up her bright red umbrella, she had followed after him.

A shudder ran through her body as she remembered the blood on his hands that night, but she let the memory drift away behind her walls, her focus turning back to the fuzzy present. Alana slipped off her black sandals and stepped from the sidewalk onto the beach, marveling at the sensation as the cool sand pushed between her toes.

With her shoes in hand, she crept silently down to the water, stopping when she reached the edge of the rising tide. She inhaled the salty ocean air, a breeze teasing pieces of her hair back from her face, and she giggled, only to muffle the sound against her arm when she spotted M, already a fair distance down the coastline. She frowned and started down the beach after him. He was walking along the strip of damp sand just above the incoming waves, and she could make out his footsteps in the light of the moon. Grinning, she followed, carefully placing her small feet where his had pressed into the sand. She lost track of time, pacing her steps to his own, occasionally teetering to the left or right.

Suddenly, M stopped.

Alana wobbled, frozen, her feet awkwardly aligned within M's longer stride. He was standing still, facing the ocean. With no one else in sight, the only sounds came from the loud crashing of the waves. She tried to see past him, wondering what had made him pause, when he let out a sharp yell of frustration. Alana jumped, losing her precarious balance, and tumbled into the wet sand. She let out a small yelp as she hit the ground.

"Who's there?" M demanded, spinning around.

"Nobody?" Alana said in a weak voice. She felt M approach and hastily climbed to her feet.

"Alana?" M stared at her incredulously as she unsuccessfully brushed sand off her black denim pants.

"Yeah?"

"What are you doing out here?"

"Following you?" She probably shouldn't have said that. Crossing her arms, she asked, "What are *you* doing out here?

You weren't in the 'Byung Ho Is An Idiot Tent'—"

He blinked at her.

"Get it? Because Byung Ho is an idiot. And a jerk. How's your head? I should have punched him…"

M just kept staring. Was that last statement too violent? She nonchalantly hid her hands behind her back.

"Don't worry, GLO's got your back. They should be taking care of it now. No one gets to treat our M that way. Not on our watch." Alana nodded at her own wisdom.

"Are you okay, Alana?"

"Yup, why?"

"Because you're switching back and forth between Korean and English."

She was?

"And you're swaying."

Now that he mentioned it, the world was moving around quite a lot. She tried to focus on making the universe stay still, but quickly gave up when everything tilted precariously to the side.

"And you just claimed to be my fan." A smile was spreading slowly across his face.

"No I didn't." She frowned.

"No? I'm pretty certain you just grouped yourself into the GLO fandom."

Oh, right. That. "I'm not your fan, but I, as well as the fans—your fans, who do not include me, even though I may seem like a fan—to the fans, I mean, because I posted it with my GLO account—"

What was she supposed to be explaining again? M's laugh was too distracting.

"I love your laugh. It makes you, I don't know, glow?" she decided to inform him, and he laughed even harder.

"You're drunk."

"Maybe?"

"How much did you drink?"

"A little…"

He was laughing again, and Alana had to smile. Today had been torture, watching M try so hard to maintain the pretense of enjoying himself while Byung Ho picked away at everything that made M, well, *Emery*. The idol had used smiles and laughter to disguise his pain, but she had recognized it all the same.

"I don't like your fake smiles."

M's laughter faltered. "My what?" He peered at her.

"You know, the pretty ones. The perfect ones. The smiles you use to hide *you*."

As if summoned by her words, his smile changed, the amusement disappearing from his eyes. "You think you know who I am, then?"

"Yes. Well, maybe…I don't know." Alana took a deep breath and tried to collect her thoughts. *Speak only English*, she reminded herself. "I know who you represent to the media. I know who you portray to the public. I know who you are to your company, to your fans…and to me."

"Who am I to you?"

"You're my fear."

The ocean breeze blew Alana's hair away from her face as she studied the idol before her. He was considering her seriously now, his gaze unwavering, before his mouth turned down into a frown. M reached out to her, gently touching the pink scar along her temple with a single finger. She jerked back, letting her hair fall forward again.

"I shouldn't have come out here," Alana whispered. She turned to leave, but M's hand on her wrist stopped her.

"You're right," he said.

She kept her head down, waiting.

"You do know me," he said. "Better than almost anyone. But you don't know everything."

"Can anyone truly know someone else?" she said, thinking of Alex and her scar now hidden in plain sight. "Everyone has secrets."

"And mine scare you?" M asked, keeping his hand gently on her arm, holding her in place.

"*Everything* scares me," she said, glaring at him. "You represent what I'm trying so hard not to want. I don't think I can survive losing anything else."

*Anyone else.*

Silence descended as M dropped his hand. The hairs on her arm tickled where he had touched her, burning a path up her arm to her heart. The tension was almost unbearable as they stared into each other's eyes.

Finally, M looked away, the wind rippling his shirt as he watched the waves bow to him on the shore. "What did you lose?"

Alana's back straightened. "I don't want to talk about it," she said shortly.

"I'm just trying to understand—"

"It's not important."

"It is to me!"

"Why? Why does it matter so much to you?" she snapped.

"Because you—your words, your actions, your music— they were what stopped *me* from losing everything!"

Alana's heart froze, and she swayed in the sudden absence of its rhythm before M's hand reached out again, this time in support.

M let out a frustrated sigh, running his free hand through his tousled hair and not meeting her gaze. "That night you found me on the Han River, it was supposed to be my last night as an idol. I had already notified Solar. I was quitting. It was over."

Alana couldn't believe it. NEON without M? She stared at him, his touch on her elbow an anchor through the turmoil of her thoughts.

"I called my parents to let them know the 'good news,' thinking they'd be happy." M let out a caustic laugh. "It was what they wanted after all."

Alana wished she could wipe away the pain from his eyes, treat the wounds eating him up from the inside. Instead, she remained still, silent, supportive—just like that night—waiting for him to explain.

"My mom was happy. I would no longer be a shameful topic at her little social functions, after all. But my father…" M smiled bitterly. "Oh no, my father was angry. Pissed, in fact. According to him, I completely wasted his money and my youth chasing after idiotic dreams. If only I had come to the realization I was a failure sooner—"

"You're not a failure!" Alana interrupted indignantly, her usual patience gone. She stepped closer to him, commanding his attention as she looked up into the shadows of his eyes. "You create meaningful music. It brings light to fans all over the world. Only GLO saw it then, but everyone sees it now! You've become one of the biggest names in Korea!"

"But I didn't know what the future would bring, Alana. Back then, cutting my losses seemed like the smartest option. The release of our first full-length album failed. Barely any fans showed up to our promotions and *fansigns*. It's not like I wanted to give up. But no matter what I did, I was disappointing the people I consider family. It was destroying me. I felt like a failure to everyone, and nothing I did was making anything better."

Alana remembered watching M punch the light post over and over again, coating his knuckles red with blood. She had thought at the time that he was venting his anger with his parents, but she was wrong. It was himself that he was truly angry with.

"So why didn't you leave?" she asked quietly. M's hand was still on her arm, both steadying and confusing her. They were so close, she could feel his breath brush against her face. Heat spiraled through her chest, as she recalled how the night on the river had ended.

"Because of you."

She stumbled back, and his arm fell to his side again. "What did I have to do with this?"

"Did that night really mean so little to you?" M spoke softly.

"I…I did what anyone would have."

"Not just anyone," M said with conviction. "Your hopes. The way you talked about what music meant to you, how you were going to attend Berklee and become a songwriter. I couldn't give up after listening to you describe dreams that had once been my own. I couldn't do that to you. I couldn't do that to the fans. The very next morning I told President Jo that I would stay. I wouldn't give up." He looked at her in earnest. "You are the reason I am here today."

"I didn't do anything, though." Alana's chest constricted with panic. Why did it have to be her? She didn't want to be the reason for another person's happiness. The irony struck sharply: fans all over the world relied on NEON and their music for that exact thing. It was one of the reasons they became fans in the first place. But that same responsibility and pressure was too much for her to handle. She knew better than most the consequences if she failed. She couldn't do it. Not after Alex.

"But you did. It was your hope that reignited my own, and your music that motivated me to try again."

"You hardly listened to my work! How could you…"

Alana's voice faltered as M tugged on the chain around his neck, pulling it out from underneath his shirt to reveal a silver USB drive dangling from the end. She stared in shock at the delicate 'A' engraved into the side, reflecting off the light of the moon. It was *her* USB, the one she used to wear around her neck. The same one she used to pass back and forth with Alex. Pain flashed across her heart, sharp and quick, and the night grew darker around her.

"It broke when you left that night," M explained. "I thought I would return it to you during our next comeback, but I never saw you..." He trailed off. "You know, I still listen to your songs all the time. It's not just your words, either. Your compositions are ingenious."

A spark of forgotten joy lit up inside her at his words.

"It's time I finally return this to its owner," M said. He took a deep breath, pulled the chain off, and held it out to her. Alana stared at the necklace in his hand, not making any move to take it. Her throat tightened. Alex was dead. She should throw the reminder of her failure away and be rid of all the memories and pain it entailed.

Seeing M's genuine, grateful expression, however, she paused, flushing as she remembered exactly *how* he had gotten hold of her necklace in the first place.

"Keep it," she said weakly, forcing the memory of their first kiss deep, *deep* down.

"Are you sure?" But M's fist had already closed protectively around the silver chain in his hand, and she smiled. She couldn't share her music with Alex anymore, but maybe, just *maybe*, she could one day share it with M again—on purpose this time.

She cleared her throat and stared down the dark coastline. She could just make out the bright lights of their hotel in the distance. "It's late."

"Or early, depending on your perspective," M said, putting the chain back on and tucking it securely underneath his shirt. A curious warmth curled in Alana's chest, and she quickly looked away.

"We should probably head back," she said. "Why did you walk all the way out here anyway?"

"I needed to clear my head," M said. "I'm surprised you followed me. Aren't we supposed to be ignoring each other?"

"I wasn't exactly thinking clearly," she muttered. "Those peach drinks apparently *do* work."

M laughed. "I noticed."

Alana felt heat return to her face, recollecting some of the things she had said…and done…

She swore.

"Alana?"

But she had already whipped out her phone from her back pocket and shakily brought up her HeartU feed.

**Giving Light to NEON:** APOLOGIZE, BYUNG HO!!! *Click to view attached media* @KByungHo @neon_solarofficial @GloForever @GloOfficialTrans @GloInternational #ICanCook #KimByungHo #GLO #NEON #M #EmeryJung #ByungHoApologize #ByungNO
*Hearts 134K, Replies 72K, Shares 98K*

"Alana, what are you looking at?"

Before Alana could hide her screen, M snatched the phone from her fingertips. She watched the amusement slip from his face as his mouth dropped open in shock.

"I'm sorry," she said miserably. "I was standing on the balcony at the hotel trying to get a picture of the ocean, and I noticed you and Byung Ho talking below. I could tell something was wrong and started to record you guys. I'm not really sure why, except I didn't like the way he was looking at you. But then, oh my god, I can't believe he actually *hit* you." Anger warred with her guilt.

"Shit. 134,000 hearts," M said, his eyes still wide as he scrolled through the comments on the post. "President Jo is gonna flip when she sees #ByungHoApologize is trending number one worldwide. And you posted this less than an hour ago... I'm impressed."

"I'm sorry," she said again. "I was drunk and angry. I'll take it down right now!"

Emery laughed. "I think it's too late for that. Hey! You think this will be enough to get me kicked off the show?" He sounded positively gleeful at the prospect.

Alana sighed. She was definitely getting fired—again. Twice in one month. That was depressing. "Why do I keep embarrassing myself around you?"

"Don't worry. Solar will handle it. The fact you posted this is rather cute, though." He handed her phone back, and she clutched it tight. If anything bad came back to hurt M's reputation, it would be her fault.

"We have very different opinions of what counts as cute," she huffed.

"True. I remember you appreciated Stu's *aegyo* in the company cafeteria. That stuff is terrifying." M shuddered in mock horror, making Alana laugh despite herself. "How are you feeling now? Any more drunken urges to protect my honor?"

Alana rolled her eyes. "Come on, let's go back."

"What if we sat here for a while?" M looked hopefully at her, following his own suggestion by plopping down onto the drying sand next to her discarded sandals.

Alana considered him as he stretched his legs out, relaxing. "Seriously? You're trending worldwide, the company is probably in damage-control mode as we speak, and we aren't even supposed to be talking to each other right now. Solar would *not* like this."

"The post is out of our hands," M said. "Also, how would Solar know what we're doing? It's not like there's any truth to the dating rumors."

"I'm pretty sure sitting alone together on the beach would add some truth to them."

"That is a very pessimistic way to look at it."

"Not pessimistic. Realistic." She had already caused— how many was it?—two internet scandals with M now. She wasn't looking for a third.

"Come on, Alana. It's been weeks since we've actually spoken to each other."

To her surprise, she really did want to talk to M. She had missed the way he could make her laugh, and alone time like this would probably never come again. It was foolish to waste it.

Seeing her hesitation, M added, "We will be back before anyone notices, I promise."

Alana sighed and sat down next to him, pushing her sandals aside. She really had no willpower when it came to M. She scrunched up her nose. "Happy?"

"Yes." His wide grin was almost blinding.

Her cheeks warmed. "You're too easy to please."

M's smile only grew. "You say that like it's a bad thing. Some of us can't be all serious and mysterious, wearing black on black on black all the time."

"Hey! I'm not that bad!"

He laughed. "Good thing I like a challenge."

"Careful, M—"

"Emery," he interjected. "Call me Emery."

"Emery," she said slowly, testing out his name on her lips.

"We can't be anything more than friends, remember?"

His eyes lit up. "So you admit we are friends now?"

She sighed, tilting her head to look up at the night sky. The stars twinkled brightly back at her, making her feel like they were sitting alone on the edge of the universe.

"Alana? Are we friends?"

She glanced over into his dark, smiling eyes, and her heart trembled. If her feelings from today showed her anything, it was that she would do almost anything to keep that smile on his face. His real smile. M's—*Emery's*—happiness was important to her. Out of all that had changed since Alex's death, that hadn't. "Yeah, Emery. I think we are."

His answering smile was everything.

# Emery
## #ImYourFan

"Hold still. This will only take a minute." Emery kept his head tilted back as Hyeran Choi, the head makeup artist, touched up his foundation. Peering into the mirror, he could just make out Jaehyun on the dressing room monitor behind him. Wearing a lemon colored suit that oddly worked with his bleached blonde hair, the eldest member was puckering his lips at the camera and holding a red lip tint close to his face. Emery would be doing the exact same thing in just a few minutes.

As the ambassadors for Pinkstone Cosmetics, NEON was the literal face of the brand. Every store was wallpapered with NEON photos, posters, and even life-size cardboard cutouts of each member. Today's shoot was for the latest "Pinkstone x NEON" Luminous Lip Stain collaboration.

"You're all set," said Hyeran. "I'll be on standby if you need a touch up."

"Thank you." Emery got up from the makeup chair and moved closer to the mirror to examine the final look. His freshly dyed chestnut brown hair fell casually onto his forehead, and the bronze shadow made his blue contacts stand out against his pale skin. He rather liked the strawberry pink lip color he was wearing—subtle and not too strong, a good match for his pastel blue suit.

"Looking good, M!" Stu called out as he entered the dressing room holding a plate of food. He had been the first one to film his close-up takes and now had a break until Jae-hyun, Emery, and Yongnam finished their shoots. Stu cleared a space on the table, moving aside empty coffee cups and water bottles before putting his plate down. Sighing dramatically, he turned to Emery and said, "I'm bored."

"Take a nap or something. We still have a few hours left. At least." Emery watched through the mirror as Stu sat in a folding chair next to the table, leaning his head back to stare at the ceiling.

"Why do these shoots always take so long?" Stu groaned, rolling to pop his neck, his alarmingly red hair—also newly redyed—not moving an inch from its careful placement across his brow, thanks to the hairspray their stylist Junho had applied.

Looking at the Australian, Emery was thankful he didn't get the orange tint himself. The color looked good on Stu, but Emery wasn't so sure he could pull it off with the accompanying peach suit the director had picked out.

"Emery, they're ready for you."

Emery turned around to see Alana standing in the doorway. She was dressed in her customary black T-shirt and jeans, adorned with a special kind of tool belt packed with makeup brushes, hairspray, and who knew what else a *coordi* might need. Her long hair was pulled into a half ponytail with some pieces left out, mostly covering the thin pink scar that spread along her hairline.

Emery gave her a quick smile.

Over the past two weeks, Alana had become a real part of

the Solar team. As her confidence grew, she started to come out of her shell around Emery and the other members. Stu had been particularly helpful in breaking the ice, due to his tendency to treat all their staff like family. Luckily, no one knew about her involvement with the Byung Ho scandal.

Emery smirked, thinking about Alana's drunken defense of his honor. Unfortunately, while her video captured their body language, she had been too far away to pick up any sound, so Byung Ho had at first tried to ignore the public outcry, citing unclear footage and fraud. However, the reality star was eventually forced to apologize for his "misunderstood" actions, and debate broke out over the reason for their fight, creating quite the uproar online.

Two weeks later, Solar was still dealing with the aftermath. While GLO had come together in full force, clamoring for an apology for the comedian's aggressive and violent actions, Emery hadn't escaped criticism. Rumors and doubt spread among *netizens* about Emery's—and by extension NEON's— lack of respect for the way things were done in the Korean entertainment industry. According to Emery's newfound haters, he must have provoked Byung Ho with rude and arrogant behavior to get that kind of reaction.

As a direct result, both Byung Ho and Emery stepped down from their roles on the show, and their scenes were cut from the episode footage. Even though Byung Ho was still the one worse off—his popularity plummeting with the scandal— it was doubtful anyone in reality TV would want to work with Emery in the foreseeable future, either. Luckily, while none of NEON's advertising contracts were affected, as a precaution, President Jo decided it would be best to keep NEON out of reality TV until after their world tour had ended.

Emery's feelings about the whole ordeal were split. Although he was grateful to Alana for defending him, as well as happy to no longer have to work with Byung Ho, he was also truly sorry for jeopardizing NEON's public image. For the most part, the other members had been understanding, but the tension between him and Jaehyun had only escalated. The day President Jo had informed NEON they would be on hiatus from TV programs, Jaehyun had lost it as soon as they returned to their dorm, yelling at Emery in front of everyone. He claimed that Emery should have avoided Byung Ho, rather than engage with his *sunbae*'s taunts as he clearly did in the video. With President Jo's rule in place, Jaehyun missed the opportunity to star in an upcoming talk show. While Jaehyun did later apologize to Emery for his outburst, he had largely been giving Emery the cold shoulder ever since.

Emery felt horrible. He knew he shouldn't have risen to Byung Ho's bait, and now he had truly hurt NEON's reputation. No matter how many times he apologized, it wouldn't make it right.

"Hey, Aly!" Stu called out in English, his mouth full of chips as he snacked on his plate of food.

"Hello, Stu," said Alana as she nodded to the Australian. "You need anything?"

"How about a kiss?" Stu said, reenacting the dance from today's commercial, complete with exaggerated puckered lips. Alana's mouth twitched into a small smile, her light brown eyes sparkling as she held back laughter.

"Put it away, Stu! No one needs that," Emery said with a glare.

Alana smiled sweetly. "I don't think I can help you there, Stu. Company rules, and all."

"Oh well. If you change your mind, you know where to find me," Stu said with a wink.

Emery cringed. "Let's go." He needed to get her away from Stu before he corrupted her.

Alana turned her attention back to Emery, a happy smile still on her pink lips, and he had a hard time keeping his grimace firmly in place as they left the dressing room together.

It was dark in the studio, all except for the main stage, which was brightly illuminated, almost blindingly so. Staff from both Pinkstone and Solar filled the room, with cameras and lighting equipment scattered around the stage. In the middle of it all was the director's seat surrounded by large monitors. There were five chairs placed behind the director's, one for each member of NEON.

Yongnam, Jaehyun, and Minhyuk stood next to the director, reviewing the cuts from Jaehyun's session. Emery spotted Sungil near the snack table in the back of the room making himself a plate for lunch. Emery's stomach growled at the sight of the food, but he ignored it.

"Hello, Director Lee," Emery said, bowing as he walked toward them.

"M, great! We're just about ready for you." The director was a tall, wiry man with a jovial smile and large silver glasses. "Take a look at Jaehyun's footage. Such smooth and fluid movements. Let's try and get some similar shots from you."

"I'll do my best, sir." Emery looked over at his *hyung*, noticing Jaehyun's proud smile.

"Great. Take a seat and we'll call you when we're ready." Clipboard in hand, Director Lee walked toward a cameraman near the stage.

"Yellow suits you," Emery said tentatively to Jaehyun.

"All colors suit me." Jaehyun smirked, not looking away from the screen.

"Even Stu's peach suit?" said Yongnam with a grimace.

Jaehyun snickered and lowered his voice. "Let's just say there's a reason I called dibs on this suit first."

"So, any poses you recommend?" asked Emery as he

glanced at the set.

"You trying to steal my moves now?" Jaehyun said, raising an eyebrow.

"No, of course not…" Emery trailed off, unsure of how to respond.

"Yongnam," Jaehyun said, turning to the leader. "I've been meaning to tell you. I can't get that new chorus you made last night out of my head."

"Thanks, but it still needs work, I think," Yongnam said.

"You were working yesterday?" said Emery in surprise. "I thought we agreed to take the night off."

Yongnam shrugged, sheepish. "I didn't want to bother you. After everything that's been going on lately, you needed the rest."

"Oh."

"I'll show you what I did once we get back to the dorm. It's not much."

"Are you kidding?" said Jaehyun. "You totally overhauled the song. I didn't recognize it."

Emery looked back and forth between Jaehyun and Yong-nam, unease settling in his stomach. It wasn't uncommon for the other members of NEON to be involved in the album-making process, but Emery was usually the first one Yongnam shared his edits with.

"Time for your touch-up, Yongnam," said Minhyuk, ges-turing for him to head to the dressing room. "Jaehyun, be sure to eat something before we do the group photo shoot in an hour. I have to step outside for a call with President Jo, but I'll be back soon."

As the two idols headed off, Emery sat down in his chair, trying to shrug off his discomfort. It was no big deal if Yong-nam and Jaehyun were working last night without him. So what if they were purposely leaving him out? It was no more than he deserved.

Emery sighed. The studio was warm, but not uncomfortably so. The weather outside was much worse. September was right around the corner, but the temperature was still in the nineties. Suddenly, a cool breeze hit the right side of his face. Turning his head, he was startled to find Alana standing almost on top of him.

"What are you doing?" asked Emery, slightly alarmed.

"I'm your fan."

He stared back at her intensely focused expression, unsure of what to say.

"Well not really your *fan* fan, but your literal fan. See?" Alana held up the mini handheld fan right in front of Emery's face. It felt nice.

"Don't you have more important things to do?"

"Actually, no," Alana said, a proud look in her eyes. "My job right now is to be your shadow. Minhyuk told me not to let you out of my sight."

Emery chuckled. "Well you don't have to stand *that* close. Take a seat."

"Oh, I couldn't," she said, glancing at the chairs marked for NEON.

"Come on. No one would care."

"Emery, do you want to get me in trouble?" She tried to look cross, but the smile hinting at her lips ruined it.

"Of course not!"

"Good, because I'm finally starting to enjoy my job. I haven't been yelled at in days!"

"Congrats!" Emery reached his hand out to give her a fist bump. She tried to reciprocate, but the gesture was rather awkward since she was still holding the fan.

Alana's resulting giggle instantly made Emery smile, his earlier worries pushed away.

"These sandwiches are good," Sungil said as he made his way over to them, plopping down in the chair on Emery's left and shaking his light brown hair out of his eyes.

"Ah, stop tempting me." Emery glanced at Sungil's plate that was stacked high with mini sandwiches. "I haven't eaten since we left at 6:00 a.m."

"Want me to make you a plate, *Hyung?*" asked Sungil.

"It's okay. I'll help myself after my close-ups."

Sungil shrugged, his light purple suit bunching up around his shoulders, and held his plate out to Alana. "*Noona*, would you like one?"

"Thanks, Eagle, but I'll eat after Emery is done."

"You should eat now. Don't wait for me," Emery said, glancing at her thin frame. He never saw her eat when she was working, and it worried him.

"No, I'm fine, really," protested Alana.

"Just have one. Sungil doesn't mind."

"Nope," Sungil said with a grin as Emery reached over to his plate and snatched up one of the mini sandwiches, holding it out near Alana's face.

"Say ahhh—"

"Okay, fine, just stop." She quickly grabbed the sandwich from his hand, her cheeks reddening.

"M, time to shine!" Director Lee approached them. Emery nodded and stood, leaving Sungil behind to finish eating. The director walked alongside him toward the set, outlining the different shots they would be taking.

As he stepped in front of the camera, Emery felt strangely nervous. To the side, he could see Alana standing, her eyes bright as she took in the set and the flurry of action from the camera crew.

"Okay, ready?" Director Lee called out. "Action!"

Emery tore his attention away from Alana and looked

directly at the camera. It was time to get to work.

"Cut! Set up the next backdrop," said Director Lee. "M, next we need a close-up of you applying the tint."

While the crew rearranged the set, Emery walked toward Alana and his stylists. Hyeran immediately dabbed powder on his face while Alana held up her little fan to help cool him down.

"It must be hot under the lights," Alana commented. "You're sweating."

Emery shrugged, but felt heat creep across his face.

Hyeran reached out with a makeup remover wipe, carefully eliminating the tint from Emery's lips. She followed up with a clear layer of lip balm.

"Okay, all done," Hyeran said while turning to look at Alana. "I need to make sure Yongnam is ready. Can you help out when Director Lee wants the color removed again?"

Alana nodded, and Hyeran headed toward the dressing room, leaving the two of them standing together.

"You look cool up there," Alana said.

"Really?" Emery said skeptically. "I'd say all the *aegyo* I'm doing overrides any cool factor I may have."

"You mean all the kissy faces you're making?" She closed her eyes, puckered her lips, and placed a peace sign over her left eye.

Emery glared at her while fighting back a smile. "Excuse me, it was more like…" He made finger hearts with both hands and moved them while he danced around Alana, making kissing noises.

Alana burst into laughter, the air around her changing. It was like a heavy veil had lifted, taking the sadness lingering in her eyes with it. Emery smiled, basking in her momentary glow.

"Seriously, though. It's exciting." A distant look came across her face. "I used to always wonder what these commercial shoots were like."

"Did you expect all the waiting? That's about ninety percent of it," Emery said, gesturing at the room around him.

"Oh." Alana's eyes widened.

"What?" Emery looked down at his blue suit self-consciously.

"You're sweating again," she said, reaching into her tool belt and pulling out a sheet of blotting paper.

"It's okay——" Emery started.

"Just a second." She reached up with a tissue to softly dab away the beads of sweat on his forehead, her light eyes focused intently on his face. Emery couldn't help but be aware of how close she was standing. He could feel her warm breath on his neck as she dabbed his skin, and it felt as if the temperature in the room had spiked twenty degrees. He clenched his hands into fists, his face flushing.

"Everything all set?" Director Lee had returned to stand next to the main camera, in position to start.

"I'm ready!" Emery called out, a bit too loudly. He darted back from Alana, stumbling on an electrical cord. Alana frowned, but he managed to keep his balance and moved into place for the shoot.

"Action!"

Following the director's voice, Emery did as he was instructed, slowly moving the applicator wand along his bottom lip. With the camera less than six inches from his face, it truly was a close-up.

"Cut!" cried the director. "Let's shoot again. This time, move a bit slower. We need to really capture the texture of the product."

Alana stepped onto the set, looking adorably nervous

under the bright lights. Emery vaguely wondered what she would look like wearing the same tint.

Without a word, she reached up with a makeup wipe to remove the still damp product from his lips. He wanted to say something, but it was difficult to speak while she was touching his mouth. The director waited for them to finish, and Alana pulled away, practically running off set.

"Okay, action!"

Emery did it again, and again, and again. Each time, Director Lee would find something he didn't like about the shot, and Emery continued to apply and remove the tint until the director was finally satisfied. After the eleventh take, Emery's lips felt raw. Not to mention that they might be permanently dyed strawberry pink.

"Great work! You're all finished, M," said Director Lee.

Emery bowed, thanking the director as he moved off set once again. He handed the lip stain to a Pinkstone staff member before moving to the side where Alana was waiting for him.

"Thanks for your help," said Emery.

"Of course. That's my job."

"True," Emery said as he tried to wipe away the excess product. "Do you have a mirror in that fancy belt of yours?"

"Here, let me," said Alana, already reaching up with her thumb, her eyes narrowed in concentration. Emery's skin tingled at her touch, and he looked down, entranced by her bare, soft lips.

"You two look cozy," Yongnam's deep voice cut through them like a sheet of ice, and both Alana and Emery jumped back. Emery could feel his cheeks flush. If he had to guess, his face was as pink as the suit Yongnam wore.

"Hey, I'm just kidding," Yongnam said, clearing his throat. "How was your shoot?"

"Over, thankfully." Emery took another step away from Alana. "The director seemed happy, at least."

"Ha. He's always happy." Yongnam was smiling, but it didn't quite reach his eyes. Of all the NEON members, Yongnam had yet to warm up to Alana. Emery had caught him on more than one occasion watching her with a frown. Emery wasn't sure what to make of the whole situation.

"I heard that after the close-ups, we have the Christmas-themed shoot," Yongnam continued. "Do you think we can make Stu be a reindeer?"

"Just convince Jaehyun *hyung* and Sungil, and it's a done deal," said Emery, glancing back at Alana. Her head was tilted down, discomfort radiating off her in waves.

"Alana, we need your help in the dressing room," Yena said as she walked by, dragging a large silver suitcase behind her.

"Okay!" Alana called, her head snapping back up. She turned away from Emery and Yongnam without a word and ran in the direction of the dressing room.

Emery stood in silence next to Yongnam for a moment, watching as the camera crew changed the set backdrop for the next shoot.

"You should get something to eat," Yongnam said finally. He jerked his head toward the food table. "There are a few sandwiches left."

"Will do." Emery turned to leave, but stopped when he heard Yongnam speak again.

"Emery, be careful, okay?" Despite the small grin his leader wore, his tone was concerned.

"Don't worry," said Emery, his lips widening into one of his trademark smiles. "I always am."

★ ★ ★ ★ ★

Emery was exhausted. As soon as the Pinkstone shoot finished, Minhyuk had ushered NEON into the van and onto their next schedule. They completed their special appearance on *2! 3! Radio!* and now NEON was finally on their way back to the dorm. Emery's head spun thinking about all the work he still had to get done before he could sleep.

The clock on the car's dashboard read 8:24 p.m. Alana— along with the rest of the Solar staff, besides Minhyuk—had been let off after the commercial finished.

The traffic was surprisingly light for a Tuesday night as they sped down the highway back to Seoul. Minhyuk was in high spirits, blasting music and conducting a sing-along that Stu and Sungil were happily taking part in. In the back of the van, Jaehyun somehow managed to sleep through the noisy atmosphere, or at least he *pretended* to sleep. M hadn't spoken to him since their conversation at the commercial shoot. Next to Emery sat Yongnam, who was playing a game on his phone. Every so often they would both chuckle whenever Minhyuk hit a particularly bad note.

Emery took out his phone, double-checked that it was still on silent, and sent a quick message to Alana. Since their talk on the beach, Emery had returned to texting her on a regular basis, but he was careful not to overstep the unspoken boundaries of their new friendship.

### August 27

Emery (8:26 p.m.) Did you eat?

Her response was almost immediate, and Emery's stomach did a small flip.

Alana (8:26 p.m.) Not yet, but soon! I'm almost home. You?

**Emery (8:27 p.m.)** Still in the van :( but we might order chicken when we get to the dorm. I'm starving! Only got to eat two mini sandwiches

**Alana (8:28 p.m.)** Yum!! Have fun!

**Alana (8:29 p.m.)** Man, now I want chicken too… I blame you

**Emery (8:29 p.m.)** I'd save you a piece but I don't think there will be anything left after Sungil gets to it

Emery smiled as he closed Tiki Talk and switched to the notebook app on his phone.

"M! Join in!" Stu called out. "*Manager-hyung* sucks at harmonizing."

"Hey!" Minhyuk said, glaring at Stu in the rearview mirror. "I'll have you know I could have been a K-pop idol if I wanted!"

"In your dreams," Stu said, his silver cross earring shaking as he laughed.

"Back in my day—" Minhyuk's eyes returned to focus on the road. "What—"

It happened in seconds: a deafening crack, an explosion of pain. Then Emery's world went dark.

# Alana

## #DripDrop

Alana wanted to break something. Preferably the water cooler, which was making a soft dripping noise every so often, the inconsistency of the rhythm slowly driving her past mad to plain psychotic.

*Deep breaths,* Alana reminded herself. Going crazy in a hospital was never a good idea. She looked around in suspicion. They might not let her leave.

Alana hated hospitals. The disinfectant smell, the artificial lighting, the overworked doctors, the uncomfortable plastic chairs—everything about the supposed "place of healing" seemed designed to repel anyone unfortunate enough to be trapped in one. Alana shifted in her seat in the hallway outside the operating room, studying the varying displays of fear and exhaustion on the faces around her.

*Drip.*

Her eye twitched. Everything had been so distressingly *normal* before Yena's phone call. Stephanie teasing her about Emery. Aunt Park cutting up fruit in the kitchen. Uncle Lim complaining about Stephanie's new hair color. It was no more than three hours ago, but it felt like a lifetime had passed.

The walls she had built to trap the night of Alex's death had crumbled at the image of NEON's crumpled black van on the news. Everything came crashing down, creating a jumble of broken thoughts and emotions, submerging her in the dust of memory.

It had been dark in the hallway the night that everything changed. NEON's comeback show had ended in the early hours before dawn, and she was on her way to wash up before finally getting some sleep. The light in the bathroom she shared with Alex was on, shining through the crack under the door. She remembered finding it strange—in retrospect, the first sign something was wrong.

Cautiously, she had approached the door, unease spreading through her as she knocked against the steady wood. All was quiet for the space of a few breaths until she heard a dull thud from within. Confused, she had softly called out her brother's name, her heartbeat spiking as the silence grew. Exhaling unsteadily, she had considered returning to her room— she was in desperate need of sleep—but something forced her to stay, standing uncertainly in the empty hall as adrenaline raced through her.

She tried opening the door, surprised to find it unlocked, and found Alex convulsing on the bathroom floor.

The rest was a blur. She was kneeling, her hands gripping his shoulders as she tried to hold him still, his limbs unconsciously flailing as he seized. She was bleeding, her head pulsing after its blow to the cabinet corner when his arm collided against her side. She was screaming, her parents rushing in, adding their own panicked cries to the tiny room.

*Drip.*

Alana took a slow, shaky breath through her nose, ignoring the haunting echo of Alex's death. This wasn't the time. Her brother was dead. He had died en route to the hospital, the paramedics unable to revive him. There was nothing she could do now to bring Alex back. But there was still hope for NEON and Minhyuk. Everything could still be okay.

*Emery, please be okay.*

She barely remembered getting into the taxi after Yena's call, or even arriving at the hospital. Stephanie had been her savior, taking over the phone to get directions and guiding them both out the door.

Alana couldn't think. She couldn't focus. Everything felt numb as her thoughts danced with her worst fears. The world around her blurred.

*Drip.*

"Aly, are you okay?" Yena's face was pale and her eyebrows knitted as she sat down next to Alana. After arriving at the hospital, they had located Yena, along with PR Manager Choi, near the first-floor service desk, and the nurses had directed them straight to the Emergency Room, where they had been told to wait with the other Solar personnel who filtered in and out. Eventually, a doctor had met with them. He had pulled his square, black glasses from his lab coat pocket and read from a clipboard. Disinterested. Detached. He listed off each patient's status as if reading out a grocery list.

*Patient Shin Sunwoo—lacerations on hands and contusions on the ribs.*
*Patient Kim Yongnam—stitches on upper right arm.*
*Patient Lee Jaehyun—whiplash.*
*Patient Lee Sungil—possible concussion.*
*Patient Jang Minhyuk—emergency surgery.*
*Patient Jung Emery—emergency surgery.*

He couldn't say more, not until an official guardian arrived. He said they were lucky, that it could have been worse, especially with that type of side collision. Each word repeated in Alana's head—*lucky, worse, collision*—until she felt like she would be sick. Since President Jo was the one listed as Emery's emergency contact in Korea, they would have to wait for her arrival to get more information. And so, the waiting continued. Manager Choi had gone upstairs to the VIP ward where the other NEON members were relocated to for the night. All the members except one, of course.

*Drip.*

Alana closed her eyes.

"Alana?" Yena's voice cut through the tornado of her emotions.

"I'm okay," she said, her voice rough and scratchy. Without opening her eyes, she cleared her throat and tried again. "How about you?"

"Yeah. Me, too."

More silence. Alana didn't exactly feel like talking, but she also didn't want to be alone. She needed a distraction from the disjointed memories swirling inside her.

*Drip.*

"I'm going to check on everyone else upstairs. Would you like to come with me?" Yena asked.

Alana slowly opened her eyes. "Someone should stay here. Just in case." Her words felt thick on her tongue.

Yena stood up slowly and held her hands against her lower back as she stretched. "Should I ask Manager Choi to send someone down to take your place?"

"I'm fine here. You go. See that they're all still doing okay."

"If you're sure…" Yena eyed her with concern.

"Stephanie will be back soon," Alana pointed out.

"Okay. Message me if anything happens."

Alana forced her lips into what she hoped passed for a smile. Judging by the sympathy in Yena's exhausted laugh, it must not have been very convincing. Alana waited until Yena disappeared around the corner before allowing the smile to slip away.

*Drip*

She stood up abruptly, eyeing the water cooler with irritation.

"Where are you off to, Aly?"

Startled, Alana looked over her shoulder to find not only her cousin, but also the one and only President Jo. Tall, thin, and dressed sharply in a powder blue pantsuit, Solar's CEO walked toward them, her short black hair neatly clipped back. With high cheekbones, flawless skin, and round eyes, she looked every bit the polished former pop star that she was. Manager Choi followed in her wake.

Catching herself, Alana clumsily bowed in greeting. "President."

President Jo nodded before cutting straight to the point. "Manger Choi has already briefed me on the situation. Unfortunately, we still don't know the full extent of Emery or Manager Jang's injuries. We've been told to wait until the surgeries are over for an update. Has a doctor come by?"

"No, not yet," Alana said, shaking her head dizzily. What could be taking the doctors so long? Surely, someone must know *something*.

President Jo's face settled into lines of worry. "Let's take a seat then. We may be waiting for a while."

"Here. I brought your tea," Stephanie said as they sat down, handing a cup to Alana.

"Thank you." The cup felt abnormally hot to her cold fingers, and she clutched it tightly, trying to absorb some of the warmth into her skin.

President Jo spoke in a low murmur to the other Solar staff present, discussing how best to handle the NEON members' families, as Alana and Stephanie listened on in silence.

Alana's fears eased a small bit watching the president take control of the situation. Gripping the hot tea, Alana leaned back against the hard plastic chair and stared blankly at the wall across from her. There was a small scuff mark rubbed into the bottom of the white paint, as if someone had kicked the wall with their shoe.

*Drip.*

With an electric hum, the glass doors of the surgery ward opened and a doctor walked out. Alana sat up so suddenly the hot tea splashed over, and she hissed as the momentary pain broke past her numbed senses. Setting her cup down, she stood, hastily wiping her hands onto her black jeans.

"The family of Patient Jang Minhyuk?" the doctor said while looking around the waiting area. He was dressed in green surgical scrubs, and when he removed his mask, Alana could see hints of grey peppering his otherwise thick, black hair.

President Jo quickly walked over to the doctor, her heels clicking against the white floor. Alana remained standing with the others, watching as the president and doctor conferred, President Jo nodding along to what the doctor said. When she returned to their side, she had a small smile on her face.

"Manager Jang is going to be okay."

Everyone let out a relieved breath.

"He had multiple fractures in his left ankle. The bone had splintered and they needed to operate before setting the break."

"W-what about Emery?" Alana asked.

"He's still in surgery."

"But he's all right?"

"I-I don't know," said President Jo, her voice faltering for the first time since she had arrived. "Still no word."

Alana took a deliberate breath through her nose, her lungs battling against her rising panic.

"Aly?" Stephanie said, resting a hand on Alana's shoulder.

Before Alana could respond, the glass doors opened again—a female surgeon this time. She wore her hair in a tight bun and a mask hid her expression from the worried faces in the hall.

"The family of Patient Jung Emery," the doctor called out.

Alana stilled, her fear crystallizing as it raced through her bloodstream, holding her frozen in place. Her ears began to ring, and the hallway blurred around her.

"Yes, we're here," President Jo said, raising her hand.

"Hello, I am Doctor Lee."

"How is he?" President Jo asked, tightness pulling around her eyes.

"The surgery was a success."

Alana exhaled, releasing the air held stiffly in her lungs, one thought echoing through her mind with acute clarity: *Emery is okay.*

"Both bones in his left forearm broke upon impact," Doctor Lee continued, speaking in a calm and serious manner. "A compound fracture like that requires immediate surgery to reduce the risk of infection."

*Emery is okay.*

"We cleaned out the injury, inserted a metal plate and screws, and managed to properly reposition and stabilize the bones in his arm. He should make a full recovery with antibiotics and a cast to prevent shifting or movement."

"Thank god," President Jo said weakly, holding a hand against her forehead as she took another deep breath in.

"We would like Patient Jung to stay overnight to watch for any complications. However, with his cast in place, he should be up and about within the next couple days."

"What about dancing?" PR Manager Choi asked. "Or traveling? When will he be able to perform again? NEON has their world tour coming up in six weeks…"

*Emery is okay.*

"I would hold off until his injury has the chance to heal more before making any decisions."

Manager Choi turned to the president. "We need to get another statement out to the media as soon as possible. The fans are panicking across social media channels."

"You have something prepared?" asked President Jo.

"Yes, my team has already written the general information. We were waiting only on word of M's condition."

President Jo rubbed her temples. "Update it, give it to me to look over, then send it out. That should be enough for tonight."

"We will be moving Patient Jung to the VIP ward," Doctor Lee spoke up. "If you need anything else, please notify one of the nurses."

*Emery is okay.*

"Thank you, Doctor Lee," said President Jo. The doctor nodded and headed off down the hall.

"I need to go meet with Sungil's mother upstairs," President Jo said, letting out a tired sigh. "Manager Choi, can you greet Yongnam's parents when they arrive? We also need to arrange for staff to stay overnight to keep an eye on NEON and Manager Jang."

"I'll stay," Alana said, her voice strained.

"Me too." Stephanie kept her hand on Alana's shoulder.

"Thank you, Alana, Stephanie," President Jo said, nodding to each in turn. "That will be helpful."

"I'll ask if some of the other staff can stay the night as well," Manager Choi added. "We'll need at least one member of the PR team to remain in case anything changes overnight."

The voices of President Jo and Manager Choi faded out as Alana focused on the only fact that mattered, shining through her doubts and fears.

*Emery is okay.*

# Emery

## #HoldMeTight

Everything felt heavy. His body and mind were weighted, pulling him down against the soft surface beneath him.

Slowly, Emery cracked open his eyes, taking in the dim lighting of his surroundings from his position—propped up at an angle—on the sole bed in the room. The walls were a neutral ivory, and there was a giant TV hanging against the wall opposite him and a couch along the window, where he could just make out a small figure nestled deeply under a grey blanket.

Everything hurt, and Emery gave in to the pain, letting his eyes fall closed. As he lay there, brief flashes of memory played before his mind—*the crescent moon shining in the night sky, the masked faces calling out, the white ceiling blurring past, the nurses hovering over him.*

Emery snapped his eyes open. He had been in the van. Something had come at them out of nowhere. There was a crash...

Panic flooded his muddled thoughts. What happened? Was everyone okay?

He tried to sit up, but his body still wasn't responding

properly. His eyes swept across the room, this time in alarm. He opened his mouth to speak, but all that came from his dry throat was a low, almost inaudible groan.

It must have been enough, however, because without warning, the figure on the sofa bolted upright, her glossy dark hair tangling around her face. As she looked over to him in confusion, he took in her familiar features.

"Alana," he said, but what he thought would be a yell came across as only a whisper.

She stood, but tripped over the blanket wrapped around her ankles. Stumbling, she caught herself on the chair to the right side of his bed, then collapsed into it.

"You're okay," she whispered, scanning him worriedly. She looked exhausted, drawn, as if she hadn't slept in days, and her skin had an ashen, frail quality to it that made the dark circles around her eyes stand out. Following the direction of her anxious gaze, Emery noticed his left arm propped up on its own pillow, held completely immobile and covered in a white cast.

Alana's face tightened as she made a move to stand up. "I need to call the nurse."

"Wait!" he coughed. He reached to stop her, but the pain that shot through every nerve ending stopped him, and he collapsed back against his pillow, wincing.

"Don't move!" Alana said breathlessly, hovering at his side. "What do you need?"

"Water," he choked out.

She poured him a glass of water from the bedside table, her hands trembling as she held the cup to his lips.

He swallowed a mouthful of the cool liquid, the water soothing his throat enough to speak. "What happened?"

She set the cup down and clutched his right arm tightly, but gently, careful not to disturb the IV in his hand. She looked even more panicked, fear shining brightly in her eyes. "An a-accident."

"Is everyone okay?" he asked, his own fear rising to the surface.

"Yes. No. I mean, more or less. You're okay." Her hands gripped him even tighter, the words spilling out from her much too fast.

"You're not making any sense."

"I'm sorry. I-I was so worried."

"What happened?" Emery repeated. He kept his tone steady, trying not to let any of his growing alarm add to her panic.

"The c-crash—on the news. You were taken to the hospital… And your van. Oh my god your van was totaled. I thought I'd lost you—just like Alex."

"Slow down," Emery said, his mind spinning.

"I thought… I couldn't stop thinking… I couldn't stop…" She gasped for breath, struggling to speak as tears streamed unchecked down her cheeks. Her hands shook as she clutched his right arm closer.

"Alana, shhh. It's all right. Take deep breaths." With one arm pinned to the mattress and the other confined in a cast, all he could do was whisper words of comfort to her. "Alana, please focus. You need to tell me what's going on."

She blinked at him through her tears. "A driver. He ran a red light. Collided into your van. A side collision."

Emery stared at her, trying to process what she was saying.

"You had surgery," she continued. "You fractured your arm. In both bones, they said. We had to wait hours before they could even tell us what happened. We were so scared."

"But what about Yongnam? Sungil, Minhyuk, everyone else? Are they safe?"

"Yes. Yes, everyone is doing okay. They are just next door."

Emery let out a giant breath of relief, finally allowing himself to sink back against the bed. While Alana continued to speak, her tears continued to fall. She didn't seem able to stop them.

"Minhyuk needed surgery, too." Her expression closed off as she looked to his injured arm once more, then became fixated on her own hands gripping the sleeve of his hospital pajamas. "He hurt his ankle pretty badly, but the doctor said he's going to be okay." With that, her fingers slowly loosened their grip on his arm, peeling off one by one.

Emery tried to think about what this all would mean for NEON. For him.

"My parents," he said hesitantly. "Do they know?"

Alana was already shaking her head. "President Jo tried to contact your family, but no one picked up."

"Right." He shouldn't be surprised, really. Last time he was in the hospital with a serious case of the flu, he had already recovered by the time his parents realized something was wrong.

"Maybe try calling them in the morning?"

He sighed. "It's probably better they don't know." Tentatively, he brought his right hand up to his hair, flinching at the large bandage across his forehead.

"They had to stitch up a cut on your head," Alana explained. "From the glass…" she trailed off.

"Does that mean we'll have matching scars?" He smirked.

Unfortunately, his weak attempt at a joke backfired. Alana yanked away, a strangled sob escaping her lips as her eyes darkened.

"Alana…I'm sorry," he said, reaching out for her hand and holding it gently in his own. "Everything's going to be okay." He gave her a reassuring squeeze.

"You're okay." She nodded and shifted her gaze to the

window, as a new wave of tears fell from her eyes.

"Yes, I'm right here."

She faced him slowly. "But you could have died…like Alex." The last part came out in just a whisper.

He studied her, taking in her quiet anguish. "Alex?" She had mentioned the name before in her panicked rambling.

Alana took a deep breath, her fingers clutching his tightly. Emery waited for her to continue. But she didn't, and the silence between them stretched on.

"Ala—"

"I'm sorry," Alana said abruptly, staring down at their entwined hands. "This isn't about me. Please forget I said anything."

"It's okay. Tell me. I'll listen."

Still, she remained quiet, unmoving. Her pain called out to him, and he let his instincts take over, giving in to the overwhelming urge to comfort her.

"Come here, Alana," he said. She looked up then, hesitantly meeting his eyes, as if seeking reassurance. He tugged her to him, and she toppled forward awkwardly, catching herself against his pillow. Emery let out a small grunt of pain that he masked with a huff of laughter. Smiling at Alana's worried expression, he scooted over as best as he could, careful of his IV, and she joined him on the bed, automatically curling into his chest. They lay there together, Emery with his good arm wrapped around her shaking shoulders as she began to cry in earnest. He squeezed her tighter, listening to her gasping sobs.

Eventually, her tears subsided and quiet returned to the room.

"You mentioned Alex…" he began cautiously, watching her reaction closely. "Who…?"

She shifted, and he could feel her take a long, deep breath against his neck.

"He…was my brother."

*Was*, past tense.

"He died last year," she explained softly, and Emery stilled before pulling Alana closer, holding her as tightly as he could as she tucked her head underneath his chin. She fit against him perfectly, like she was meant to be there.

"Alana, I'm so sorry."

"No, don't apologize."

"How…how did he die?" he asked, speaking slowly, choosing his words carefully.

"Suicide. Overdose." She brushed her fingers against the scar along her temple. "I was there. I watched him die."

*Damn.*

His heart clenched and sorrow washed over him, overwhelmed by Alana's revelation. To have her brother not only die by suicide, but to witness it herself…it was no wonder she seemed so changed, so broken. He felt paralyzed.

"It's been over a year now, but it feels like it happened just days ago," she whispered, drawing a shaky breath. Emery traced circles soothingly against the soft skin of her arm as she continued. "If I had gone in even one minute sooner, if I hadn't hesitated…" She finally met his eyes, making his breath catch at the unadulterated grief shining in hers. Then she blinked and looked away again.

"I should have been there for him. I should have stopped him. I should have—"

He felt her shake her head against his chest.

"I'm trying my best, to move on, to move past it, but it's so hard. So incredibly hard…"

He continued to draw soft circles on her arm with his fingertips, letting her speak her grief. Minutes slowly ticked by, her sobs gradually decreasing in intensity as she lay curled against him.

"I don't want to lose anyone else," she said, her voice breaking. "I can't lose you, too."

He clutched her even closer. "I'm here. I'm not going anywhere."

"You're special, Emery. You know that, right?" she whispered into his neck, tickling the skin there. He liked the way she called him by his full name, as if that part of him, the true part of himself others rarely saw, was somehow just for her. "The world would be a darker place without you. Don't ever forget that."

He resisted the urge to kiss the top of her head. "You're pretty special, too."

She took his right hand in her own, giving it a small squeeze, not letting go.

A quiet moment later, he spoke. "I'm so sorry about your brother."

She squeezed his hand again.

"I'm here for you, Alana, if you ever need to talk."

She didn't say anything as she sat up slowly, shifting so that Emery could see her face. She was so close, just inches away. He could see teardrops still trapped against her eyelashes, reflecting off the dim light. His eyes shifted to her soft pink lips as she smiled sadly up at him.

"Alana, I—"

A terse knock sounded at the door. Alana lunged for the chair as Emery fell back, doing his best to smooth out the blanket on the bed with his good hand. The door slid open a split second later, and a nurse in white walked into the room.

"Patient Jung, you're awake." She spoke in a no-nonsense voice. "I'm Nurse Min."

Alana stood, wiping her eyes before clutching her hands politely in front of her and backing away from Emery's bed. Her gaze darted around the room, looking everywhere except at him. From his left side, the nurse checked his status on the monitor. "How are you feeling?"

*Overwhelmed*, he thought as he looked down at his arm, his emotions running amok.

Instead, he answered, "Okay. I think."

"Any pain?"

Emery gave a small shrug, ignoring the throbbing ache radiating from his arm. "It's manageable."

"Good." She made a note on her clipboard. "Let me know if you need us to increase your pain meds. Be sure to rest." She gave him a pointed look.

"Yes, Nurse Min." Emery allowed himself to sink into his pillow, doing his best to appear obedient.

The nurse looked toward Alana. "Miss, I understand you're with his company. It's almost four in the morning. Doctor Lee should be in around nine to check on his condition."

"Y-yes, thank you," Alana said, her eyes rimmed with redness.

The nurse nodded and left, the door giving a soft click as it slid back into place. A long silence filled the room as Alana stood hesitantly by his bed.

"I don't actually need to sleep just yet…" Emery said with a gentle smile, patting the space next to him.

Alana gasped out a small laugh, her eyes lightening despite the sadness etched into her face. "I think you'd better listen to the nurse, Emery." She folded her blanket into a neat square, ignoring Emery's gaze as she moved about the room.

Without warning the door slid open again, but only by a small crack. Emery and Alana stared at the opening for a moment, until Jaehyun's head peaked into the room. He wore the same white and blue button-up pajama set as Emery, but he sported a blue brace around his neck.

"Is she gone?" he whispered.

A wave of relief washed over Emery and his face stretched into a wide grin. "*Hyu—*"

"Shhh! Don't let the nurse hear. She's ruthless. I've already been yelled at five times by her. *'Patient Lee, get back in bed!'* I swear, she has it out for me." He gave a playful smirk that didn't quite mask his worry.

In the distance came the sound of an echoing clatter, then muffled swearing. Jaehyun held up his finger before disappearing from the doorway. A moment later, he was back, bringing the rest of NEON with him. Yongnam, Stu, and Sungil, all in the matching hospital pajamas, crept in soundlessly after Jaehyun, shutting the door quietly behind them.

"*Hyung!*" Sungil whisper-yelled, running to his side. He jumped into the spot on Emery's bed that Alana had previously occupied, causing both idols to wince as the movement jostled their injuries. "You're awake!"

"Ah, careful!" Emery half-scolded while giving the *maknae* his best attempt at a one-armed bear hug.

"We could hear the nurse talking from our rooms. Figured you must be back in the land of the living," Yongnam said with a fond look from the foot of Emery's bed.

Sungil grinned from underneath the white bandage wrapped around his brown head of hair. "We snuck out," he whispered conspiratorially.

"Like they could keep us away." Jaehyun let out a fake, haughty laugh, and Yongnam rolled his eyes.

"Keep it down, or we'll be kicked out again," the leader reminded them.

Emery's gaze shifted to Stu, who stood uncharacteristically silent to the left of the bed as he watched Emery closely. His red hair was matted to his forehead, and both of his hands were wrapped in thick gauze. Meeting Emery's eyes, his lips pulled into a tight line.

"You okay, mate?"

"Yeah, and you?"

Stu nodded. "You had us worried there for a bit."

Emery finally took a good look at his group members and felt a pang as he noticed their assortment of bandages and bruises. Their haggard expressions were a far cry from their polished idol selves. "I'll be okay," Emery reassured them all.

"You were unconscious, *Hyung*," Sungil whispered, and Emery patted the *maknae*'s back. "There was blood everywhere, and your arm…"

"It didn't look good," said Yongnam with a grimace.

"You weren't responding, even when the ambulance arrived," said Stu, shaking his head, as if to force the image from his mind.

"I'm sorry," said Emery, moving his focus to his injured arm. With the heavy white bandages and the splint that extended past his fingers, it looked almost three times its normal size.

Sungil chuckled weakly. "I feel like we're filming a drama."

"At least no one's in a coma," said Jaehyun as he fought back a smile. "Or woke up with amnesia, for that matter."

Everyone groaned.

"Not now, Jaehyun." Stu reached over and gave the blonde a weak admonishing tap on his butt.

Emery looked up and caught a glimpse of Alana slowly moving toward the door.

"Alana!" he called, much louder than he anticipated.

She froze as everyone turned to look at her, then gave them a small wave.

"Are *you* doing okay?" Yongnam asked her.

Emery frowned.

"I'm fine. Just glad everyone is all right." Her voice sounded surprisingly steady. "I'm going to step out for a minute. You guys keep Emery company until I get back."

"You should have seen her earlier, M," Jaehyun said as the door closed behind her. "She barely spoke, practically jumping every time someone mentioned your name." He pretended to be spooked, making an exaggerated gasping sound before sitting down at the foot of Emery's bed.

"What about you? You didn't care about me at all?" Emery nudged Jaehyun with his foot. Inside, he was genuinely relieved that the eldest member seemed to be speaking with him again, given the way things had been between them since the mess with Byung Ho.

"Oh, he did. He was crying," Yongnam said. After a slight hesitation, he continued. "We all were."

A heavy silence filled the room. Emery's stomach dropped as a series of *what ifs* started running through his head.

"Minhyuk's going to be okay, too," Yongnam added. "We saw him after he got out of surgery."

"But he's going to have a hard time chasing us with his beat-up foot," Stu said, a reluctant smile slowly spreading across his face, looking more like his usual self. "He'll be on crutches for *ages*."

"Oooh, right. Maybe we'll actually have some breathing room for once." Jaehyun was also back to grinning before he reached up to check his neck brace.

"Solar wouldn't switch our manager, would they?" said Sungil, sitting up from the bed in alarm.

"No way. Minhyuk's ours. I won't let them." Stu tried to cross his arms over his chest, cursing as the bandages on his hands hampered his movement.

Fatigue slowly enveloped Emery as the conversation turned to Minhyuk and the various ways they could tease him. He nestled further into his pillow, enjoying the sound of their light banter, letting their voices wash over him as he drifted off.

When he woke again, NEON was gone.

There, curled up in the chair next to his bed, was Alana, sound asleep under the grey blanket. Through a crack in the curtains, Emery could see the sky just beginning to lighten. He watched Alana, enjoying the chance to study her unguarded face. With her black hair swept back and the soft smile ghosting across her delicate lips, she resembled the Alana he had first met two years ago.

He never *had* come across anyone like Alana before. The fact she was still here, still trying to make sense of her life after everything…it was inspiring. He couldn't begin to comprehend how hard the past year must have been for her. While her pain was still raw, he was touched she had confided in him. It spoke of a trust he wasn't sure he deserved. All he knew was that he would do whatever it took to keep it—to keep her close. Somehow, her quiet presence in his life had become important to him, more important than he ever would have imagined.

Looking at her peaceful expression as she slept, he smiled. "You're special, too, Alana. Never forget that."

# Alana

## #MoonlightAgain

"Finally! NEON's on!"

Alana looked up from the studded blue leather jacket she was cataloguing in Solar's inventory closet.

Emery sat cross-legged on the floor of the storage room, leaning against the wall with his laptop open in front of him and his phone clutched in his right hand. His left arm was still in its cast and sling, immobilized against his chest. Alana rolled her eyes at the hot pink leopard fur coat draped around his shoulders. She was pretty sure it was a remnant from President Jo's solo career.

"You know, Emery, there's a perfectly good table with chairs in the other room," Alana told him once again, her voice trailing off as Emery shushed her and turned the volume up on his laptop. The opening *MR* for "Forever Alone" blasted through the room, and Alana couldn't help but mouth silently along with the sound of the fanchants coming from the speakers.

She set the leather halter in her hands onto the folding table and moved next to Emery, watching the performance over his shoulder. NEON, now just four members, gracefully began their choreography, Eagle coming forward to sing Emery's opening verse—or lip sync it, and rather poorly at that.

Alana smiled. There was a reason NEON preferred to sing live.

"Our little Sungil, so cute." Emery held his phone at an angle nearly perpendicular to the computer screen and snapped a picture of the *maknae*.

"You know you can just screenshot it on your laptop, right?"

"Yeah, but it looks better this way." Emery showed her the picture before snapping a few more photos.

"Eagle looks like an alien from that angle, though," Alana felt obligated to point out.

"Yup. It's art." He continued to take shots of his group mates, each picture more unflattering than the last. "Ha! Perfect! I'm posting this one for GLO." Emery looked down at his phone. "How does this sound for the caption—'Kyaaa handsome Jaehyun *hyung*'?"

Alana glanced at the blurry, enlarged head of Jaehyun on Emery's screen and laughed, making Emery grin proudly up at her. She felt her cheeks heat at the warmth in his gaze and quickly broke eye contact, returning to reorganize the inventory.

It had been like this between them for a month, ever since she confessed the truth about Alex.

She shook her head, remembering how she'd lost control of her emotions in the hospital. It had been embarrassing, and yet finally sharing about Alex had eased some of the grief she'd felt since his death. Perhaps because it was Emery. He had been incredibly understanding and considerate, holding her while her anguish poured out. The pain was still there, of course, but it no longer felt quite as ragged. The shadows had loosened their tight grip around her heart, allowing her to breathe a bit more easily, at least for now.

As "Enlighten" played through the speakers, she looked over at Emery once again. His eyebrows were pulled together in concentration while he furiously typed one-handed into his phone, his gaze alternating between his computer and phone screens.

Alana was happy to see him in good spirits. She had worried he would feel depressed, being forced to stay behind in Seoul to recover while the rest of NEON performed at Music Now in Bangkok. The doctors had advised him against international travel so soon after his surgery, and Solar had agreed, hoping that more rest would allow him to participate in NEON's upcoming world tour. Unfortunately, Emery seemed to have also found a new outlet for his abundance of free time—annoying Alana as she worked.

Emery sighed as the sounds of "Enlighten" and cheering faded from his laptop.

"The performance is over?" Alana hung up a black-and-white striped blazer on a rack in the back of the room.

"Yeah." Emery sighed again as he shut his computer with an audible click.

"And you're finished posting your picture?"

"Excuse me. *Pictures*. Plural. Some of us can multitask, Alana."

She could hear the teasing smile on his lips, but didn't take the bait. "Good. So I guess you're heading home then?"

"Trying to get rid of me?"

"Yes," she said simply.

"Sorry, but I think I'll just keep chilling here. I'm comfy." Emery leaned back against the wall, the fluffy pink coat engulfing his lithe frame.

"You must have something more important to do right now." Alana held up a race-car driver jumpsuit, uncertain how to categorize it.

"Nope." He leaned over onto his right arm, burrowing deeper into the jacket as he watched her work.

"Really?" She put the jumpsuit down for the moment and crossed her arms. "What about those song edits you were complaining about?"

Emery sat up, pretending to be offended. "That was yesterday. How do you know I haven't already finished it?"

"Have you?"

"Basically." His gave her a cheesy grin. "Just need to tweak it a bit, and it'll be ready."

Alana snorted. "Are you stuck? Alex used to say the same thing when a track was giving him trouble."

Emery's eyes softened. "He wrote music, too?"

"Yeah." Alana was surprised she had mentioned her brother aloud, but even more so that she didn't feel the need to change the subject. "He was actually the one who taught me the basics of composing. He was the keyboardist in a band back in Chicago and spent all his time at local gigs instead of studying. My parents hated it." She looked away sadly, remembering the many late-night arguments she had overheard at home.

Emery carefully stood and walked over to her, the pink fur coat still hanging loosely from his shoulders. "What did your parents think about your songs?"

"They were supportive, at least more so than with Alex. They were proud when I got into Berklee." She sighed. "But it doesn't matter anymore. I'm done with that part of my life."

"But why? What made you want to give up music?" Emery took a step closer, looking worried.

"It was just too...much. Too difficult, after Alex died," she said, avoiding his eyes. They were now less than a foot apart.

"Alana?"

She let out a deep breath. "Look, he wasn't just my

brother. He was my mentor in music. Everything I created, I gave to him to check, to help guide me through the process." She paused, focusing her gaze on the silver chain she could just make out underneath his sling. "You know that USB around your neck? Alex was the one who gave it to me." She turned to the rack of miniskirts as she tried to get her emotions under control.

"He was gone most evenings playing gigs when I was in high school," she said. "We didn't see each other very often, so we left USB drives of our latest projects on each other's desks, which we would later go over together. We did it for years, all the way up until I went to college... I tried to keep up the tradition, but Alex stopped sending any of his work back. I should have known..." Alana's eyes stung as her voice wavered.

Emery put his hand on her shoulder and pulled her around. Finally, she looked up to meet his eyes, relieved when she saw no pity there.

"Music reminds me of Alex," she whispered. "Remembering him—it's too painful."

Alana's choked sob got lost in Emery's warmth. He held her close in a one-armed hug, his absurd jacket tickling her nose, and she could smell oranges and sandalwood, along with a hint of fresh soap, his own unique scent.

Alana felt the vibration of Emery's voice against her cheek as he spoke. "I'm so sorry."

Slowly, she let herself relax into his embrace, resting her head against his chest.

Emery cleared his throat and pulled back to look into her eyes. "Do you think you will ever create music again?"

"It just doesn't seem right anymore."

His eyebrows drew together. "But you're so talented. Perhaps music could help..."

Alana averted her gaze and stepped away from Emery's

embrace. He just didn't understand. Music was the problem, tied directly to her guilt and grief.

"Have you thought about what you want to do instead? Not that you aren't a great stylist or anything. I mean, you could just be my assistant forever."

She let out a small, unhappy laugh. "I'm still working on that part. My main goal right now is to keep busy—to keep going and not mess up."

"But at some point you'll have to stop running—"

"No," she cut in. "Don't judge the things I do to survive."

Emery opened his mouth, then shut it. "You're right." There was a moment's silence before he hesitantly added, "It's just that I hate to see you lose yourself like this."

His words stung. It was a comment she had heard many times from her family and friends. But it felt different coming from him. Even more shameful, somehow.

"I should go."

He winced. "Alana, I'm sorry. I won't mention it again."

"It's not that. Work ended hours ago," she said with a tired smile, suddenly feeling exhausted to her bones. Stephanie had already left the company around 5:00 p.m. for an appointment with a new fashion brand. "If you aren't going to work in your studio, you should take a cab home soon."

"What?" Emery brushed past Alana to pick up his phone from the ground. "It's almost ten-thirty. Why didn't you say something earlier?"

"I promised Minhyuk I'd babysit you while he was out of commission." Their manager had been taking time off to recover from his surgery, but was expected back to work on Monday.

"Babysit?" Emery pouted, a mischievous glint in his eyes.

"I'm just doing my job." Alana crossed her arms again.

"Right." Emery smiled. "Well, I need coffee if I'm going

to finish that track tonight." He put his laptop and the rest of his things in his backpack.

"Do you want me to make you some before I go?" Alana started for the hallway, where there was a coffee machine.

"No, I want real coffee. From a coffee shop."

She paused. "Um, all right. If you wait here, I'll go buy you a coffee and bring it back? Iced Americano, right?"

"That's okay. You don't have to do that." Emery slung his backpack over his good shoulder.

Alana exhaled in relief. She really just wanted to go home to her bed.

"I'll go to the café by myself," he added nonchalantly.

Alana spluttered. "You can't go alone! You shouldn't go at all!"

"Why not?"

"Because you'll be recognized! And you're still injured. And it's late. And…you can't go out dressed like that!"

Emery looked down at his furry pink jacket and laughed. "Wouldn't be the first time I wore something ridiculous in public." Her expression must have looked pained, because he set his backpack down, slipped the coat off his shoulders, and placed it on the folding table. "There. Better?"

"No!"

"Well, at least you're honest." He laughed again. "See you later, Alana!"

Alana watched in shock as Emery casually picked his bag up once more and walked out of the room. She couldn't just let him go on his own, could she? Technically, she was off the clock as of two hours ago. She was *also* supposed to keep her eye on him, but hopefully, *surely*, Emery could buy coffee on his own without getting into too much trouble.

She stared at the black leopard spots on the pink coat.

"Wait!" Alana shouted, snatching her bag from the corner

as she rushed from the room.

Emery paused by the elevator, eyebrows raised.

"I'm coming with you," Alana gasped. "I can't let you just walk around by yourself."

His answering grin made her blush head to toe.

*I'm going to regret this*, she thought.

Alana couldn't believe what she was doing.

She looked around the theater nervously as she carried popcorn to the dark figure hunched over in the back row. The theater was largely empty, with only three other couples occupying the middle rows for the midnight showing of *Come Back To Me*, the Korean movie starring Hyun Soo Jun that had come out more than a month ago.

"Did you get the popcorn?" the figure whispered as she slid into the seat to his right.

"Here." She shoved the bowl at Emery, inspecting his outfit closely. He was dressed in the same black sweats and shirt he'd been wearing all day, but he had added a black cap and face mask. It would be hard to recognize him with the added darkness of the theater, but it was still reckless. GLO *could* recognize him. The fandom didn't need to see his face to know. They could tell by the shape of his hands, the sound of his laughter, or even the way his eyes seemed to dance when he smiled. She knew from experience. Also, his cast was a dead giveaway. If they hadn't been spotted yet, it was just a matter of time.

"What about the chocolate?" he asked, looking at her now empty hands as he pulled his mask down to eat some popcorn.

"What?" Alana groaned and stood up. "You didn't say anything about chocolate."

"Not for me." He grabbed her arm and pulled her back down next to him. "For you. I know how much you love it."

She blushed, then caught herself. "We're not here for me!"

"Forget the chocolate then." He let go of her arm and focused back on the advertisement playing on screen. "If you want to go home, you can, Alana. I don't mind staying by myself. I've been wanting to see this movie for forever. I don't get a lot of opportunities to go out like this."

At the reminder of Emery's demanding lifestyle, Alana's irritation left her as quickly as it had appeared. "No. I'm fine. Let's just watch the movie and go home."

"Sure." He smiled before eating another handful of popcorn.

Alana sighed. He had been saying that all night. Sure, they would just go to the café, then home. But after she bought his iced Americano, he plopped down at a table in the back corner, and Alana had no choice but to follow, keeping him out of sight as best she could while he took forever to finish his small drink, chatting aimlessly about music and the other NEON members. Afterwards, Emery insisted on taking a walk. Sure, he'd clear his head wandering the backstreets of Gangnam and that would be it. Twenty minutes later, Alana found herself buying tickets to a midnight movie.

*Sure. Yeah, right.*

She sent a quick message to Stephanie, telling her not to wait up since she would be who knew how late, and let out another tired sigh as the advertisement on screen ended and the theater darkened. If she fell asleep during the movie, would Emery wake her?

Something brushed against her hand, and Alana jumped. She glanced at Emery in the dark to find his eyes on her, reflecting the light of the screen.

Gently taking her hand in his, he asked softly, "Is this okay?"

She swallowed, and diverted her gaze forward as her heart beat wildly in her chest.

"Alana?"

Not trusting her voice, she nodded, and he squeezed her hand in response. She continued to stare at the screen, unseeing, as the movie started.

Afterwards, Alana couldn't describe the plot even if she wanted to, her mind solely focused on the feel of Emery's hand holding her own. Conflicting emotions warred inside her. She knew he had held her hand before, but that was an act of comfort. Without panic or sorrow clouding her mind, this was an entirely new sensation.

When he drew slow circles against the back of her hand with his thumb, her breath caught, and she shivered.

"Cold?" Emery's breath tickled her ear as he leaned closer.

Keeping her eyes locked safely on the movie, she frantically shook her head. No, she was anything but cold.

"Are you sure? You have goosebumps."

"Fine," she squeaked.

"Okay, just let me know if you are." She could hear a smile in his voice, but she didn't dare glance over to check.

Throughout the movie, Alana kept waiting for him to drop her hand, especially once her fingers grew numb and sweaty. But rather than pull away, Emery adjusted his grip, and never let go. She sat there in a daze, her eyes only registering her surroundings when the lights came on and the couples in front began collecting their things.

"That was pretty good," Emery said, looking over at her. "I'm not sure how I feel about the ending, but Hyun Soo *hyung's* acting was awesome. What'd you think?"

"The movie is over?" she wondered aloud. She barely remembered any of it.

Emery laughed and finally pulled his hand back to tuck

a piece of hair behind her ear. She felt her face flush and immediately stood up.

"Okay, time to go," she said, picking up the nearly untouched popcorn. Seeing it made her blush even harder. He had sacrificed eating popcorn to hold her hand.

Emery also stood and stretched his right arm into the air. Alana looked away at the glimpse of skin showing below his shirt. Quickly making her way past the rows of seats in the theater, she glanced back only once to check that he was following.

As they stepped outside into the cool evening air, she took a deep breath. The street was almost empty, a rare sight for Gangnam. Everyone was doing much more rational things with their time like sleeping, not cuddling with celebrities in movie theaters.

Alana raised her arm, spotting a taxi down the road, only to have Emery step in front of her.

"What are you doing?" he asked, pulling his mask over his face and waving at the taxi driver to keep going when it slowed down.

"Getting a taxi to take you home. What are *you* doing?" She looked at him incredulously.

He watched the taxi disappear around the corner before answering, "How about we go for a walk?"

"We've already *done* that. We walked here, remember?"

Emery had the nerve to laugh. "Please, Alana. Just to stretch our legs." His tone quieted when he added, "I don't want to go back to my empty apartment just yet."

She stilled. "Is this your first time staying there without NEON?"

"Excluding last night? Yeah." He started walking down the street, and Alana hurried to keep pace. "I've slept alone at the studio while working, but never at our home. With them in

Bangkok, it's just too quiet."

Her heart clenched. "Good thing they'll be back tomorrow," she said, trying to comfort him.

"True." His eyes smiled at her above his face mask, and he reached out to grab her hand.

"Emery," she whispered furiously. Now his eyes seemed to smirk. Alana glanced around anxiously, but seeing no one else, she said nothing more, and allowed herself to enjoy the comforting warmth of his skin against hers.

They walked around the empty Cheongdam neighborhood, still holding hands. Alana didn't comment as Emery chose their direction, but when they turned a corner, she faltered, recognizing their destination.

"Emery," she said again in warning, planting her feet firmly underneath her and yanking him to a stop.

"We're already here. Let's just look at the water. That's all." He stared back at her, his expression pleading. She hesitated, and he gave her hand a squeeze, dropping his voice. "Just a few minutes. I promise."

Sighing, she started walking again, pulling Emery along the path to the surprisingly well-lit underpass leading to the river.

"We'll head back after this," Emery said into the night.

She rolled her eyes, but her lips curved into a smile. "I need to learn to say 'no' to you."

He pulled his mask down to reveal a frown. "We don't have to go."

Feeling herself soften, she kept walking. After a few moments, they stepped out of the tunnel and onto the open walking path that ran alongside the Han River.

"I like being with you, Emery." As soon as she said it, she was taken aback by the intensity of her own feelings. Before she could withdraw her own statement, happiness flashed across Emery's face, and Alana decided to let it be. It was the truth, after all.

She gently let go of his hand, heading toward the path's edge to look out across the river. No matter how many times she saw it, the view was beautiful, especially at night with the moon and city lights winking in the rippling surface.

"This is the same bench, right?" Emery asked mildly. Alana turned from the water to survey their surroundings as Emery sat.

She nodded. "I recognize the light post. But please try not to pick another fight. I didn't bring any bandages."

He laughed, the sound radiant and carefree. "Come here," he said, patting the open space on the bench before holding out his hand. She took her place beside him, gripping his hand with her own. The light post overhead illuminated them both, Emery's eyes shining especially bright.

"Thank you, Alana," he said quietly, after they'd enjoyed the scenery for a minute. At her questioning look, he added, "For tonight. And for before. I never had the chance to properly thank you for what you did for me that night."

"Emery, you don't—"

"No, I do. I'm only here now because of you."

"Not just because of me," she denied. "You're the one who ultimately decided to stay. To keep trying."

Alana's heart hurt. She hadn't meant to be his savior. She had only wanted to ease his pain, to help him just as his music had helped her and countless other fans. How could she not step in when she saw him hurting? Any GLO would have done the same, but this—she never meant for any of this to happen.

"How are things with your parents? Better, I hope?" said Alana. She couldn't be the only support in his life. She wasn't enough. She would fail again. She knew it.

"With my mom, it's all right. She's disappointed, but deep down I think she cares." His gaze drifted out toward the river. "I don't speak to my father anymore. I'm a lost cause as far as he's concerned." He let out a long sigh. "At times, I really feel bad for my fans."

She tensed. "Why would you say that?"

He didn't answer at first, instead watching the city in the distance. "It must have been disappointing, having me as your idol. I make mistakes. I can't do anything properly. I can only smile stupidly—no matter what people say about me, or NEON, or GLO. I'm not who they think I am. I don't deserve the love they give me."

"No, Emery," she whispered, her heart breaking at the defeat she heard in his voice.

"It's true," he said softly. "The most I can do is apologize—for every little mistake, misunderstanding or not. Why would anybody idolize that?" He shook his head. "I can't even love someone else without being forced to hide it. To apologize for it. And over what? For having feelings? For being human? What's wrong with being human?"

At that, he met her gaze, and Alana's breath caught at the turmoil in his dark eyes.

"But you have a voice," she told him, putting as much conviction as she could into her words. "Your fame may cage you, but it also gives you power to make real change. Your lyrics inspire people every day to overcome their fears, to push through their pain, to dream, because there's hope waiting on the other side. That's why your fans love you. Not because of your perfect image, but because of the humanity of your message."

"But what good is a message if it's missing half the truth?"

"Everyone has secrets, Emery. Parts of themselves they want to hide. In the end, no one can truly keep you from sharing yours. If your fans stop loving you for being true to yourself, then they never really loved you in the first place."

His whole demeanor softened. "And if my secrets involved you?"

Alana's heart skipped a beat at the words he wasn't saying. "Emery?"

"Have you honestly not realized by now?" His eyes studied her face closely before dropping to her mouth as he leaned in closer.

"We can't," she said desperately. His warm breath caressed her face as she put her hand lightly on his chest, holding him back.

He looked back into her eyes, accepting her denial with a smile of self-mockery. "Am I not human to you, too?"

How could he think that? After everything they had been through together, everything she had shared with him, it was impossible.

"No, Emery," she whispered. The truth was before her. She had to recognize it now. "You are everything to me."

At her confession, Emery closed the distance between them, and Alana gasped as his lips brushed against hers. He pulled back briefly, watching her reaction, and then met her lips again, gently coaxing a response from her mouth. Alana felt her eyes close, and she kissed him back, pressing up against his body. He groaned, and she dug her fingers into his shirt to steady herself as he wrapped an arm around her, holding her tight against him. A hard shudder ran down her spine when he deepened the kiss, and she lost herself to sensation, moaning as he explored her mouth.

Abruptly, they pulled apart, and she struggled to right herself at the sudden loss. Everywhere he touched, her skin was on fire, as if he had ignited all her nerve endings, sparking them to life. They were both panting, tangled around each other on the bench, as they looked at each other, and Alana found her gaze falling back to his mouth in longing.

She watched as Emery's lips curved into a smile, and suddenly he was laughing.

"Don't laugh. That was only my second kiss." She pouted at him playfully, turning red as she remembered her first kiss in this same spot.

All of a sudden, he kissed her again, giving her another quick taste and leaving her breathless. "Now here's your third." He looked at her with such fondness that she didn't think there was any part of her that *wasn't* blushing.

"Cute," she said, struggling to keep a straight face.

Emery laughed again. "Come on, let's get you home before I do something rash."

"That doesn't sound so bad." She grinned at him. "I'm beginning to like it here. Let's never leave."

"Alana," he groaned, abruptly standing. "Don't tempt me."

"Or we could go back to your place…" She flushed, voice trailing off, at the look he gave her. "Or not. It was just a thought. Unless you—no pretend I never said anything. Really I—"

"Alana," He said, cutting her off. "Are you sure?"

As she gazed into his dark brown eyes, she knew she was. She wanted this. They could be together, just Emery and Alana, leaving their pain and grief behind, if only for one night. He cared for her, and she trusted him. She knew she'd be safe by his side.

"Yes."

He held out his hand and she took it without hesitation, letting him help her to her feet.

They never let go.

★ ★ ★ ★ ★

It wasn't until later, when Alana was lying in his arms as Emery slept serenely beside her, that it hit her.

Emery had feelings for her. Real, honest feelings. Feelings that she had accepted by her words and actions.

Alana wasn't sure when their relationship had changed from admiration and friendship into something more. She'd thought she had her emotions under control, yet somehow they had grown wild, reaching past her walls and consuming her whole, acting according to their own agenda.

*I love him*, she thought, her lungs tightening as tears came to her eyes.

With the realization, overwhelming dread filled her. Their relationship could never be. She knew this. She had always known this. Emery was an idol, and she worked for Solar. Not even President Jo could smooth things over if anyone found out, because they were no longer pretending. No, this time, the rumors would be true, and the scandal would break Emery. He would lose his fans, his career, his life. She couldn't let music be taken away from him, too.

She curled herself tighter around him, surrounded by his familiar scent, as she deliberately locked her feelings away, planning out what she had to do next.

Her days at Solar Entertainment were numbered.

# Emery

## #YouAndMe

" "Five, six, seven, eight."

Emery slumped against the mirror, watching NEON perform their opening segment for what felt like the hundredth time that day. Everyone in the room was covered in sweat— NEON, the backup dancers, and even their head choreographer Hyojoon Kang. Everyone, that was, except Emery.

He wanted to support NEON, but watching them practice without him was painful. He knew all the steps, the motions ingrained in his muscle memory, but all he could do was tap his foot from the sidelines and act as an extra set of eyes for the staff.

With Emery's injury still healing, NEON had re-choreographed many of their performances for the concert, doing their best to fill in for his absence. While he would still be on stage and singing his parts, he wouldn't be performing any of the more intense dances. Instead, he'd be sitting on a stool for the majority of the show.

The concert was just three days away, and everyone was in full prep mode. Tomorrow was the first day of dress rehearsals at the venue, and Emery could feel both excitement and apprehension coursing through him. It was their first dome concert—more than twenty thousand people would be there on Saturday night.

Emery's stomach twisted. He hated that he couldn't be fully part of it.

Inevitably, as so often happened these past few days, Emery's thoughts drifted to Alana. He checked his phone for the time—4:27 p.m. She should be back by now, after spending all day at the venue helping set up the backstage area with the other *coordis*. As if on cue, Emery's phone buzzed with a new message.

*October 2*

**Alana (4:27 p.m.)** Just got back to Solar. Do you have time to meet later?

Emery felt a smile tug on his lips. That night together had been perfect, freeing. It had felt so right being with her, like she understood him completely. Afterwards, he had spent every moment wishing to see her again. With their hectic schedules, however, his attempts to speak with her over the past few days had yet to work out. Catching glimpses of her around Solar and having to hide how he felt only made it worse.

**Emery (4:28 p.m.)** Still in practice. But I should be able to get away soon!

"Stop!" called out Hyojoon and the music cut off abruptly. "Jaehyun. You were a second behind. Remember, you now follow Emery's part, not your old one."

"Yes, *Seonsaengnim*," said Jaehyun, his face flushed from exertion, his brown hair dripping sweat onto the floor as he took steady breaths through his nose. Both Jaehyun and Stu had switched back to more muted hair colors for the upcoming world tour, since brown dye required less upkeep.

"I know how hard it is to make all these last-minute changes," Hyojoon said, pulling his long hair back into a ponytail.

"Guys, we got this," Yongnam said, determination glinting in his eyes. He wiped his sweat on the sleeve of his grey T-shirt.

"Let's take a ten-minute break. Then we'll run through it again." At Hyojoon's announcement, everyone broke apart.

Emery turned back to his phone, scrolling through social media until Stu sat down and tackled him from the right side.

"Watch the arm!" Emery yelped. "And my phone!" Emery carefully put his phone away in the pocket of his baggy zip-up hoodie and adjusted his sling.

"I'm nowhere near it!" Stu held his hands up. "I just missed you, that's all."

"I'm right here. You can't *really* miss me."

"You know what I mean." Without his usual colored lenses, Stu's eyes reflected black in the fluorescent lighting.

"At least I'm not all sweaty like you," Emery said, elbowing Stu in the side. Beads of sweat dripped down from the Australian's chocolate-brown hair and onto Emery's arm. "Grab a towel or something!"

Walking toward them, Sungil threw his own towel right at Stu before collapsing spread-eagled on the floor. "Is it dinnertime yet?" he groaned.

"You just had a snack," Jaehyun pointed out as he sat down on Emery's left, a good four feet of space between them.

This inexplicable distance had become typical of Jaehyun's behavior, as of late. Immediately following the car accident, the eldest NEON member had shown concern for Emery and his injury, but as the days wore on, Jaehyun had started avoiding Emery when possible and watching his words carefully when not. Emery didn't think his *hyung* was still mad, per se, about the *I Can Cook* incident, but something was off with their relationship.

Watching Jaehyun now, Emery resolved to talk things out with him, at least before their world tour started. He missed how things used to be with his *hyung*.

Sighing, Emery looked down at his cast. He missed a lot of things lately.

Yongnam was the last to join them, taking a seat in front of Emery and steadily drinking from a water bottle. With his eyes scrunched closed, tight lines appeared between his brows. He looked exhausted.

"You guys are killing it." Emery gave them a thumbs up with his good hand. "The concert is going to be amazing."

"Oh yeah, does anyone have extra tickets?" asked Jaehyun, texting on his phone. "I forgot to get one for my cousin's girlfriend and now my aunt and mom are both pissed." He snorted. "Grandma's cool with it, though. Says the girlfriend is too uppity." With two brothers, three sisters, and a large extended family, it wasn't surprising that Jaehyun had run out of tickets.

"Sorry, I gave all mine out already," said Yongnam, placing his water beside him.

"You can have mine," said Emery, jumping at the chance to bridge the gap between them. "I only need a couple for friends."

"Ooh, I want in, too!" Stu interjected. "Jaehyun can't get all your extra tickets."

"How are your parents, *Hyung*?" Sungil raised his head, shaking the sweat from his sandy brown hair as he looked at Emery. "Didn't they want to come to the show?"

"Oh, you know, flying all the way to Seoul would be too much." Emery kept his voice light. "Especially since I won't really be performing."

"Hey! You're performing!" said Stu. "You still need to carry us with your amazing vocals." He hugged Emery's right arm, turning up his *aegyo*. "What would we do without you?" At his insistent kissing noises, Emery shoved Stu off, laughing.

"Seriously, though. We need you, M," Yongnam said with a tired smile.

"Okay, okay." Emery grinned in surrender before pulling his arm out of Stu's grip and standing up. "I'm going to head up to the studio. I'll be more use to you all up there. Text me if something interesting happens."

"Bye Emmie!" Stu called out, and without looking back, Emery held up his uninjured arm in a wave before walking out.

Emery pushed the button for the elevator. He hoped Alana would be free soon. He had been working on a special project for the past few weeks and he couldn't wait to share it with her. He tapped his foot, wishing the elevator would move faster.

When he arrived on the fourth floor, he was greeted by a whirlwind of chaos. It looked like every *coordi* that worked for Solar was packed into the common area. Suitcases, clothing, and accessories had been laid out in neat piles on every available surface. On the table to his right, Emery noticed the familiar sequin jackets that NEON would be wearing in the third segment of the concert.

Alana was in the back of the room, focused intently on the rows of shoes laid out before her. With six outfit changes for each of the members, the stylists were responsible for keeping track of more than thirty unique looks. For the last few weeks, NEON had been having costume fittings nonstop, making sure that everything would be ready for the world tour. Emery's head spun just thinking about all the coordination and planning needed to pull it off. Luckily, that wasn't his job.

He quietly went back into the hallway, not wanting to distract the *coordis* or draw attention to himself. Instead, he took the stairs up to the fifth floor, intent on getting some work done while he waited for Alana to finish.

In contrast to the bustling floor below, the fifth floor was deserted. With everyone's focus on the concert, recording new music had been put temporarily on hold. Even their sister group NEPTUNE wasn't in the studio this week, since the sound engineers were assisting with the concert setup. Emery and Yongnam were still working on their new tracks, but the pace had slowed down considerably. Recording wouldn't officially start for another two months, only after they finished the first leg of their world tour and returned to Seoul in time for the end-of-year award shows.

Emery opened the door to his own studio with a sigh of relief. While the room wasn't big, it was more than enough for him. Similar to his setup at the dorm, his studio centered around his computer and keyboard. Two monitors took up most of the desk space, flanked on either side by state-of-the-art speakers. In the corner stood his recording mic, and a full-sized keyboard was easily accessible under his desk. His favorite part though was his shelf of limited-edition Punk the Pom figurines. He had started collecting the dogs when he was a trainee, and thanks largely to his fans, he had amassed upwards of a hundred Punk dolls, in every size, shape, and color possible.

Emery turned on his computer and sat down on his swivel chair, casually spinning from side to side while waiting for everything to fire up. He took out his phone and messaged Alana.

**Emery (4:42 p.m.)** When you're free, come find me in my studio. No one's up here

Alana (4:43 p.m.) Sorry! I should be done in about 30 minutes. Wait for me?

Emery (4:43 p.m.) Of course ^^

In fact, Emery was grateful for the extra time. He'd been working on a new song ever since the accident, drawing mainly from the time he had spent with Alana while he recovered. It was just about finished.

He flipped the switch to turn on the large floor lamps scattered in three of the four corners of his studio. As an afterthought, he also turned on the string of white lights tacked along the top perimeter of the room, illuminating everything in a warm and inviting glow.

Emery put on his headphones and played the song again, wanting to make sure there weren't any last-minute tweaks to make. He hadn't let anyone listen to this song yet, not even Yongnam. Alana would be the first.

Forty-one minutes later—Emery had been counting— there was a knock on the door.

"Come in!" he called out and watched as Alana cautiously stepped into the room. For once, she wasn't wearing all black. Rather, she had on a pair of light wash blue jeans with a classic rose-pink V-neck shirt. Her hair was pulled back in a messy ponytail, flyaways sticking out at odd angles around her face, yet her eyes glowed in the light of the room.

Emery had to remind himself to blink.

"Hey Emery," Alana said quietly, shutting the door behind her. She looked around the room, avoiding his gaze. "So strange…" she muttered.

"What?" Sometimes Emery felt like he could sense exactly what Alana was thinking, their psyches synced to the same wavelength, but other times, like now, he had no clue what was going on in that head of hers.

"I mean, I'd seen it in videos, but it's surreal to actually be inside the M Studio."

Right. She was talking about his studio.

"Now you know all my secrets," Emery teased. "Here, take a seat." He gestured to the leather couch along the right side of the room, quickly moving aside his Punk pillows to make space for her. "Sorry, my obsession has gotten a bit carried away," he said sheepishly.

Alana let out a small, but genuine, laugh. "Don't ever change."

In return, Emery smiled. "I'll keep that in mind." He swiveled his chair around to fully face her. She had already slipped off her shoes and was making herself comfortable by sitting cross-legged on the sofa.

Alana picked up the summer limited edition Punk the Pom doll wearing a watermelon inner tube and hugged it to her chest. "How's your day been?" she asked, as if as an afterthought. "Things must be crazy for you with the concert so soon."

"Yeah, but not as much as everyone else. I mean, NEON is certainly busy…" Emery shrugged.

That got her attention. "Hey, you're part of NEON, too!" she said indignantly.

"I know. I know. But, still." He couldn't help but glance at his cast again. "I'm not used to being on the sidelines."

She gave him a sympathetic smile before her eyes caught on something behind him.

"Whoa. Is that the newest model?"

Emery watched as her face lit up while she admired his studio setup. "Yep. I bought that synth as soon as it was released. Definitely worth the investment."

"Ah, I always wanted to work with one." A flicker of

sadness crossed her face. "I mean, back when I was still making music."

"Do you want to try it out now?" Emery gestured vaguely to his desk.

"I don't know," she said, apprehension creeping into her voice.

"Come on, Ms. Berklee, show me what you got." Emery stood and offered his hand to Alana. She took it automatically, making Emery grin, and switched places with him.

"Oh, I love your widescreen monitors! Alex would have flipped." Her eyes sparkled as she took everything in.

"Here." He reached around and pulled up his digital audio workstation so she could test out the equipment. "Now the real fun begins."

Emery stood behind Alana while she started playing around with different modes. She picked up everything quickly and naturally, her gaze one hundred percent focused as she lost herself in the sample project. Emery felt a pang in his heart as she worked. He could envision many more moments like this one, watching her while she created something from nothing.

After about thirty minutes, Alana played back the small clip she had made by layering in different elements and melodies. The finished product was rough, but he could see how it would develop, given more time.

"Can you play that again?" he asked, feeling the whispers of a song start to form in his mind.

She refreshed the sample, sitting back in his chair as the music started again. After a few beats, Emery joined in, singing along with his own made-up lyrics.

*Light eyes flash with hidden glee.*
*I'm in heaven—just you and me.*

He turned to Alana, only to find her sitting completely frozen, staring at him wide-eyed. "What do you think?"

She didn't move, not even to blink, a glazed look in her light brown eyes.

He cleared his throat and ran his fingers through his hair. "I'm sorry. I was just messing around…" He knew his voice was a bit scratchy from all the rehearsing, but was he really that bad?

"Oh my god," she whispered.

"Forget I—"

"That was so—oh my god," Alana repeated. "I can't believe you just sang to me!"

Emery shrugged, suddenly self-conscious, as Alana continued to stare in awe. "It's no big deal. I sing all the time."

"Yes, but not like—I'm sorry. Just ignore me while I curl up into a ball with my inner fangirl. We need a moment." Her cheeks were glowing.

He laughed. "Can I sit down, then? I have a surprise for you."

Alana looked up at him, still flustered. "Emery, I'm not sure… I came here for a reason." Apprehension slowly crept into her features.

"Relax. It's just something I've been working on in my free time."

Emery didn't trust himself to say anything more, so he pulled up the saved file and hit play, hoping the song would express his emotions better than his own words. As the opening bars played, Alana sat still and unmoving, her face impassive. They listened together as the chorus began.

*Your light pulls me in*
*And I know we'll survive.*
*Pain's just a memory.*
*Together, we're alive.*

"I...I mean...we—" Alana's expression gave way as she began to cry.

Emery leapt to her side on the couch. "Shhh, it's okay," he said while pulling her in for a hug, holding her close.

They sat together while the song continued to play, Emery hugging Alana tight while she quietly cried into his chest. As the song came to an end, Emery drew back until he could clearly see her face. Pain was etched into her eyes, but he was glad to see her tears had stopped.

"You mean so much to me, Alana," he murmured.

"Emery... I'm so sorry," she said brokenly.

"You have nothing to apologize for," he said, embracing her and kissing her hair. "If anything, I should be apologizing." He took a deep breath. "I'm sorry for pushing you too fast. You'll come back to music when you're ready. We have time."

"That's not it. I—"

Without warning, the door to the studio opened.

"Emery, we're about to order dinner. What do you..." Yongnam stood at the threshold, shock lighting his face as he took in Alana and Emery. "What's going on?"

Emery abruptly let go of Alana and stood up, holding his one arm out placatingly. "Yongnam, let me explain."

Yongnam glanced at Alana. "Looks pretty self-explanatory to me."

"I was just getting her opinion on a new track."

"Don't lie to me." Yongnam's expression morphed into anger, his hands curling into fists at his side. "You promised. You told me to trust you."

"This doesn't change anything." Even Emery could hear the pleading tone in his own voice.

"Of course it does! It changes everything!" Yongnam's obsidian eyes were livid. Emery had never seen him lose his calm like this. "What were you going to do?! Keep everything a secret until it all explodes in your face? And then what? Leave NEON?"

Trying to keep his voice level, Emery said, "I'm not going anywhere, Yongnam."

"You've given up before!"

Emery blanched.

"I know, M," Yongnam said. "I've always known. The day you had decided to leave, I overheard Minhyuk *hyung* on the phone with President Jo. You were all set to quit!"

"But I didn't!" Emery couldn't believe this was coming up now. He thought his secret had been safe from NEON.

"But I can't trust that you won't try again." Yongnam's gaze moved to Alana. "Especially with *her* added to the picture."

"That's not fair! You know I always put NEON first!"

The leader glared at Alana, and then back at Emery. "Clearly, you don't."

She flinched, and Emery lost the tenuous hold he had on his temper. "Get out," he snarled, his voice cold.

"See? You're already taking her side!"

"I–I have to go," she said, terribly softly, and stumbled past Emery toward the door.

Yongnam blocked her path. "Solar trusted you. With M, I can understand. But you? How do you justify this to yourself?" Yongnam demanded.

Emery stepped forward, intending to intervene, when Alana's response froze him in his tracks.

"You're right. I can't control how I feel, but I can control how I act. I've made plenty of mistakes, but I would never come between Emery and NEON. If he feels pressured to leave the group, that's all on you. Not me." She looked at Yongnam fiercely, her eyes still red from crying.

Yongnam stared at her for a moment, confusion crossing

his angry features, until, at long last, he stepped out of the way. Silence filled the room as the door shut behind her.

"You asshole," Emery growled. "If you have a problem, take it out on me, not her."

"I might just do that." Yongnam took a step closer to Emery, looking him up and down. "I would punch you if you weren't already injured."

"Well, go on then, hit me!" Emery held out his arm, begging Yongnam to act.

But he didn't. Instead, Yongnam deflated, collapsing on the sofa, head in his hands. After a long, tired sigh, he spoke. "We can't lose you, M."

"I told you, I'm not going anywhere," Emery said defensively.

Yongnam looked up, holding Emery's gaze, fear evident in his eyes. "But how can I trust you?"

"I guess you can't." Emery pointed to the door. "And I'm done trying to convince you. Get out."

# Alana

## #Encore

"GLOoooooooooo!"

The cheers reached a whole new decibel at Stu's shout as Alana watched from the sidelines backstage. NEON, dressed in leather pants and white silk shirts embroidered with intricate beading, had started the final *ment* of the concert. She glanced quickly behind her to check, once again, that everything was in place. The last outfit change of the night, ripped jeans and the official black tour T-shirt, was already prepped for each member to change into for the encore performance.

"Everyone, raise your GLOsticks high!" Stu shouted again, making Alana look back to the stage.

The audience, already glittering with light, grew even brighter as every lightstick twinkled, a galaxy of orange stars surrounding NEON.

"So brilliant…" Stu said into his mic. "No matter how many times I see it, I don't think I'll ever get used to this. Thank you, our lovely GLO. You gave us light when we had none, shining a spotlight on us and showing the way when we were lost in the dark. It's all thanks to you and your beautiful light. Thank you and I love you!"

Alana smiled sadly. Even Stu had his thoughtful moments. It was true that GLO gave NEON their light, but it was Stu who reflected it most brightly, his positive energy so strong it touched all those around him, piercing into even Alana's dark mood.

Her phone buzzed, and she sighed. Her cousin had been texting her incessantly from her seat in the audience. Stephanie's role for the concert was already over, having primarily been involved with designing and sourcing NEON's outfits, so now she was free to enjoy the show.

Glancing down at her phone confirmed Alana's suspicion.

### October 5
**Stephanie (8:44 p.m.)** Are you sure about this?

She ignored the message and watched as Jaehyun gave his last thoughts of the night.

"Again, thank you, GLO! We are where we are now, performing in front of you all together, because of your love. NEON and GLO are like one big family that will never be apart in our hearts," he paused as the fans screamed in agreement. "Also, I want to mention my other family. They were able to come to NEON's concert for the first time today, traveling all the way from Jeolla Province, and I'm especially grateful."

A chorus of *aww*s filled the dome stadium, along with the occasional "you're so handsome, Jaehyun!" as the eldest member continued. "I especially want to thank my grandparents, who raised me. I promised I would mention them tonight, and I'd just like to say I wouldn't be who I am today without their unconditional support. Grandpa! Grandma! I love you!"

Alana's phone buzzed again as the fans yelled in support.

**Stephanie (8:46 p.m.)** Aly, please. You're not thinking straight.

An echoing *ca-caw* from the crowd erupted through the stadium, and she looked up. The other members were laughing as Stu flapped his arms and ran around Eagle, who waited with a shy smile for everyone to quiet down before speaking into his mic.

"I was only fifteen when NEON debuted. At that time, I hadn't experienced much yet. All my life I knew I wanted to be a singer, and my wonderful mom signed me up for dance lessons. I practiced hard every day, but I never had time to make any friends or do the things people my age normally did."

Alana sometimes forgot how young Eagle was. Surrounded by his older members, the *maknae* came across as mature for his age, especially in comparison to some of the things Stu and Jaehyun did.

"When I joined Solar Entertainment, I was nervous about meeting my *hyungs*, but instead of judging me, they helped me. Since I didn't know anything, I learned from my members, and they became my first friends, influencing me the most as I grew into who I am today."

At this, the audience broke their attentive quiet to cry out in adoration. The simple but honest words of the youngest member were bringing out GLO's indulgent, protective side.

"That's why, after our debut, I could see how worried they had become. My *hyungs* were struggling with their own fears, and I think that was the hardest thing for me. I didn't know how I could help them, like they had helped me." Eagle looked at his band mates, visibly choked up. Into the mic, he addressed them haltingly, saying, "Thank you for raising me, and I will work harder as the youngest to make sure you don't have to worry so much anymore."

Stu walked across the stage to wrap an arm around Eagle as tears fell down the *maknae*'s face. Jaehyun had started to tear up as well and he hovered closer. Both Yongnam and Emery looked sadly at Eagle, but stayed where they were on stage. Their sweat and jewelry glinted under the spotlights.

**Stephanie (8:49 p.m.)** What happened, Aly? Please, talk to me

Alana turned her phone on silent and put it in her back pocket. It was Emery's turn. She held her breath as he raised his mic.

"As we prepared for our first dome concert these past few weeks, I had the time to look back on all the memories we've shared together, with NEON and with GLO." Alana noticed Yongnam had his head turned toward Emery, watching him closely.

"Honestly, there were many times I questioned if we would make it. There were moments I truly felt like giving up."

Her lungs tightened, and the sound of the fans' sympathetic protests reverberated through the stadium. During the concert, Emery had seemed himself, smiling and interacting with the audience and the rest of NEON as he sat through most of the performances, singing his parts, but Alana was still worried—the usual brightness in his eyes was missing.

"But, each time I saw our fans' faces, heard how our songs had impacted your lives, I felt the responsibility to you all to keep trying. No matter what happens, GLO and NEON are my family, my true family, and I will never give that up."

A tear slid down Alana's cheek. She quickly brushed it away, but more only took its place. She realized she wasn't the only one struggling. Eagle had started crying again, and Stu looked like he was trying his absolute hardest not to join in. While Jaehyun stared at the floor, Yongnam wore a pained expression as he kept his focus on Emery.

"Most recently, when we were in the accident, I was truly scared I would lose everything. Even when I found out NEON was okay, I worried what would happen if I couldn't recover enough to step on stage again, or see GLO again. I would lose the only true family I had."

He turned away from the audience to collect himself, giving Alana a clear view of his expression without the monitors. Tears fell unchecked down his face, and her heart broke when he covered his mouth to sob.

Yongnam took a faltering step toward Emery, but it was Stu who blocked her view as he placed an arm around Emery's good shoulder in comfort. The audience roared with pain that echoed Alana's own and began to chant, "Don't cry! Don't cry! Don't cry!"

When Emery recovered his composure enough to speak, he turned back to the audience. Starting and stopping a few times, it took him a few tries, but he finally managed to finish his speech.

"I know…I know we put you through a lot over the years, and I…just want to say thank you, GLO… From the bottom of our hearts, truly, thank you… Let's walk this path together forever. And I will do my best to give you more music that brings hope to your lives, just as you have brought hope to mine."

GLO's answering cheer was deafening, and Alana doubted there was a dry eye in the entire audience.

Last came NEON's leader, Yongnam. He turned his gaze from Emery to the crowd.

"First of all, I would like to thank GLO for supporting us through our long journey from debut to tonight, the first stop of our Enlightenment Tour. Being able to perform in front of twenty thousand fans, we feel truly honored. It wouldn't be possible without the love we get from you guys, and we'll continue working hard to bring you good music."

Yongnam faced the camera closest to him. "I also want to thank Solar Entertainment, the staff, producers, Kang Hyojoon *seonsaengnim*, and President Jo for making all this possible and believing in our potential. I trust you to always do the right thing, and I feel lucky to have you all supporting us. Thank you."

As she watched, Alana felt like he had spoken directly to her. But Yongnam didn't need to worry. She meant what she told him in the studio: she would not come between Emery and NEON.

"Lastly, I want to thank my members." Yongnam looked at each of them as he spoke, and now he, too, looked to be on the verge of tears. "I'm so grateful that we are able to be here together in this amazing arena. I know, as your leader, I'm not always perfect. I make mistakes. Just know that I want you all to be happy, and I will work harder to show you a better version of myself."

Yongnam held his arms out as the rest of NEON joined him for a giant group hug, the crowd crying out their love to them.

"Okay, now, it's time for the last song of the night," Yongnam said into his mic, breaking apart from the emotional hug.

"Are you guys ready?" Stu cried.

The answer was obvious, but GLO gave it anyways, cheering all the while.

"Let's *wake up!*" Eagle called into his mic and the audience erupted with even more excitement.

The stage lights went dark, and GLO lit up the arena with a mesmerizing ocean of orange lightsticks as NEON got into place and Emery moved off to the side. Alana turned away from the stage as the music began, tears still flowing down her cheeks. Her emotions had been a wreck ever since her night with Emery. She needed to get ahold of herself. Pulling her phone out and wiping her eyes, she realized she had missed more messages from her cousin.

Stephanie (8:50 p.m.) Why aren't you responding??

Stephanie (8:51 p.m.) I'm worried

Stephanie (8:53 p.m.) Meet me as soon as the show's over

Typing quickly, she sent a reply to Stephanie and put her phone away.

Alana (8:55 p.m.) Okay

The sound of fireworks shot from the stage, and she knew it was almost time.

"Get ready!" Yena called out to the stylists. "Eight minutes for the last costume change! It's going to be tight—no room for mistakes!"

Meanwhile, NEON sang through the final lines of "Enlighten."

> Wide awake, dawn has come.
> I look to the light, now enlightened
> Because of you.

The song came to an end with an explosion of more fireworks and cheers. The stage lights faded, and Alana's heart beat wildly in anticipation. As NEON stepped backstage, handing their mics off to the staff, the stylists burst into action, ushering the members into changing areas with alarming speed.

"Sungil, over here! Quick!"

"Here, Yongnam, put this on first, and then I'll fix your hair!"

"Careful of your earpiece, Stu! It's caught on your shirt!"

Alana made eye contact with Emery, motioning for him to hurry. As he jogged up to her, she could make out the slight redness around his eyes.

"Last change," she reminded him. "Everything's laid out for you."

He nodded, giving her an exhausted grin.

"Be careful with your—"

"Cast. I know." He smiled again to soften the interruption. "Relax, Alana. It's almost over."

She felt stricken as he strode quickly away to get changed.

*"Encore! Encore! Encore! Encore!"*

The fans' chanting roared backstage, serving only to remind her there wasn't much time left.

Less than two minutes later, Emery rejoined her, and her eyes scanned his outfit from head to toe, checking for any oversights. When her gaze made it back to his face, she blushed at the laughter dancing behind his eyes.

"Like what you see?" Emery teased in English.

*"Encore! Encore! Encore! Encore!"*

Acutely aware of their proximity, she bit her tongue, holding back a retort. "Your hair's fine, but we need to retouch your makeup—Hyeran!"

The head makeup artist looked over from where she was redoing Jaehyun's eye shadow. "Yeah?"

"Emery needs a touch up too!"

Hyeran rolled her eyes, grinning. "They all do! That's what happens when they sweat and cry all over stage, ruining my perfect work!" She used a towel to wipe more sweat off Jaehyun's forehead before it dripped down to ruin the eyeliner she'd just fixed. "Like, seriously."

"Hey!" Jaehyun protested. "My sweat is a gift. You should feel blessed to be in its presence."

"Gross," Eagle commented in passing as his *coordi* led him to get his hair fixed by Junho, the head hairdresser.

"Respect your elders, Sungil!" Jaehyun said with a mock scowl, but otherwise holding still for Hyeran.

*"Encore! Encore! Encore! ENCORE!"*

"At least *I'm* not sweating everywhere for once," Emery mused, as Alana pulled out her own set of foundation and began applying more coverage around his eyes and nose. "I guess that's a plus."

"Very true," Yena said, overhearing Emery's comment as she came over. "How's everything over here?"

"Just need to touch up his eyes and he'll be ready," Alana reported, pulling back to re-examine her work.

"Good job, Aly! You're the quickest one so far." Yena's eyes scrutinized the commotion of stylists, managers, and members again as she spoke. "How about you, M? You have everything you need?"

Emery gave a bright grin. "Yup. Alana is doing a great job. By the end of this tour, she'll be a pro."

*"ENCORE! ENCORE! ENCORE! ENCORE!"*

"I wish. It's going to be hard without her," Yena said sadly.

Alana's stomach flipped. He wasn't supposed to find out this way.

"What do you mean?" Emery asked Yena, speaking up to be heard over the fans' increasing volume.

Yena looked to Alana in surprise. "You haven't told him yet?" Turning her attention back to Emery, she said, "Alana turned in her resignation letter on Monday. Today is her last day."

*"ENCORE! ENCORE! ENCORE! EN—"*

Screams overwhelmed the stadium as the final concert *VCR* could be heard starting on the stage screens.

"Two minutes—*aish*! Watch the clothes, Stu!" Yena called out as he spilled water on his shirt. "Thank god the tour shirt is black this year," she muttered.

"Alana?" Emery stood frozen, staring at her.

Alana's heart thundered in her chest. It wasn't supposed to happen like this, but there had never been a good time to tell him. Something had always come up. Alana opened her mouth to speak just as Hyeran appeared.

"I'll add more shadow and clean up the eyeliner, but that's all there's time for," the makeup artist said, making quick, efficient work with her brush.

"One minute!" Yena shouted.

"Done," Hyeran said, already on her way to check on Yongnam.

Alana didn't move, and neither did Emery. She kept waiting for him to react, to say something, anything, but all he did was watch her, the growing disbelief in his expression begging *her* to be the one to react, to speak up, to deny it. But what could she say to make this less painful?

"Emery. Your mic."

Alana could see the muscles in Emery's neck straining as he forced every unspoken word and emotion back. By the time he looked at the staff member holding his mic, there was a smile on his face—the same smile he had once worn for Byung Ho. Only this was a million times worse.

This one was all her fault.

Her insides shrinking, she watched as Emery took his custom orange mic, checked his members were in position, and stepped on stage—smiling.

The screaming of the fans was just an echo to the screaming of her heart.

★ ★ ★ ★ ★

"One, two, three!"

Alana hung back, watching, as Emery posed with NEON. They were piled together on a black leather sofa in the backstage waiting room, each holding up an Enlightenment Tour in Seoul fan banner as Sohee the social media manager took their picture.

"Okay?" Jaehyun asked, wiping sweat from his brow with the towel around his neck.

"One more," Sohee said, looking at the last shot on her camera. "Sungil, your banner is upside down again."

Without dropping his V-sign pose, Eagle casually flipped his banner right-side up, the words "Together let's hold hands into brighter memories" now matching the others.

"One, two, three!" Sohee took another round of pictures. "Okay, *now* you're done."

"Yesss!" Stu jumped up from the sofa in triumph, the others following suit, while Emery's smile dropped from his face like it had never been there to begin with. He still hadn't noticed Alana standing in the hall, and she wasn't sure if that was a good thing or not. Her cell phone buzzed.

Stephanie (9:49 pm) I'm slowly making my way through the crowds. Where are you?

Once the concert ended, Alana had officially signed off on her last night as a *coordi*, but she remained backstage, wanting to find Emery. She needed to explain. Not that there was much to say, but she couldn't just leave things the way they were.

Alana (9:50 p.m.) Backstage

**Alana (9:50 p.m.)** I have to talk to Emery

**Alana (9:51 p.m.)** I'll message when I'm done

"Make sure you take some *selcas* to post on your account later!" Sohee called out to the members, who nodded, already preoccupied with collecting their bags, jackets, and various electronics from around the room.

A sudden commotion down the hallway stole Alana's focus. She looked up to find Minhyuk leading a group of people, forcing her out of the way from her position at the door. As they drew closer, she stepped even farther away, realizing who the guests were.

"NEON, look who's here," Minhyuk announced into the waiting room, turning awkwardly thanks to the walking cast on his left foot, to reveal who was standing behind him.

"Mum!" Stu shouted, tackling the woman wearing a breezy yellow dress and bright orange scarf in a hug before she'd even fully entered the room.

"Congratulations, Stuart!" his mother exclaimed in English, her Australian accent even stronger than Stu's. "I'm so proud of you!"

Alana watched as they embraced, and the sound of families reuniting clamored throughout the waiting room. As Stu started taking a *selca* with his mom, Alana stepped quietly into the room. Each of the members was speaking and laughing with his parents and siblings, or in Jaehyun's case, his entire family clan.

Emery, however, stood alone, watching NEON with a blank look on his face. Alana's chest ached, and she fought the urge to go to him. She could understand his parents not being able to come, with them living in Los Angeles, but seeing him like this, without anybody at all…it was heartbreaking.

**Stephanie (9:54 p.m.)** You haven't told him yet?

Alana grimaced. She didn't want to continue creeping awkwardly along the wall, but she couldn't figure out how to pull Emery aside without drawing unwanted attention.

The members slowly migrated out of the room as more friends and family came backstage. Thankfully, no one paid her any attention.

"Great show, M!"

Alana looked away from watching Yongnam take pictures with his little sister, who was adorably dressed in head-to-toe neon orange, to see HI5's Jaden giving Emery a friendly hug.

"Jaden!" Emery said, genuine surprise on his face. "I didn't know you were coming. I thought HI5 was promoting in Japan."

"We are." Jaden grinned, sweeping his mint-green hair back from his eyes. "I have a flight back to Osaka tonight, but Director Ku swung us all tickets. I couldn't pass up the chance to see NEON's first dome concert. Seriously, dude, you all were awesome!"

"'Us'?" Emery said, looking around Jaden to see the rest of the *I Can Cook* cast approaching.

"Good show, M," Director Ku said, shaking Emery's hand. "I understand now why my daughter and wife are such huge fans of yours."

"Thank you, Director," Emery said, his eyes wide.

"Hey, kiddo," said Byung Ho as he stepped forward, meaty shoulders straining against his white button-down shirt as he uncrossed his arms.

Alana felt herself inching closer to Emery. What was Byung Ho doing here? She looked around, growing frustrated that no one seemed to realize his presence.

"That was some concert!" Byung Ho exclaimed. "Lots

of tears."

Alana cursed whoever thought it was a good idea to give the *I Can Cook* team tickets.

"Your voice is really unique," Director Ku said to Emery with a grin. "You seemed like a good kid during filming—too bad we didn't get to work together more. You know I tried to keep you on the show, right? But President Jo was so insistent."

At last, Alana saw Yongnam glance over towards the commotion around Emery, eyes tightening at the sight of Byung Ho.

"Let's see if we can get a picture." Scanning the crowd, Director Ku spotted Alana lurking along the wall. "Hey, could you take a photo for us?"

She froze as everyone turned to her—including Emery. She watched what little expression he had on his face disappear, a careful nothingness in his eyes as he looked at her. Her breath hitched. "O-okay…"

"Great! Here, you can use my phone."

Taking the director's phone carefully with both hands, Alana waited for everyone to get in position before rapidly snapping a few pictures. She noticed Jaehyun was also observing the group out of the corner of his eye as he conversed with his grandparents.

"Okay?" she said, handing the phone back to the director, who swiped through the photos. She glanced back up only to see Emery quickly turn away.

"I never got the chance to apologize in person for that misunderstanding we had," Byung Ho mentioned loudly to Emery.

"Apologize?" Emery asked wearily.

"Sorry kiddo," Byung Ho continued in an airy tone. "I can see now that you're quite the trend."

"Not just a trend. NEON's going to take over the world,"

Jaden said brightly, clapping Emery on the back.

"Byung Ho was adamant about apologizing to you," Director Ku said, smiling proudly as he slid his phone into his pocket.

"Not that there's much to apologize for, right kiddo?" Byung Ho let out a loud laugh. "We all know how *netizens* exaggerate."

"I—" Emery started.

"It's okay," Byung Ho continued. "I know you're normally a respectful kid. Filming for variety shows is stressful, isn't it? I remember how it was when I was just starting in the industry."

"I'm glad you two can finally work this out," Director Ku said, patting them both on their backs.

Across the room, Jaehyun shared a look with Yongnam before excusing himself from his conversation and approaching the *I Can Cook* group around Emery. He stood unobtrusively behind Jaden.

"It must have been tough sitting out most of the show, but I have to say, the concert was surprisingly decent," Byung Ho said casually, elbowing Jaden for agreement. "It seems NEON didn't really need M during the show, did they?"

"You're right," Emery said abruptly, locking his gaze on Alana. "I'm not needed."

Alana felt her heart, already throbbing wildly, start to crack against the pressure.

"Wow," Byung Ho said with a laugh. "Someone needs to learn to take a jo—"

"No. You're right, *Sunbae*. I'm useless. Worthless. Unnecessary. You're always right, aren't you?"

The group fell quiet at Emery's outburst while he continued to stare at Alana.

"It wasn't meant to be taken seriously, M." PD Ku tried to smooth over the situation as Byung Ho's face reddened.

"Byung Ho wasn't seriously suggesting you don't belong in NEON."

Emery let out a sharp bark of laughter.

"M, you okay?" said Jaehyun, who had stepped forward and put his hand on Emery's shoulder. He stared at Byung Ho with an overly polite expression.

Still, Emery didn't look away from Alana. "Never better," he said, his smile wide and eyes blank.

Alana backed away from Emery, her lungs burning, her heart pounding.

"Is everything all right over here?" Minhyuk said as he limped his way toward them.

Emery finally looked away, and Alana was free. Without a second thought, she turned, followed her racing heart, and ran.

Hall after hall, room after room, everything became a blur. She had no destination in mind, only escape, until her gasping breath caused her to stumble to a stop in a deserted hallway.

"Somebody, Alex, please," she choked out, sinking to her knees and clutching her head tightly. "Make it all go away."

Her eyes closed, she felt the seconds tick by, trying to get herself back under control, trying to forget the look on Emery's face as he yelled out his pain. She knew it was her fault he was spiraling. It was all her fault.

"Are you just going to run away from all this? From me?"

Alana slowly lifted her head. There was Emery, standing in front of her, staring at her with hurt and disappointment.

"You were really going to leave without saying goodbye? After everything?" he asked incredulously.

"I can't stay here," she said, begging him to understand. "Don't you see? We can't do this. It isn't right!"

Emery shook his head and pulled her to her feet, glancing around before guiding them both to a secluded corner.

Stepping closer, he cupped her face with his hand. "Not right, Alana? How could this be wrong?"

He didn't get it. Emery was caught up in the false security they felt whenever they were together. He hadn't yet grasped the complications, the repercussions, not even after they had been caught by Yongnam. Looking into his eyes now, she knew he would never let her go. She had to be the one to end it, to make things right.

Alana swallowed painfully, pushing his hand away, and she felt a cold, empty veil envelop her as she forced her feelings behind her walls. "I'm not right for you, Emery. We don't belong together."

"No, Alana. Don't say that."

"Us. You and me. It can't work. It will only end up destroying us both." She was broken and would only break Emery too if she stayed. She couldn't be the one to ruin him.

"Is this about what Yongnam said?" A dark look crossed Emery's handsome face.

"No, it has nothing to do with Yongnam. He just made everything more real."

Emery ran his fingers through his hair, his face drawn tight. "Yena said you turned in your resignation on Monday," he said slowly. "How long have you been planning this and never said anything? Days? Weeks?"

"I *tried* to tell you," she said, her voice breaking slightly. She took another deep breath and focused on the numbness spreading through her.

"In the studio…" Realization dawned in Emery's eyes. "That's why you were crying. It wasn't because of Alex."

That thought distracted her. He thought she was upset that day because of Alex? No. It was the prospect of breaking Emery's heart that had scared her. And she had every right to be afraid. Too many feelings were involved. She needed to put a stop to their relationship before she hurt him even more, before it was too late.

"Where will you go?" Emery suddenly asked. "Do you have something lined up?"

Still unsettled, Alana answered without thinking, "I'm going to figure things out from home."

Emery sighed. "I know I'm leaving on world tour soon—and this is horrible timing—but when I come back to Korea, I really think we can work this out."

"No," she said. "I mean I'm going to my *real* home. Back to Chicago. My dad already purchased the plane ticket."

Emery tensed. "You're leaving Korea?"

"Yes. On Monday."

"You're leaving," he repeated. Raw, unfiltered pain crossed his features, and the cracks in her heart widened.

Speaking slowly around the pain, Alana said, "Being with you was like a dream, Emery, but it's time to wake up."

"That's bullshit!" Emery quickly ran his hand through his hair again. "You're scared. What we have is real, and it's made you feel something you're too scared to face!"

"Real? I'm the only one here trying to face reality, Emery! What did you think would happen to us? We would secretly date for years while I worked as your stylist, breaking company rules left and right?"

He glared at her. "I don't care what you do, Alana, as long as you're happy! But this? Ending things between us without even trying? You really are a quitter."

Pain tore through Alana, sorrow and anguish and shame spilling over. She thought of all she had given up after Alex's death, everything she had done to survive the constant guilt of knowing she had failed her brother. How could Emery say that? She had trusted him with her secrets. Now he was turning them against her.

Emery's expression fell at the sight of whatever he saw on her face. "Alana, I—"

"No, you're right," she spat, latching onto her anger to displace her pain. "I *am* a quitter. But do you want to know *why*? Why I gave up on my music? Why I dropped out of school? It's the question you've been asking all this time."

He watched her wearily, conflicting emotions warring across his face. "Why?"

"It was because of *you*. If I hadn't been a fan of NEON, Alex would still be alive."

He jerked back from her, as if she'd struck him, but she kept speaking, unable to stop the words as they poured out, finally letting free all the buried guilt surrounding her brother's death.

"That night—the reason I wasn't with my brother for his final show, the reason I wasn't there to see the warning signs, the reason I wasn't there to save him—was because I stayed home to watch *your* comeback. I cared more about NEON than my own family, and now I have to live with the consequences every single day of my life."

Seeing the horror on Emery's face, she looked away. She had to rein in her own heartbreak, force herself to say what was necessary for him to let her go, even if it wasn't entirely true. It was time to end this.

"You see?" she said, calming her emotions by trapping them once again behind her walls. "Every time I look at you, every time I hear one of NEON's songs, I see Alex dying on my bathroom floor, and I can't bear it. Not anymore."

Emery's face was white, his right hand clenching into a fist at his side.

"You're going to be okay," she said, regaining her outward composure even as her insides trembled. "NEON needs you right now. And your fans—your fans need you, too."

"But what about what *I* need?" Emery asked frantically. "What about what I *want?*" He took a hesitant step forward.

"You don't want me, Emery. Not really." She took a step back, then another, as Emery watched her with hopeless defeat in his eyes. Pulling away felt like she was personally ripping her heart to shreds.

"Don't do this," he whispered haltingly. "I love you, Alana. Does that mean nothing?"

All her walls shattered at his words, and the flood of pain came surging forward. She was drowning. She could never be trusted with something as precious as his love. Some things were never meant to last.

*It's time to go.*

She turned her back on him, hiding the tears she could no longer fight, and walked down the hallway, refusing to look back.

# Emery

## #Reflection

"Mom..." said Emery, his voice low and restrained.

"It's just that your father's already committed to his golf trip."

"Of course he has." Emery gripped the phone tighter, resisting the urge to snap at her.

"And I'd love to come, but Friday nights are usually when I get together with the girls. And I just hate driving into the city, especially on the weekend."

Emery couldn't deal with this tonight. He couldn't handle his mother's excuses, not now. The concert would be his first time back to Los Angeles in more than a year, and his parents made zero effort to attend. He knew he should have expected this, but it still cut deep. How could he mean so little to them? His cheeks grew hot with disappointed anger. "Do whatever you want, Mom."

"You understand, right?"

Her nonchalance was what finally set him off.

"Do I understand that my parents can't be *bothered* to see their only son? Yeah, I understand. I hear you loud and clear." He paused for a second before biting out, "I don't want you to come anyway."

"Emery, that's not—"

"Don't speak to your mother like that."

Emery froze at the sound of his father's deep, gruff voice.

"After all we've done for you, all the opportunities we've given you, show some respect. Your mother cares for you, and I won't stand by listening to you yell—"

"Well, why the hell not?" Emery cut in sharply. "You talk to me for the first time in two years and expect me to care what you think?"

"Watch your tone."

"No. I'm done trying to please you. I only called to let Mom know I'd be in town for our concert, but I see now how pointless that was."

"The world doesn't revolve around you, Emery. You may want to fool around on stage and throw your life away, but that doesn't mean we have to watch."

"Yes. You've made that painfully clear." Swallowing heavily, he couldn't help but ask. "What do you want me to do? What will make you happy? If I have power? Money?" Emery laughed bitterly. "I have more money now than I'll ever need. Is that what you want from me?"

His father snorted. "Keep your money. God knows how you earned it."

Emery felt his blood run cold. "You know *nothing* about my life."

"Your life? You think *your* life is so special? What does it matter if you know nothing about the real world? Forget college—you never even graduated from high school! I'm ashamed to call you my son, do you hear me? So don't come crawling back home when you fail."

The words shouldn't have hurt. He knew how his father saw him. Still, pain from old and new scars alike consumed him. His father continued his tirade, ranting on and on, but Emery was no longer listening. He was done.

"This conversation is over," Emery said, interrupting his father mid-sentence, and hung up the phone with shaking hands. A moment later it rang again, "Mom" flashing on the screen, but Emery swiftly declined the call, then threw his phone across the bed and into the hotel pillow. Anger churned within him, frothing and swirling. He had hoped, just this once, his parents could see the success he had found with NEON. If they would only—but no. He shook his head violently. They didn't care. Clearly, he meant nothing.

Emotions gave way to nausea.

Lurching, he ran to the bathroom and emptied his stomach into the porcelain toilet before sinking low to the tiled floor.

The past month had been a blur, ever since Alana had left. Every day was a struggle, especially with NEON's world tour now underway. It was becoming harder and harder to force his smile into place, to pretend everything was okay, even for the fans.

Their six-city tour in Latin America had wrapped up in Mexico City the day before, and they had arrived in New York just a few hours ago. In the coming three weeks, they would have seven concerts in seven different cities across the U.S. But with his arm healing, Emery still couldn't fully participate, and the stress and guilt from being forced to the sidelines was slowly getting to him. It didn't help that his relationships with the NEON members were strained at best, especially with Yongnam and Jaehyun, who were both avoiding him offstage, but watching him when they thought he wasn't looking. Lately, Emery had found it easier to just keep to himself.

He missed Alana. He missed her quiet presence. He missed her small smiles. He missed being able to talk with her about anything and everything. Mostly, he just missed *her*. At least she had made it home safely—Stephanie had let him know. But he hadn't spoken to Stephanie since, keeping his distance from Alana's cousin just as he kept his distance from everyone else.

He knew it was foolish of him to think their relationship could have worked—he *knew* that—but he hadn't been able to give up hope, to stop himself from wishing, even when it was doomed from the start. She was his friend, and he didn't want anyone else but her, but he couldn't blame her for leaving, not after everything she'd been through.

Flushing the toilet, he grimaced. He didn't understand how Alana could have ever tolerated his presence, now that he knew she linked NEON to Alex's death. He should never have pried, should never have chased her. It was no small wonder she left.

Everything was his fault. Not Alana's. Not Yongnam's. Not his father's. It was his own damn fault. No one could stay by his side once they knew the real Emery.

He stumbled to the sink, rinsed his mouth out, and splashed water on his face, then stood back to take a hard look in the mirror. The baggy black sweatshirt drowned his features, hiding the cast on his left arm. While he no longer had to use the sling every day, his movements were still limited. Against his pale skin, his cheekbones stood out sharply, but it was the eyes that threw him. They stared darkly back at him— hollow, broken, defeated. He forced a smile to his lips, but the eyes never moved, as if immune to his actions, as if belonging to someone else.

He let out a sardonic laugh, and at that, his eyes did change. But it was worse. They turned cruel, mocking his efforts.

"Who could ever love you?" he muttered to himself. His mouth twisted, and he slammed his hand against the mirror, the sound reverberating in the tiny space. Still, the eyes laughed back at him, cold and bitter.

"Goddammit!"

He hit his reflection again. Harder. Enough for his palm to sting, sparking feeling through his fingers and down his arm into his very bones. He curled his hand into a fist and looked into those eyes. Everything he saw reflected there—the fear, the doubt, the guilt—he *hated*.

His fist collided with the mirror, sending a small crack through the glass, dividing his reflection into two. Gritting his teeth, he stared at both halves of himself and wondered which side was more real.

*Who am I?*

He hit the glass once more, throwing all his weight into it. He felt his knuckles tear and welcomed the rush of painful warmth.

"I'm a lie."

More cracks splintered outward as he struck out, fracturing his image into broken shards of resentment.

"I'm a failure."

Again and again he punched until he could no longer see his face through the spiderweb of black crevices and red blood.

"I'm *nothing*."

Tears sprang to his eyes as pain exploded in his fist. Finally waking from the haze of anger, he looked in alarm at the rivulets of blood dripping down his arm and into the sink.

He hurried to grab a white hand towel from beside the door, and tried to maneuver his left arm to wrap the torn knuckles of his right hand, his "good" hand. Blood smeared onto his cast while he choked back a sob.

He slid down to the floor, holding his throbbing hand against his chest and letting the tears fall. Time passed as he gave in to the abyss of pain and hate. Nothing else seemed to matter.

A knock on his hotel room door called him back.

"Hyung! *It's me, Sungil!*"

Emery groaned as the knocking continued, growing louder and more insistent.

"*I have your food!*" Sungil said, his voice muffled through the door.

With detached interest, Emery glanced around him, taking in the blood and fractured mirror.

"Hyung? *Hello?*" Sungil called again.

He knew that if he continued to ignore the *maknae*, Minhyuk would likely come to personally open his door. He pulled himself up by the sink and replaced the bloody towel around his fist with a smaller washcloth, tugging the sleeve of his sweatshirt down to cover the new injury. He avoided his crushed reflection in the mirror as he left the bathroom, closing the door firmly shut behind him.

With a shaky breath, he slowly opened the main door.

"We got you a burger!" Sungil stood alone with a bright smile on his face, wearing a blue hoodie and jeans, his brown hair hanging messily into his eyes.

"Thanks," Emery croaked, making no move to take the bag of food. He cleared his throat. "You can have it though. I'm not hungry." He tried to close the door, but Sungil's foot shoved between them, holding it open.

"*Hyung*, you need to eat." Sungil looked at him more closely, and his eyes widened. "Are you okay?"

"I-I just need to sleep…" started Emery, but it was no use. In his moment of hesitation, Sungil had already pushed his way into the room. He sat down on the floor by the window with their food and gestured for Emery to join him.

"Eat first, then sleep," Sungil said with a pointed look.

Emery wordlessly took a seat across from the *maknae* on the floor, tightening his grip on the washcloth hidden beneath his sleeve.

"This is the place you took us last time we came to New York. I've been dreaming about it ever since." Sungil dug into his own bag of food, unboxing a juicy hamburger and licking his lips in anticipation. Emery awkwardly used his left hand to pick at some of the fries, chewing, but not tasting anything.

"Where's everyone else?" said Emery after Sungil swallowed a mouthful of his burger. Of all NEON's members, the *maknae* was the least likely to eat alone.

Sungil took another huge bite and finished chewing before responding. "They went back to their rooms. Everyone was pretty tired, I guess."

Just then, there was another knock on the door.

"Coming!" Sungil said, immediately jumping up to answer it.

"Oh hey, Sungil!" said Stu, also holding a takeout bag from the same restaurant. "Did you guys steal all the tomato sauce? You know I can't eat fries without it."

"Ketchup? You can have mine," Sungil chirped, leading Stu into Emery's room.

"Nice set up, M," Stu said approvingly, adjusting his glasses as he looked at the mini studio on the desk.

Emery didn't even glance at it. Composing with his portable studio in hotel rooms was how he spent almost all his free time. But everything he'd created recently felt overwhelmingly empty.

Stu joined them on the ground, sitting down in his black sweats and orange T-shirt. "I think Yongnam's working right now, too."

Emery shrugged as he ate another fry.

"Can we hear it?" asked Sungil. He was once again smiling brightly, his hands tapping a steady rhythm against his legs. "You've been working so hard this whole tour. I bet your songs are awesome."

"Another time," said Emery, shifting back a bit, putting distance between them. "It's... they're not ready yet."

"Oh. Okay, sure," said Sungil, exchanging a look with Stu, who set his burger down slowly and faced Emery head on.

"Mate, you can't keep ignoring us," he said. "I feel like we haven't actually *talked* in weeks. What's going on with you?"

Emery kept his gaze downcast, playing with a fry in his left hand. "I'm fine. Just tired, that's all."

"Sure, and that's why you and Yongnam can't even make eye contact?" Stu raised an eyebrow.

"Or why Jaehyun is constantly shooting you guilty looks?" added Sungil.

Emery looked up. His members' carefree expressions were gone.

"What's wrong, M?" Stu asked, his eyebrows now knitted in concern behind his glasses.

A loud knock on the door saved Emery from answering.

"*Sungil! You in here?*" The voice was unmistakably Jaehyun's.

"Shit," Stu cursed in English before yelling back in Korean, "Go away, *Hyung!*"

The knocking grew more and more frantic with ever louder cries of "let me in!"

"Hold that thought, M." Stu sighed and got up to open the door.

Jaehyun came sauntering in, dressed in a hotel robe over flannel pants and slippers. "I was looking everywhere for you, Sungil. Aren't we going to watch the finale of *Moonlight, Again?*" He sat down on Emery's king-size bed, surveying the room. "Oh, you guys still eating?"

"Shhh! Not now, *Hyung*," said Sungil from his place on the floor, holding a finger to his lips.

"As I was saying," continued Stu, "what's wrong, Emery?"

Understanding crossed Jaehyun's face, and he looked to Emery too.

"Nothing. I'm fine," said Emery, frustration leaking into his tone.

"We're not stupid. Something has been off with you for a while now," said Stu, throwing a meaningful glance from Emery to Jaehyun.

"Come on, you two. It's obvious M wants to be left alone," said Jaehyun. "Let's just watch the drama and leave him be."

"Yongnam needs to be here," Sungil said to Stu, ignoring the eldest member's words.

"I agree."

Emery stifled a groan. "Really, guys? What's Yongnam have to do with this?"

"Everything!" cried Stu, throwing his hands up in exasperation. "We hoped things would get better on their own, but looks like we have to step in."

Sungil nodded. "This can't go on any longer."

Before Emery had time to react, Stu jumped up and flew across the room to grab Emery's phone on the bed. "Keep M back!"

On cue, Sungil tackled Emery to the ground, pinning him down by essentially lying on top of him.

"Get *off!*" Emery winced as his freshly injured hand slammed against the floor.

"Sorry, sorry, *Hyung*, please don't kill me later," Sungil apologized as he held onto Emery.

"Hold on. What's his password?" Stu muttered, his glasses askew.

"Zero, six, zero, two," said Sungil without any hesitation. "Hurry, he's struggling!"

"Got it!" Stu cried. "Good work, Sungil. Okay, opening Tiki Talk and… ha! He's listed as Captain Yongnam."

"Get on with it," Sungil grunted as Emery kneed him in the stomach.

"Typing...typing...and sent!" Stu said triumphantly.

Sungil promptly released Emery, and sat back, breathing heavily. Thankfully, Emery had kept hold of the washcloth throughout the struggle. He re-adjusted his sleeve, making sure his injury stayed hidden, but otherwise didn't move from his position on the ground. Jaehyun remained perched on the end of the bed looking alarmed.

"Hey, let me see!" Sungil grabbed the phone from Stu and snorted at the message. "Really?"

"Couldn't resist," Stu said with a smirk.

As Sungil grinned in response, Emery's phone started to buzz, and the *maknae* jumped in surprise. "*Hyung*, your mom's calling," he said, immediately holding the phone out to Emery.

Emery stood up, taking his phone back with his left hand and quickly shoving it into his sweatshirt pocket. His food forgotten on the floor, Emery moved to sit in the chair at the desk, anxious for some space.

Watching him, Sungil frowned. "Hey, M, why are you only using your left hand?"

As everyone's attention turned to his broken arm, a sharp knock sounded at the door.

"What did you tell Yongnam?" Emery said, tugging on his sleeves as adrenaline pulsed through his body.

"Nothing important..." said Stu, but Emery knew better than to trust his innocent expression.

"I'll get the door!" offered Sungil.

"We're not leaving until you guys work it out!" said Stu.

As the *maknae* opened the door, Yongnam strode in, his expression livid. "What's going on?" he demanded as soon as the door slammed shut.

"*Hyung*, come in," said Stu, spreading his arms in a welcoming gesture. He had returned to sitting on the floor and munching on his ketchup-covered fries.

Emery rose from his seat, holding his right hand behind him, and said stiffly, "I'm done with this. Everyone needs to get out!"

"Are you kidding me?!" Yongnam's voice shook and his eyes flashed.

"Woah, *Hyung*." Sungil looked at their leader with fear in his eyes. "Calm down."

"This is exactly why I can't trust you!" Yongnam directed his rage entirely at Emery. "How dare you!"

"What?" said Emery, stepping forward in defiance. He had no clue what Stu wrote in the message to get Yongnam so worked up, but his leader's anger had reignited his own. "Go on! Don't stop there."

"This is ridiculous! You're acting pathetic," Yongnam said, moving closer until they were mere inches apart.

"I'm fine. I can take care of myself."

"What the hell is this about?!" said Jaehyun in disbelief.

Stu shook his head, stunned. "There's no way M's message was *that* bad. All I said was that we needed to talk and that things were going to change with NEON. Oh. Maybe I used a few too many swear words…"

Yongnam's dark eyes flared as he looked at Emery. "Sure, you can take care of yourself until one of your secrets come out to ruin us all. How many more do you have?"

"So I'm not allowed to have my own thoughts and feelings now?!"

"Secrets?" said Stu. "What secrets?"

"M is dating Alana," Yongnam said in a matter of fact tone.

At the mention of her name, Emery snapped. He yanked Yongnam's white T-shirt with his hands and shoved the leader back, the washcloth falling to the floor.

"Don't bring her into this!" Emery shouted, shaking with fury.

"Blood," Sungil interrupted in a small voice, pointing to the rag at their feet.

Everyone froze, looking from the bloody washcloth on the ground, to the red stain on Yongnam's shirt, and then to Emery's torn fist now hanging at his side. Emery paled as he hurriedly pulled his sleeve back into place.

"M?" Yongnam said quietly.

"How many times do I have to tell you? I'm *fine*." Emery's eyes darted around the room, looking for an escape as his heart pounded wildly.

"What happened?" the raven-haired leader took a hesitant step forward.

"Get out," Emery pleaded, his voice breaking.

"No," said Yongnam calmly, taking another step closer. "Tell me."

"I can't," Emery whispered in defeat. His whole body trembled as he let out a stifled cry.

Without another word, Yongnam gripped Emery in a tight hug, holding him close as Emery's sobs tore from his chest, echoing throughout the room.

"I'm sorry," Emery said into Yongnam's shoulder. It seemed to be the only thing he *could* say. "I'm sorry. I'm sorry. I-I'm sorry."

"It's okay." Yongnam pulled back to look at him, the tears on his face matching Emery's own. He led Emery to sit on the bed next to Jaehyun, keeping his arm around Emery's shoulders. Sungil approached hesitantly, a bottle of water in hand. Emery took a shuddering breath and avoided their eyes as tears continued to stream down his face. He drank a few gulps of the proffered water, feeling NEON's collective gaze fall to his bloodied hand. Setting the water bottle down on the floor, he moved to wipe his tears away with his sleeve, ignoring the pain in his torn knuckles.

"I'll get another towel," Jaehyun said into the quiet room, moving quickly from the bed to the bathroom, halting as soon as he opened the door. "Ah. The scene of the crime."

Stu stood up to see what Jaehyun meant, taking in the damage, his face ashen. "M, what's going on?"

"I'm sorry. You weren't supposed to see this." Emery kept his attention focused on his injury, trying to stop the blood from dripping on the white bedspread as his hands shook harder. The wounds were mostly shallow, his knuckles just scratched by the glass, but there was one cut that ran deeper, slicing across his fingers and making a mess of his black sweatpants.

"Don't apologize," Stu said bluntly, coming back into the room to Emery's bedside. Jaehyun followed with a fresh towel and handed it to Emery. "Just talk to us, M. Please."

"Keep the pressure on that cut," said Jaehyun, returning to his spot and eyeing Emery's knuckles critically. "That's going to take some time to heal."

"Why didn't you say anything? We were right next door." Sungil hovered in front of them, wide-eyed.

"Is this about Alana?" Yongnam asked carefully, removing his arm from Emery's shoulders to study his face more closely.

"No," Emery said quickly. He looked awkwardly to the floor, unable to meet anyone's eyes. "I mean, no, not really... We broke up."

No one spoke for a moment.

"Bloody hell," muttered Stu in English.

"How long was this going on?" Jaehyun choked, his eyes flickering back and forth between Emery's face and his injured hand.

"Nothing was *going* on. It ended before it really began." Emery pressed the towel tighter against his throbbing knuckles.

"I was hoping you two would work out," said Sungil, taking a seat on the floor in front of Emery.

"You knew?" Emery said, looking down at the *maknae* in surprise.

"It was kind of hard not to…" Sungil glanced at the other members for support.

"*I* didn't know!" Stu said, and Jaehyun nodded in agreement.

"Well, I could just tell, you know? From the way they acted." Sungil shrugged and clasped his hands. "They were adorable together."

"But wait," said Jaehyun, turning to Yongnam. "Why were you so mad?"

Yongnam remained silent for a moment, a strained expression on his face. "The text message. It scared me." He faced Emery, meeting his eyes directly. "I thought you were leaving, this time for good."

"Leaving? Why would M leave?" Jaehyun asked in alarm, pulling his robe closer around him.

As his group members looked at him, their eyes full of fear and confusion, Emery realized he couldn't continue the charade—the lies, the secrets. NEON was his family. Why the hell was he still keeping this from them?

"I almost quit," said Emery, letting out an unsteady breath. "Two years ago when we were struggling. I…I was ready to leave." Emery raised his right hand to run it through his hair, but Jaehyun caught his forearm, adjusting the towel and re-applying pressure to Emery's wound.

"Why?" Yongnam said. "I mean, sure, it was rough then, but I thought we were making it through together. You never even said anything."

Emery hesitated, the shame of his past weakness, his *failure*, overwhelming him.

"You can tell us, mate," Stu said softly, crouching down next to Sungil.

Taking another deep breath, Emery said, "My family... They hate what I do. They never wanted me to come to Korea..."

Emery faltered, feeling all their eyes on him. Yongnam placed a reassuring hand on his shoulder, urging him to continue.

"My father, he basically gave me a choice. I could quit and come home, or I could never come home again." Emery shook his head. "I wasn't doing anyone any good. I thought if I went home, I could at least make my parents happy. I could finally do *something* right. So I did it—I quit. But when I told my father, he *still* wasn't happy. I had already proven myself worthless in his eyes."

Emery paused, a tired laugh escaping his mouth. Jaehyun carefully moved the towel, checking to see if the bleeding had stopped before holding it back down against the wound, frowning apologetically when Emery winced.

"Even now, we don't speak—not until tonight, at least." Emery laughed again. "He's still the exact same. He won't forgive me for staying with NEON, for chasing impossible dreams. He doesn't care that those dreams came true. To him, I'm nothing."

Emery's voice broke, and he could feel his eyes stinging again with fresh tears. "Do you know how hard that is?" He didn't wait for them to answer. "No matter how successful we become, my parents are never going to approve. I'll never be good enough," he whispered, his words falling heavily into the tense atmosphere of the room.

"Why didn't you say anything?" Stu was the first to break the silence, rocking back onto his heels and popping the knuckles of his left hand.

"I didn't want you to worry…"

"M, we're here for you," Stu said emphatically. "You just always seem so happy. How are we supposed to know something's wrong if you don't tell us?"

"You guys have enough to worry about…especially recently. Lately, all I've been doing is causing trouble…"

"God, I've been such an asshole," Jaehyun spoke abruptly, putting reassuring pressure on Emery's hand. "I should have never given you so much crap about the Byung Ho thing. I knew it wasn't really your fault, but I still blamed you."

"No—"

"Let me finish." Jaehyun eyed him seriously, and Emery shut his mouth, nodding once.

"I've been putting this off for way too long." Jaehyun let out a harsh sigh. "I'm sorry, M. I shouldn't have taken my anger out on you. I've felt guilty for the way I've treated you ever since our accident, but I didn't say anything. I was too… embarrassed."

Stu snorted.

"Anyways." Jaehyun blushed. "I'm really sorry, M. I should have apologized sooner…"

"I'm sorry, too," Emery said again, a tear falling down his cheek.

"Okay, now you have to stop beating yourself up," Stu said, glancing at Emery's hand. "Literally. We know you hate being on the sidelines, but that doesn't make you any less a part of NEON."

"Bleeding's stopped," Jaehyun observed as he checked under the bandage again.

Yongnam gently took the bloody towel from the oldest member before examining Emery's wounds more closely. "How did this happen?"

"I don't know… Everything was just too much. I felt so…

alone." At his words, Yongnam pulled Emery in for another all-encompassing hug. Stu, Jaehyun, and Sungil quickly followed as they threw their arms around the pair and joined them on the bed.

"NEON is everything to me..." said Emery raggedly. "Please never doubt that."

"I'm sorry, Emery," said Yongnam. "I'm so sorry."

Emery hugged Yongnam back even tighter.

"Man, now I'm crying too," said Stu, and Emery felt Sungil nod against his cheek. They all hugged for longer than they would probably ever admit to.

Finally breaking apart, they sat together on the bed, observing the fresh tears in each other's eyes before erupting in heartfelt laughter. For Emery, the action was cathartic, soothing away the past few weeks of isolation and loneliness.

"Thanks for being my family, guys," Emery said hoarsely, after everyone had settled down. "I'm in this until the end."

"But, *Hyung*..." Sungil tapped his fingers against the bedspread, his face furrowing. "What made you come back? After quitting? I still don't understand."

"Alana..." said Emery, glancing down at his cast.

"Yes, Alana," said Stu with a smirk. "Your secret ex-girlfriend."

"No, I mean Alana is the one who helped me."

"Wait. I'm confused," Jaehyun said. "Alana didn't start working for us until this summer, so how did she keep you from quitting?"

"Because she's our GLO," said Sungil matter-of-factly.

"You're right." Emery looked at the *maknae* in disbelief as the others started at the statement. "She was our fan. I ran into her the last day of our *Luminescence* promotions, after the *fansign*. She made me realize that I wasn't ready to give up on our dreams..."

"This explains so much," Yongnam said, staring at the ceiling with a grimace.

Jaehyun let out a groan. "I still can't believe you were secretly dating! How could you?"

"I'm sorry. I should have never let it happen." Emery looked down in shame.

"No!" said Jaehyun quickly. "I'm not mad that you guys dated. I'm mad that you never told us."

"Oh?" Emery was confused.

"Mate, we don't care if you date," said Stu. "Well, maybe you shouldn't date our staff, but she's not staff anymore, so…"

"We just need to all be on the same page," Yongnam clarified.

"We got your back, *Hyung*," added Sungil.

"So…what actually happened with Alana?" Jaehyun shoved his hands in the pockets of his robe.

"She left. She didn't want to get between me and NEON."

An awkward silence took over, and Emery let out a sigh, his heart hurting at the memory of Alana's departure.

"I'm sorry I barged in on you two." Yongnam watched him guiltily. "I didn't mean those things I said. I really do trust you, M. I just wish you trusted us enough to help you."

Emery swallowed. "I let things get out of hand. I know I should have told you before you found us like that."

"Found you like what? Just what exactly were you doing with Aly?" Stu said suggestively, wiggling his eyebrows.

"Hey!" Emery felt a small smirk tugging at his lips. "I don't kiss and tell."

They all dissolved into laughter. With a genuine smile, Emery looked around at NEON, his true family, and a forgotten warmth spread through his chest.

He wasn't alone.

# Alana

## #Liar

Alana stretched up as far as she could reach, leaning forward on the tips of her toes to place the last brightly colored bag of *jjajangmyeon* on the top shelf. Standing back, she took in the aisle of every type of ramen imaginable—pork, miso, spicy—now fully stocked and organized.

She sighed, tired from a long day of helping out at her parents' grocery store, the job she took on after her return to Chicago. Spending day after day unpacking and shelving food was an adequate distraction, making the last four months in Korea seem like they had almost never happened.

*Almost.*

She tried not to think about why she left. About Emery. She tried not to remember the look on his face when she had shattered both their hearts. Working at the Korean grocery store, she focused on unpacking each item of food with care, as if every bag of ramen were a memory she was trying to store away and forget.

But as usual, she was failing. She couldn't help but worry. Her imagination constantly tormented her. She knew better than most how Emery reacted to stress. Balancing NEON's world tour with…well, *everything else* wouldn't be easy. She hoped he was managing okay. She hoped he was moving on, like she so desperately wished she could. Every day that went by without seeing his face, without hearing his voice, without feeling his warmth was slowly killing her.

She shook her head. She couldn't think about that.

"How's it going with the ramen, Aly?"

Alana looked over to see her mom standing at the end of the aisle, a green apron over her simple black dress and concern evident on her face. Like Aunt Park, she was a petite woman with short, straight black hair, but her once-polished appearance had grown visibly lined by recent stress and heart-ache. Alana tried not to notice.

"*Eomma*." She gave a tired smile. "I just finished," she said casually in Korean.

"Good. Your shift ended twenty minutes ago. You should head out now. There's a surprise waiting for you."

Alana gave her mom a wary look. "Surprise?"

"You'll see. Your *appa* and I will meet you at home in a bit."

"*Eomma*…"

"Don't worry. I think it will help cheer you up."

Alana quickly flicked through the possibilities, her stomach sinking as she remembered what day it was. Tomorrow was NEON's Chicago concert, and the group was likely already in town. On her way to work, she couldn't help but look twice at every person she passed, thinking that she'd seen Emery—the bright smile on his lips, the graceful shape of his hands, the laughter in his dark brown eyes. He couldn't be here, could he? No. She snorted at the absurdity of the idea.

Her parents didn't know about Emery, but they did know something was wrong—*different*. They'd hovered around her ever since she came home, watching her worriedly. She imagined they thought her current mood was because of

Alex, unaware of her disaster of a relationship, and like usual, they avoided talking about it. That's not how the Kims dealt with their problems.

"Okay… Then I guess I'll see you and *Appa* later."

She ignored her mom's scrutinizing look and headed to the back room to put her apron away and collect her things from her locker. She pulled on a black peacoat and tucked a grey scarf securely around her neck.

"I'm off!" Alana called out as she walked by her mom at the register. This late at night, only a handful of customers were in the store.

She made her way to the parking lot, taking a deep breath of fresh air and looking up at the starless night sky, and shivered. It was growing colder outside, the Chicago winter fast approaching.

Pulling out her keys, she froze at the sight of the figure leaning against the side of her silver hatchback. Dread coursed through her veins, anticipating the coming confrontation. When her mom said there would be a surprise, she had hoped it meant there was ice cream cake at home, not this.

"Hey, Aly. Long time no see." Stephanie waved from beside Alana's car, her posture relaxed.

"Steph…"

"What? No hug for your favorite cousin?"

Alana smiled in apology and embraced Stephanie. Her cousin's hair was pulled back in a tight bun, hot pink streaks now threading through her ash grey locks. She was bundled up in a soft pink down jacket and a navy-blue scarf wrapped tightly around the lower half of her face.

"How long have you been waiting out here?" Alana asked.

"Only a few minutes. Uncle Kim picked me up from the hotel an hour ago." Stephanie studied Alana. "How are you?"

"I'm fine."

"Liar."

Alana's eyes narrowed, and they both watched each other carefully. Wind blew Stephanie's pink bangs across her face, and her cousin let out a frosted breath.

"Can we talk in the car, Aly? It's ridiculously cold."

Alana smirked and unlocked the car doors wordlessly before climbing into the driver's seat.

They both sat in silence for a moment, Alana pointedly not looking at her cousin as she started the car and got the heat going.

"It feels like way longer than a month since I saw you... This world tour has been crazy. It's basically a new city every two days. You'd think that'd be cool, right? But all I've seen so far are hotels, concert venues, and airports. I'm so glad I at least had the night off to come see you and Aunt and Uncle Kim." Stephanie loosened her scarf, blowing warm air into her fingers. "Okay, no more small talk. I have to ask. Did leaving solve everything you thought it would?"

Alana kept her gaze firmly on the steering wheel. "It was the right thing to do."

"Really?" Sarcasm dripped from her cousin's voice. "You know, M has been a mess since you left."

Alana glared at her hands. The burn from that first night at Music Now had long since healed. "Leave it, Steph. There was no future for the two of us—only scandals and heartbreak."

"You don't know that for sure," Stephanie countered.

"I do!" Alana looked up to direct her glare on her infuriating cousin. She didn't want to have this conversation, not now, not ever. She had done what was needed. "A dating scandal would ruin Emery, and it would have been all my fault! I couldn't hurt NEON, not any more than I already have."

Stephanie raised an eyebrow. "Last time I checked, it takes at least two to make a dating scandal."

Alana rolled her eyes. "But it only takes one mistake to cause it, and I know I'd be the one to do it."

"Why do you think that?"

"I obviously have some serious issues."

Stephanie let out an exasperated breath. "Everyone has problems, Aly."

"Yeah, but mine aren't going away anytime soon."

"That's why you should be with M! You can work through your problems together—"

"It's *over*, Steph. Just drop it."

"No, I won't just drop it," her cousin huffed indignantly. "I saw you two together, Aly. For the first time in forever you were finally yourself again. You're good for each other."

"You don't know what you're talking about…"

"Well, if I don't know something, it's because you never say anything!" Stephanie's voice grew to a shout. "Honestly, Aly, you need to talk about this! This isn't good for you. Stop being such a coward!"

"Shut *up*, Stephanie!"

"Why did you run? What were you so afraid of that you broke that boy's heart?"

Alana flinched. "I never wanted Emery to get hurt," she said quietly.

"Well, you failed at that."

Alana was back to glaring, her hands tightening into fists. "I was right to break up with Emery. Things would only have gotten worse if I stayed."

"I'm not so sure about that. Things are pretty bad now."

Alana's head snapped up and she took in her cousin's grim expression. "Wait. What do you mean?"

"Let's just say M's got some anger issues to work through. But if you want details, you're gonna have to ask him yourself. Minhyuk's been super hush-hush about it." Stephanie waved a dismissive hand. "But back to my point. You can fix this. NEON is *here*. This doesn't have to be the end for you two."

"No. He must hate me. I already hate myself. I *lied* to him, Steph. Even if I apologized, I know he'd never trust me—not after what I said."

"You don't know how he'd react. M should decide that for himself."

"Ha, and then what? We get back together?"

A sly look crossed Stephanie's face. "If that's what you both wanted…"

Alana remained silent, crossing her arms in annoyance.

"No one's perfect," Stephanie continued. "You are going to mess up—that's just a fact of life. It's how you handle your mistakes that makes the difference."

"Leaving Emery wasn't a mistake," Alana said defiantly. "Starting a relationship in the first place was the mistake. I should have never gotten close to him. Then he would have never gotten hurt."

"You can't change the past, Aly. You can't save everyone, no matter how much you want to." Stephanie took a deep breath and faced Alana head on. "Emery's not Alex."

Alana's heart constricted. Her brother didn't belong in this conversation.

"Steph, don't—"

"No, I'm done keeping my mouth shut. I know it's hard, but you *need* to talk about this."

"I can't!"

"You can," Stephanie said calmly, her face tight. "What do you think Alex would say to you right now? What would he want you to do?"

Alana stiffened. "He can't say anything. He's *dead*."

"I know," Stephanie said. Silence descended as she waited for Alana to answer. The clock on the dashboard counted the minutes as they passed.

"Talk to me, Aly," Stephanie finally whispered.

Alana met her cousin's determined gaze and knew there was no getting out of this. Moisture pricked at her eyes. She couldn't seem to stop crying lately. After leaving her heart in Seoul, she hadn't found the strength to build her walls back up, and the tears kept spilling out. She wiped her face on the back of her hand, drawing a shaky breath before whispering, "Alex... I think he would want me to be happy. He always wanted me to be happy..."

Stephanie nodded sadly. "Yeah, I think so, too. Alex wouldn't want you sacrificing yourself for the sake of his memory."

"But it still hurts, Steph. I don't think it'll ever stop."

"I know," Stephanie said thickly, resting a hand on Alana's shoulder. "But it's time to stop playing the martyr. Both for Alex and for Emery."

"I was trying to do the right thing," Alana breathed, tears now falling in earnest. Stephanie handed her a tissue from her purse.

"You aren't responsible for the happiness of the world, Aly. You're grieving, but it's also okay to move forward in your life. As long as you're happy, I think Alex would be, too."

Emery had said the same thing, standing in the backstage hallway pleading with her not to go. He'd wanted her to be happy, even as she was breaking his heart. Alana blinked the tears away from her lashes, letting them fall onto her lap.

"Trust yourself, Aly. You *can* do this. Don't let fear stop you from living."

But her life had been put on hold, her survival plan taking priority. She thought about everything she had given up— her music, her education, her friends...*Emery*. But Stephanie was right. No matter what she lost or who she protected, Alex would never come back. She had nothing left but her own grief and guilt.

What was the plan now?

★ ★ ★ ★ ★

Alana stood in front of the door, her heart throbbing as she stared at the bronze doorknob.

She was obviously a masochist. She should turn around, go back to her room, and forget she ever had this crazy impulse.

After her painful conversation with Stephanie the day before, Alana had tried to go back to *not* thinking about anything related to Emery or Alex, but she'd failed spectacularly. Her cousin's words ran through her mind all night, and she couldn't stop the doubt from creeping in. Should she have acted differently? *Had* she made a mistake leaving Emery? She certainly wasn't happy with how everything had played out.

She'd woken up after a sleepless night irritated with herself, and with her cousin for prying, all the while avoiding the answers to the questions plaguing her…right up until this moment where she found herself standing outside Alex's bedroom door. She hadn't been in his room since the night before he died. Until now, she hadn't been able to work up the courage.

Her poor heart hitched into her throat as she placed her hand on the doorknob, her numb fingers unfeeling against the cold metal. Taking a deep breath, she pushed, and the door opened with a small creak as she stepped inside.

Alex's room looked exactly the same as it always had. The early afternoon light was muted through the curtains, casting shadows on the band posters that covered the cream walls. Alex's backpack lay next to his bed, his headphones peeking out of the open zipper. Paper and pens littered the desk.

Her throat closed. There was a black sweatshirt with his band's logo folded over the back of the chair, and she let her fingers brush across it, feeling its soft texture. Alex used to wear it whenever he worked on his music late into the night. She had gotten it made for him years ago, using her first official paycheck from working in their parents' store.

A sob ripped from her and she dropped to her knees, pulling the sweatshirt down with her as she cried.

Breathing raggedly, she barely heard the soft clink when something fell against the floorboard beside her. Alana blinked away her tears and stared at the small, silver object next to her—at the USB drive that had fallen out of the sweatshirt pocket.

She gasped, the pain twofold as she recalled both the music she had shared with Alex and the memories she had shared with Emery. Her heart throbbed remembering the way Emery would hold his necklace, as if it were something important to him, as if *she* were someone important to him.

Picking up the USB with trembling fingers, she contemplated it. Which of Alex's songs did this contain? What was the last track he had given her?

She tensed when the memory didn't come.

She couldn't remember. She couldn't even tell if this USB was his or one of her own.

Moving on autopilot, she turned on the dusty computer and inserted the USB stick into the port. Still clutching the sweatshirt in her arms, she sat down at his desk, her heart beating wildly as she waited for the monitor to light up.

She stared at the drive—labeled 'ALEX KIM 5'—that appeared on the computer's desktop. So it was Alex's after all. Her lungs constricting, she hovered the cursor over Alex's name, hesitating for only a moment before tapping the mouse twice, opening it. She felt her mouth curve into a sad smile as she scrolled through his old songs and projects. He had created so much, put so much of himself into his music.

She scrolled further, and her eyes latched onto her own name—*Aly*—titling a track at the very bottom of the folder.

Her breath caught in shock that quickly turned to horror. It had been saved to the drive on the day of Alex's death.

Had this always been here waiting for her? Had Alex expected her to find it?

Her hand shook as she clicked on the file. She adjusted the volume on the computer and waited, her heart pounding.

*"Aly, I know you're probably confused and hurting right now."*

She inhaled sharply at the sound of Alex's voice speaking her name.

*"You're probably wondering why I did it… I never wanted you to find out. I wish you didn't have to. You were so happy this summer, creating music and listening to those K-pop guys you love so much. I didn't want you to lose that."*

Gripping the sweatshirt tightly in her hands, she sat, hanging onto his every word. She could picture him recording this, huddled over the mic at his desk. Where had she been? Probably in her room streaming NEON music videos.

*"I know how upset you must feel, but I'm not like you, Aly. For me, music has always been my only escape, from our parents, from school, from life. That's over for me now. I guess I wasn't ever really as good as I thought. But you—you create music like you were born to do it. And you've only just begun. I know you're going to do amazing things."*

What would Alex think about the mess her life had become? What would he say if he saw her now—her dreams and ambitions in limbo? Would he care?

*"I can't do this anymore. I know you won't understand, but you'll get through this. You always were the strong one."*

A sob broke free from Alana's throat.

*"No matter what, I'll always be your brother. I love you, Aly."*

The recording ended, and the room fell silent but for Alana's cries as tears overtook her.

"I love you, too, Alex," she whispered into the quiet, curling in on herself. "So, so much."

Pain pulsed through her veins as she took in his words, replaying them over and over in her mind. He thought she was strong? No. A strong person wouldn't have treated Emery the way she had. She wasn't the Alana her brother had known.

Stephanie was right. She was a coward.

An image of Emery's sorrow-filled face came unbidden to her mind's eye. She needed to start living again. No one else could save her from herself.

She needed to fix this.

Somehow, Emery had slipped past her walls with his kind smiles and gentle teasing, holding her in her grief. Instead of fearing her pain, he had acknowledged it, sat with her through the tears, and helped her heal. But once her pain lay bare between them, there was nothing left for her to hide behind. She had run—but no more. She was done with that. It was time for her to be brave.

First, she needed a ticket. To a sold-out concert. Five hours before the doors opened.

Pulling out her phone, still holding Alex's sweatshirt in her arms, she sent a quick message.

### November 2

**Alana (1:27 p.m.)** Hey. I need your help.

# Emery

## #CHICAGLO

"Hello Chicago!" Sungil cried as excited screams filled the theater.

Yongnam led them in their official greeting. "One. Two. Three. We are—"

"NEON! Shine on!" all the members said together while bowing to the audience. This was one of Emery's favorite parts of the show—their first chance of the night to see GLO up close. Looking out into the sea of orange GLOsticks always filled his heart with joy.

"So good to be back!" said Stu while waving an arm above his head.

They had just finished their opening segment with four full songs. Sungil was wiping his face with a towel and Yongnam had already chugged an entire bottle of water. Even without dancing, Emery could feel sweat pooling on his forehead from the bright, heavy stage lights.

Each member took turns introducing themselves to the fans, and the cheers grew louder and louder. They stood in their usual order—Emery, Sungil, Yongnam, Stu, Jaehyun—facing the crowd. While much smaller than their dome concert in Seoul, Chicago's show was quite impressive, and Emery still couldn't believe how popular they had become in his home country. The theater held more than five thousand packed seats. Apparently, the tickets had sold out within minutes—seconds, if you didn't count the lag time.

Finally, it was Emery's turn to introduce himself. He pulled out his custom earpiece, wanting to hear the full roar of the crowd, and took a moment to let their screams wash over him.

"Chicagooooo!" he yelled, and the fans went wild.

"ChicaGLOoooo!" Stu echoed, Emery laughing along with his members as everyone in the theater lost it.

As the two English speakers of the group, Stu and Emery took over most of the talking when they went overseas, acting as makeshift translators when the other members gave up trying to speak in English. Luckily, Stu was a natural emcee, and Emery was happy to let him take the lead.

Emery looked out into the audience, exhilarated by the unending bright smiles from their fandom.

"Hi guys, I'm Emery! Nice to meet you." He waved with his right arm, his knuckles carefully wrapped in a white bandage while his broken left arm hung at his side. "Let's have fun tonight!"

GLO screamed back in greeting.

"I'm sorry I'm not able to fully participate in all our songs today." Emery looked to the far right of the theater, scanning the crowd while he listened to the fans' repeated cry of "it's okay!"

"I'm—"

He blinked. No, it couldn't be… He looked again, but he had lost her. There were too many people in the audience. His mind was playing tricks on him.

He shook his head, reminding himself to stay focused.

"I'm resting well." Emery had to pause again, this time

because the cheers were too loud. "And I'll return to the stage with performances even better than before! Thank you GLO!"

Emery peered into the crowd again, but he still couldn't catch any sign of her.

★ ★ ★ ★ ★

"Good job everyone!" Minhyuk said as NEON reentered their dressing room backstage. The staff were all applauding and patting the members on the back.

The show had been a big success. GLO had loved the encore, especially when Stu had forcibly restrained Emery to show off his bare stomach. Emery glanced down self-consciously. His abs had nothing on the Australian rapper's eight-pack.

"We have deep dish pizza waiting for you at the hotel."

"Sweet!" called Sungil. He was taking a *selca* with the show's banner next to Stu, who still hadn't put his shirt back on. Emery chuckled thinking how GLO would react tonight on social media.

Yongnam had his camera out, snapping shots of some of the staff members. Emery made brief eye contact with Stephanie, confused by the playful wink she gave him. Outside of her official duties, she usually pretended he didn't exist, at least since Alana had left.

"Get changed and let's get going," said Minhyuk, walking with a slight limp as he helped the staff pack up the room.

Emery busied himself by grabbing his street clothes—a white T-shirt, his now-clean black zip up hoodie, and jeans—and changing behind a curtain. He would wait to take his makeup off until they got back to the hotel.

"Guys, we have a special guest today!" Emery heard Yena call. "You won't believe who I found."

Cries of surprise and greetings rang throughout the dressing room.

*"What are you doing here?!"*

*"Long time no see."*

*"Couldn't stay away, huh?"*

His stomach dropped. Stepping out from behind the curtain, he stopped dead in his tracks. He blinked—once, twice.

*Alana.*

She looked nervous, yet animated. Her cheeks were red, but whether from embarrassment or excitement, he wasn't sure. Her light brown eyes widened as soon as they found Emery's, her gaze intense, almost challenging, and Emery had to fight to maintain eye contact.

"Hi…" she said, her voice trailing off.

"Aly!" Stu rushed forward and tackled her in a bear hug.

Emery instinctively took a step toward them, but forced himself to stop, glancing around the room in growing panic. Sungil and Jaehyun were both laughing and making their way to Alana, but Yongnam was looking directly at Emery, an eyebrow raised as he mouthed the words, "You okay?"

No, he most definitely was not okay.

He wasn't ready. Seeing her so suddenly had caught him by surprise. What was he supposed to do? Yell at her? Embrace her? Kiss her?

His heart burned, with both longing and fear. It was too soon, his wounds too raw. Emery felt his head spin and nausea spread outward from the pit of his stomach.

An expectant tension filled the air. It was as if he had a flashing sign above his head that read "romantic fool" and everyone was waiting for a dramatic reunion. NEON knew how he felt about her, after all. After opening up to them in New York just two days ago, Emery felt relieved, the weight of his secrets finally lifted. He still struggled to voice his true thoughts aloud, but he was working on it, his members catching him when he slipped up.

Despite NEON's renewed closeness, Emery continued to miss Alana, his feelings left unresolved. It was the little things he missed most—her love of chocolate, the way her eyes sparkled, her inability to multitask. He yearned to hold her tight, talking with her into the night about everything and nothing at all. He missed the way he felt when he was around her, never having to pretend. But he couldn't keep chasing her. Not anymore—especially if being near him brought her more harm than good.

This was his chance to act. But instead of feeling joyful, he felt paralyzed, completely overwhelmed.

"I'll be outside," Emery heard himself mutter as he grabbed his backpack, walking by Alana without a second glance. He refused to give in to the ache in his heart.

Only after he got into their hired van did he let himself collapse, pulling his knees to his chest and resting his head on them. A wave of sorrow hit him full force and he couldn't help but let out an audible cry.

★ ★ ★ ★ ★

"You doing okay?"

Emery looked up to see Yongnam entering the van. He hoped the darkness hid his red-rimmed eyes.

"Just tired," Emery said while averting his gaze.

Yongnam let out an exasperated sigh.

"Actually, no…" Emery admitted, shifting uncomfortably. "I wasn't ready."

The leader took a seat next to him in the back row. "For what it's worth, Alana looked devastated when you left."

Emery groaned. "Please don't tell me that."

"What happened?" Yongnam's voice was calm and un-judging.

"I-I don't know." Emery fidgeted with the strings on his sweatshirt. "I was afraid, I guess."

Yongnam remained silent, waiting for Emery to continue.

"I don't want to hurt her. I just don't see how we can make 'us' work. I didn't want her to reject me all over again, especially not in front of you guys…"

"Don't worry what we think. You need to stand up for what you want. This is your life, M. If you want to date, then date. I'm not standing in your way." Yongnam paused before finishing. "I trust you. We all do."

Through the darkness, Emery could just make out the sincere smile on Yongnam's face.

"That…that means a lot," said Emery, as the van door slid open again, revealing the rest of NEON.

"Ugh, so hungry," said Sungil as he took the seat in front of Emery.

"Hey!" said Stu. Instead of sitting in one of the open seats, he squeezed himself in between Emery and Yongnam, making it entirely way too cramped for them all in the backseat.

"How are you holding up, M?" said Jaehyun from the seat in front of Yongnam. "We're here if you need anything."

Emery shook his head at the evident support from his members.

"I blew it," he admitted, burying his face in his hands. "Sorry you guys had to witness that."

"Mate, you didn't *totally* blow it," said Stu. "You just need a pep talk. If anyone can still salvage it, it's you—M from NEON! What *can't* you do?" Everyone chuckled as Emery elbowed Stu lightly in the stomach.

Emery frowned, his mind racing through the possibilities and discarding them just as quickly. "It's over, guys. Can we pretend this never happened?"

Focused on his phone, Yongnam gave a half-hearted grunt of what Emery hoped was agreement.

"Maybe you'll feel differently after you eat?" said Sungil with a hopeful look.

Emery resisted the urge to roll his eyes. "Just drop it. *Please?*"

They fell into silence as Minhyuk got into the front passenger's seat and the van departed for the hotel.

★ ★ ★ ★ ★

His room smelled like pizza. Two giant slices of deep dish cheese pizza sat on the desk, completely untouched. Emery wasn't in the mood to eat, not when his stomach churned with embarrassment and regret.

*"Tiki Tiki!"*

Emery grabbed his phone from the bathroom counter, checking the new message.

### November 2

Captain Yongnam (11:14 p.m.) Can we talk?

Emery (11:15 p.m.) Sure

Captain Yongnam (11:15 p.m.) I'll come to your room in a few minutes. Room 1215?

Emery (11:16 p.m.) Yep, see you soon

Emery was in the middle of getting ready for bed. He had just showered and his hair was still wet. It felt good to wash away the makeup, sweat, and hairspray from the show.

He stood in the bathroom, studying himself in the pristine mirror. His brown hair hung damp around his face, covering the faint remnant of his scar from the accident. With his lean muscles visible through his T-shirt, he looked stronger, his eyes tired and sad, but no longer cold. He tried a smile, relieved when his reflection softened. Running a towel through his hair, he turned away from the mirror.

Less than a week had passed since his "incident" in the bathroom. After alerting Minhyuk, the manager had swiftly stepped in, handling the hotel damages and taking Emery to the hospital to get his injury cleaned and bandaged. Things had settled down, although Emery had lost the privilege of having his own hotel room for the rest of the tour. He didn't mind though. After everything, it was rather nice to be surrounded by steady support and reassurance. Tonight he was sharing with Jaehyun.

"Hey M," the oldest member said, appearing in the open doorway of the bathroom. "Sungil needs me for a second. Is it okay if I step out for a bit?"

"Sure, no problem. I'm just about to go to sleep." Emery smiled in encouragement.

Despite his words, concern briefly flashed across Jaehyun's eyes. "I'll be right next door. Let me know if you need me."

"Thanks for checking in, *Hyung*."

Jaehyun's face morphed into a proud grin. "Be back soon."

As the door closed, Emery continued going through the motions of his skincare routine. Toner, essence, ampoule and serum—he applied them without much thought, keeping his mind as blank as possible. Just as he dotted on his moisturizer, there was a knock on the door.

Expecting Yongnam, Emery hastily rubbed the cream into his face as he reached for the door.

He careened to a stop. "*Alana?*"

She was dressed in the same outfit she had worn to the show, jeans and a black sweater, but she looked more frazzled, her eyes wide with surprise.

"Em—Emery?" she said cautiously. "Where's Yongnam?"

"Uh, not here."

"Oh." She shifted uncomfortably. "I'm supposed to meet him."

"Huh? This is my room." He looked at the door to confirm. "Room 1215."

"Oh," she said again, pausing awkwardly. "Do you know where he is?"

"Actually, he should be here any minute."

"Umm, then I'll just wait out here," she said as she started to turn away.

"No!" Emery said a bit too loudly. "Eh—no. Come in before someone sees you."

She looked over her shoulder, her expression uncertain. In the distance, Emery could hear the ding of the elevator. Without hesitating, he reached out and pulled her into the room. The door closed behind them with a *click*.

Instantly, he dropped her hand. They stood awkwardly in the entryway, neither one moving.

"Uh. You can take a seat if you want," Emery said to Alana, gesturing toward the chair near the window. As she perched on the seat, he sat at the edge of his bed, unsure of what to say.

There was a moment's silence.

"You're not a fan?" Alana said at last.

"What?"

She pointed to the pizza left on his desk. "A fan of our pizza."

"Oh. I actually love it. I just wasn't feeling so great earlier."

"You're sick?" Her eyes widened.

"No. I was just…*off*." He looked toward the door. Where was Yongnam already?

"Because of me?"

Emery didn't speak, not trusting himself to answer.

"I'm sorry. I shouldn't have come."

"Why?" He met her eyes again. "Why *did* you come?"

"I told you. Yongnam wanted to meet—"

"No, earlier. Why did you come to the concert?"

"Oh right." She paused. "I wanted to apologize."

"For what? Breaking my heart?" The words slipped out before he could stop them.

She recoiled, and Emery's anger flared.

"You quit. You're the one who pulled away," he accused sharply. "You made everything seem like it was one sided. It wasn't—it never was. You weren't the only one in this relationship. I—"

"I know."

"—what?" Emery stared back at her.

Alana took a deep breath, her eyes fluttering closed for a moment. "I know," she repeated. "I messed up. I'm sorry. I'm so sorry for hurting you."

Emery shook his head. "Associating me with your brother's death—I can't win. Not against that."

Alana bit her lip. "That's not true."

"But you said—"

"I lied."

His mind went blank.

Alana seemed to curl in on herself. "I needed to push you away. It's true that I watched your comeback the night he died, but I never blamed you or NEON. I blamed myself for not being there for my brother. But I can't keep living like this. Alex wouldn't want me to. I finally realize that now."

"Oh." Emery didn't know what to say. He had fixated on

her words from that night, constantly replaying them in his mind. Her revelation had haunted him, and he resented that he had unintentionally caused her so much pain. He felt another flash of anger—her lie had cut deep—but relief quickly took its place. He was thankful to have one less burden on his shoulders.

"I'm sorry," she repeated. "I went too far, and I regretted it as soon as I said it. I…I just didn't know how else to break away from you."

"But why? Why did you push me away?"

She looked at him with a sorrowful expression. "I didn't believe we would have worked out."

"I wanted to try. You didn't give us a chance!"

"I wasn't ready. But…but I am now."

"W-what?" sputtered Emery.

"You're the one who must hate me. You have every right to, but I had to tell you. I couldn't let you leave Chicago without telling you."

His heartbeat pounded in his ears.

"I love you, Emery."

Staring at her wide-eyed, he tried his best to process her words.

"I needed you to know that," finished Alana.

*"Tiki Tiki!"*

At the sound of an incoming message, Emery took out his phone from his sweatpants pocket, thankful for an excuse to look away.

Yongnam (11:29 PM) You have another chance. Don't mess it up. Good luck ;)

Emery suppressed a groan before looking up at Alana. "Yongnam. He isn't coming…"

He ran his hand through his hair. It was almost dry now and extra fluffy. He wished he had known Alana was coming. He would have styled it and worn better clothes.

"Okay, I'll leave now." Alana stood up and grabbed her bag from the floor.

"No, wait!" Emery shouted. She stopped, but didn't sit back down.

He couldn't mess this up, not again. He didn't want anyone else but her. They deserved to give their relationship a fighting chance. Alana needed to know he was all in. He wasn't going to back down.

"I love you, too."

She looked taken aback, her eyes wide.

"How? After everything…" She trailed off. "How could you trust me again?"

Emery paused, considering her pained expression. "You're not the only one who's made mistakes. We can work through this—together."

"It's risky…"

"Sometimes you have to take a chance for the people you love." He watched as tears began to form in Alana's eyes, and he felt his own eyes start to sting. "Trust what we have, Alana."

"Okay," she breathed shakily. "I can do that."

"We need a fresh start," he continued, holding out his bandaged hand. "Hi, I'm Emery. Nice to meet you."

She looked at him with uncertainty, tucking a piece of hair behind her ear. With her scar now visible, she wiped away her tears, took a deep breath, and played along. "Hi, Emery. I'm Alana."

Their hands met, and the touch of skin against skin sent a shiver down Emery's spine and an explosion of butterflies up into his heart.

*Screw it.*

He pulled Alana in for a hug, or at least he tried to. His sudden tug had sent them both off balance, causing Alana to collide with him. They collapsed together in a heap on the bed, Alana awkwardly draped across Emery's legs.

"I'm so sorry," Alana said breathlessly as she tried her best to untangle herself.

"There's nothing to apologize for." Smiling brightly, he pulled her towards him once again, savoring the feel of her pressed against his chest. Seated together on the bed, he finally felt whole, the ache in his heart fading into a distant memory.

Fate had brought them together, but it was up to them to make it work.

"Oh," she said with a small gasp. "You're still wearing it."

Emery felt her cool fingers skim across his neck as she slowly pulled the chain of his necklace out from under his shirt, the USB dangling in the subdued lighting of the hotel room.

"It's my good luck charm."

She rubbed her thumb lightly against the "A" engraved on the metal casing, her expression thoughtful. Reaching for her hand, he wrapped it with his own, holding the USB together before brushing his lips against her fingers.

"What happened here?" she said, taking in the bandage around his knuckles. She turned her gaze upward, her eyes worried, but with a teasing glint to them. "Punch another lamp post?"

Emery smirked, doing his best to act nonchalant. "Something like that."

She scowled. "We really need to work on that."

A rush of joy flooded through him at her simple use of 'we,' and he kissed her hand again. "Okay."

A sweet smile danced on her lips, and she let out a sudden, soft laugh. "You know, you have some cream on your face." She playfully pointed at his forehead.

He let out a groan. "Are you telling me that was there the whole time?"

Alana reached up to gently wipe it away. "All fixed."

"Thank you," said Emery, and pulled her in for a deep kiss.

# Glossary

**Aegyo** - a display of intense, childish cuteness, e.g. speaking in a baby voice and making cute facial expressions and gestures, often requested of Korean celebrities on reality TV shows and live broadcasts to amuse fans; literally "charms" in Korean

**Ajumma** - a Korean title used for middle-aged or married women; the typical stereotype of an *ajumma* consists of a fierce older woman with short, black permed hair

**Appa** - "dad" in Korean (informal)

**Baksu** - "applause" or "clapping" in Korean, often said in congratulations

**Banchan** - a small side dish; traditionally provided with every Korean meal, common *banchan* include *kimchi* (pickled cabbage), *kongnamul* (soybean sprouts), *danmuji* (pickled radish), and *eomuk bokkeum* (fried fish cake)

**Bulgogi** - a type of sliced and seasoned barbequed beef; literally "fire meat" in Korean

**Chodang soondubu** - a style of soft tofu popular to Gangneung, known as their representative food; rather than salt, this tofu is made out of seawater, creating a softer texture

**Chuseok** - the Korean harvest festival holiday celebrated on August 15th of the lunar calendar on the full moon; literally "autumn eve" in Korean

**Coordi** - "coordinator" of a K-pop group in Konglish; a *co-ordi* is typically female and fills the role of stylist, manager, or staff member support, often doing any task needed

**Dubu** - "tofu" in Korean

**Eomma** - "mom" in Korean (informal)

**Fancafe** - an online forum designed specifically for Korean celebrities and fans to interact, post updates, and share information with the official members of the fanclub

**Fancam** - a fan-taken video of celebrities, usually during live performances and events

**Fansign** - an autograph signing session for Korean celebrities open to a limited number of fans; in K-pop specifically, attendees are often picked through a lottery system by purchasing albums, where one album equals one chance for entry

**Fighting** - (also spelled *hwaiting*) an encouraging word of support in Konglish; some common English translations are "let's go" or "go, team"

**Gochujang** - a type of red chili paste used in most signature Korean dishes, recognizable for its bright red color and spicy flavor

**Heol** - a sound of disbelief or nonspecific meaning in Korean, often used to express mild shock or surprise to non-positive statements or situations

**Hoobae** - a Korean title used for a "junior" in an educational or professional setting, usually designating those who have less experience or time spent in the business, school, or organization

**Hotteok** - a sweet Korean pancake that is fried and often filled with brown sugar, cinnamon, and nuts

**Hyung** - a Korean title used by males to address their older male counterparts; literally "older brother" in Korean

**Imo** - "aunt (on mother's side)" in Korean; compare to *gomo*, or "aunt (on father's side)"

**Jjajangmyeon** - a Chinese-Korean black bean noodle dish

**Jjigae** - "stew" in Korean, often consisting of tofu, meat, seafood or vegetables in varying broths and served piping hot

**Kimchi** - a traditional Korean side dish, or *banchan*, consisting of spicy pickled cabbage or other fermented vegetables

**Maknae** - a Korean title for the youngest member of a family or group

**Ment** - the time between performances at a Korean event or concert when the idols on stage speak directly to the fans, often introducing themselves, talking about the venue location, and closing the show

**MR** - the instrumental accompaniment to a song; literally "music recorded"; compare to *AR*, or "all recorded," which includes both the instrumental accompaniment and the singer's voices used for lip syncing

**Naengmyeon** - "cold noodles" in Korean

**Netizen** - a person who is actively involved in online communities; literally a "citizen of the internet"

**-nim** - a suffix attached to the end of a name or professional title to make it more deferential in Korean

**Noona** - a Korean title used by males to address their older female counterparts; literally "older sister" in Korean

**Nugu** - "nobody" in K-pop slang, often used by international fans to describe the brand new, lesser-known, or unpopular groups in the entertainment industry; literally "who" in Korean

**Omo** - an expression short for *omona*, meaning "oh, my" or "oh my gosh", in Korean

**Oppa** - a Korean title used by females to address their older male counterparts; literally "older brother" in Korean

**Samgyeopsal** - a type of grilled pork belly often eaten at Korean barbeque restaurants

**Selca** - "selfie" in Konglish, shortened from the English loanword "self camera"

**Seonsaengnim** - "teacher" in Korean

**Soju** - a type of Korean distilled beverage traditionally made from rice, wheat, or barley

**Sunbae** - a Korean title used for a "senior" in an educational or professional setting, usually designating those who have more experience or time spent in the business, school, or organization

**Unnie** - a Korean title used by females to address their older female counterparts; literally "older sister" in Korean

**VCR** - a pre-recorded video at K-pop concerts shown in between sets while the artists are preparing backstage

# Acknowledgements

Wow. We can't believe we wrote a BOOK.

And a K-pop book, of all things.

This project started out as a joke—two friends on the way to a KARD concert, bored and trapped together on the train. To pass the time, we tested our K-pop knowledge by imagining ridiculous names for a fictitious boy group—along with all the cliché K-drama moments we could throw at them.

However, as we began to flesh out the scenarios, challenging ourselves to make them as realistic as possible based off our own experiences living in Korea, we quickly realized we would LOVE to read that book. But the problem was, it didn't exist.

And thus, NEON was born.

There were so many amazing people, as well as sources of inspiration, that helped us give life to this new world. From all the K-pop artists and songs to the fandoms and online communities, without your constant passion, dedication, and creativity, we could never have turned our dream into reality.

To our beta readers—David, Erin, Melanie, Lisa, Katie, and

Jiwon—your support from the very first draft was invaluable. To "Food Interest Group," in particular, thank you for putting up with our endless stream of messages full of brainstorming, ranting, and fangirling—both book and non-book related. We count ourselves lucky every day that our love of K-pop and Korean food brought us together in Nanjing. You're all awesome. Never change. *WeChat chuckle emoji*

To our families, your love and support mean everything to us. Thank you for indulging our fangirl whims, feeding us when we're lost in our imaginations, and encouraging all of our world travels, even though you wished we lived closer.

To Paul Rosenstrock, thank you for taking on the unofficial role of our secretary, business mentor, and airport limo chauffeur. Your endless advice and assistance have been truly invaluable along this winding journey to self-publish our book.

And, to our four-legged, furry friends—Ted, Argos, and Elsi—you're the best! Thanks for keeping us company through all the late-night writing and editing sessions.

We also had a great team of editors helping us behind the scenes. Thank you to Pam Anderson and Blair Thornburgh for your insightful perspectives, comments, and determination to make this story the best it could be.

A HUGE thank you is also due to Jauni (Lin Xie) for her beautiful cover art. Please be sure to follow her on Twitter @jaunini to see her amazing artwork. Her BTS fanart is phenomenal!

We are also grateful to Patrick Knowles for his expertise in finalizing our cover's layout and to Jennifer Toomey for helping us bring our words to life with her formatting skills.

Finally, to all our readers, thank you from the bottom of our hearts for reading *Comeback*. Never be afraid to take chances and follow your own crazy dreams—you never know what will happen!

Thank you. 谢谢. 감사합니다.

Lyn & Rachel

# About the Authors

## Lyn Ashwood

Lyn likes to think of herself as an incorrigible wanderer—through cities, cultures, and stories. After acquiring her degrees, traveling from place to place, and eavesdropping on random strangers with her hard-won language skills, she finally made the somewhat irrational decision to move to Korea to work as a writer and editor, because apparently she didn't get enough of that in grad school.

When not trapped in her own mindscape, Lyn can be found queuing for concerts, hunting down the best chocolate ice cream in Seoul, or hiding in her tiny apartment streaming music videos because it's too "peopley" outside.

## Rachel Rose

Rachel has studied and worked across Asia, jumping from Taiwan to China, and then onto Korea where she currently resides. Her Instagram is almost entirely about food, and she annoyingly insists that the camera must always eat first. Her favorite K-drama tropes include contract relationships and drunken piggyback rides, although she'd hate for them to actually happen to her in real life. For more than 25 years, Rachel assumed she was exclusively a cat person until her parents adopted Ted, the Pomeranian who doesn't know he's a Pomeranian. Her life has never been the same since.

*To stay up to date on NEON and our upcoming books, follow us at **@ashwoodandrose** and visit our website* **ashwoodandrose.com.**

Made in the USA
Coppell, TX
12 August 2021

60399475R00173